Author and screenwr... ...writes crime novels and prime time TV drama for the BBC, ITV and US TV. He is also Writer in Residence at HMP Grendon. His TV credits include BBC1's *Inspector Lynley Mysteries*, *Holby City* and *The Mrs Bradley Mysteries*; ITV thrillers *The Stepfather* and *The Blind Date*; and *Perfect Strangers*, the CBS romantic comedy starring Rob Lowe and Anna Friel. Simon lives in London and Deal. His partner is fellow crime writer and Killer Women co-founder Mel McGrath. They often discuss murder methods over breakfast. *Three's a Crowd* is his first contemporary fiction novel.

SIMON BOOKER

THREE'S A CROWD

**SIMON &
SCHUSTER**

London · New York · Sydney · Toronto · New Delhi

First published in Great Britain by Simon & Schuster UK Ltd, 2021

This paperback edition published 2022

1 3 5 7 9 10 8 6 4 2

Simon & Schuster UK Ltd
1st Floor
222 Gray's Inn Road
London WC1X 8HB

Simon & Schuster Australia, Sydney
Simon & Schuster India, New Delhi

www.simonandschuster.co.uk
www.simonandschuster.com.au
www.simonandschuster.co.in

A CIP catalogue record for this book is available
from the British Library

Paperback ISBN: 978-1-3985-0477-6
eBook ISBN: 978-1-3985-0405-9

Typeset by M Rules
Printed and bound in Great Britain by
CPI Group (UK) Ltd, Croydon, CR0 4YY

MIX
Paper from
responsible sources
FSC® C171272
FSC
www.fsc.org

For Abigail

TOM

What would happen if an estranged father and son fell in love with the same woman? It's not something I'd considered – until it happened to me. Who would win? Could there *be* a winner, or would the whole thing end in tears and sick? If you'd asked these questions a few months ago I'd have told you to stop being an idiot, but life has a way of teaching us lessons we don't want to learn. Especially when it comes to what I can only describe as my father.

'If you love someone, set them free. If they don't come back, hunt them down and drown them in a sack.'

I think he was joking when he sent that text on the day Mum left in search of 'some space' but given his oddball sense of humour I can't be certain. We haven't spoken for a year. Our last phone call was typical.

'Are you blaming me for your mother's behaviour?'

'No, Dad, but let's face it – you *are* difficult to live with.'

I heard him light a cigarette before uttering the harshest insult in his lexicon – the B-word.

'Don't be boring, Tom. You want to know what's difficult to live with? Haemorrhoids. Me, I'm a day at the beach.'

If you think my father sounds a zillion years old, Jewish and American you'd make his day but he's none of the above. Truth is, he's more Cricklewood than Hollywood but as a fan of Jerry Seinfeld and Larry David he sometimes likes to mimic the way they speak. Nudging fifty, he's, like, six-foot tall – a fedora-wearing silver fox, improbably fit for a lifelong smoker and seldom seen wearing anything other than a Paul Smith suit. I once saw a woman walk into a lamppost, distracted by his bum.

'How's the great British musical coming along?'

His question oozed sarcasm. I can't blame him. Two years ago I made the mistake of telling him I was writing another musical, my fifth attempt – or was it sixth? By working evenings and weekends I'd notched up four and a half songs and a patchy libretto without a satisfying arc or resolution. The show is about dysfunctional families. God knows where I get my ideas.

My excuse for such slow progress was the day-job. Unlikely as it may seem, churning out articles for *Double Glazing Monthly* involves the same part of the brain needed to write a hit West End show, which means I'm out of creative juice by the end of the working day. So sue me, as my father might say.

'I'm hoping to finish it soon,' I said.

'And I'm hoping for lunch with Scarlett Johansson. How soon is "soon"?'

'Like, end of the year.'

'This year? Next year?'

'This year.'

'I won't hold my breath.'

I'm used to my father throwing shade at me. The worst day of his life was when I beat him at tennis. I shit you not. I was eleven. I know he thinks I'm, like, gay because, well, musicals, but I happen to be straight.

'I've had a terrific idea,' he said. '*Depression: The Musical.* What do you think?'

'Are you okay, Dad?'

'Never better.' I heard him drag on his cigarette. 'So why did you call?'

'Mum told me she's taking a sabbatical in Goa. She said I should look after you.'

'I don't need looking after. Especially by someone who thinks I'm difficult.'

'Mate, you *are* difficult. That doesn't mean I don't, like, *care* about you.'

'Care-schmare. And for God's sake, stop saying "like" every five seconds. It makes you sound like an idiotic American schoolgirl.' Then came the kicker. 'And don't call for a while. If your mother can go off the radar, so can I.'

His voice had fallen to a whisper.

'Dad?'

No reply.

'Dad?'

But he was gone.

*

That was a year ago. I phoned every day for, like, weeks. Left a dozen voicemails, maybe more. I cycled to his flat, the top two floors of a grand white-stucco house in Belsize Park, a leafy enclave for bankers who think proximity to Hampstead lends an air of intellectual respectability. Dad bought the flat years ago, before the London property market went nuts. Lucky bastard.

The lights were on and his car was parked outside, its engine still warm, so I knew he was at home. There's no mistaking the classic Jag – a 1964 red E-Type, number plate: RY 1. I rang the doorbell a million times. No response. Over the next couple of months I paid more abortive visits, left scores of messages and sent dozens of emails. Finally, I gave up and I guess we're now officially 'estranged'.

I know he's alive because I sometimes hear the first few minutes of his show. Every so often, at noon on a weekday, I find a pretext to nip out of the office and hold my mobile to my ear to catch him introducing the first 'lunchtime love song' on Silk FM. Then I know he's okay, just being Dad. Which is fine.

Absolutely fine.

Actually, it's an improvement. When I turned six, he barely spoke to me for over a year, except to ask me to tell Mum something, like he'd be away for the weekend or the school said I had nits. He stopped speaking to her for that same year – literally not a word – but never explained why. Neither did she. Go figure.

As for Mum, I receive monthly emails from the Blue

Moon Yoga Retreat on Patnem Beach along with copious instructions on how to breathe. I refrain from reminding her that I've been breathing fine for twenty-five years. I also resist the temptation to ask what she's playing at.

Okay, so she too will soon hit the Big Five-O and deserves some me-time, especially after seeing her beloved LadyKabs go bust (thanks Uber!) and putting up with Dad, but leaving him alone for, like, *a whole year*?

I glimpsed him once, a couple of months ago, on his birthday. I was cycling past the Silk FM studios on Shaftesbury Avenue and saw him getting into a taxi. He was with a blonde woman in sunglasses. I could pretend I was just passing, but my office is on the Embankment, in an ugly seventies block overlooking the Thames, so there's no getting away from the fact that I was checking up on him.

God knows how things will be when he's old and can't wipe his own arse. Given our history, no one could blame me for letting him rot but I won't, even if Mum stays away forever. He may have been a rubbish dad but at least he was *there*, which is more than can be said for his own father, last heard of fleecing wealthy widows in Monaco and Palm Beach.

Meanwhile, there's a pain-in-the-arse new editor at work and no sign of Ms Right, or even Ms Right-Now. Last week, I had a haircut I didn't need, just to feel a woman's hands running through my hair. I had a crescent moon tattooed on my forearm for the same reason, to feel a woman's touch. If that's not tragic (okay, borderline creepy) I don't know what is.

On the bright side, the barista at the New Dalston Café is worth paying over the odds for below average coffee. She's older than me – I'm guessing mid-thirties. Her name's Harriet. She has long chestnut hair and the most beautiful green eyes I've ever seen. This morning we bantered while she sprinkled extra cinnamon on my cappuccino. Great smile, gorgeous voice.

Not gonna lie, I think she likes me.

HARRIET

Dear blokes, on behalf of women everywhere, you have no idea how little you need to do to impress us.

A) Learn how to listen.

B) Don't be a fuck-nugget.

C) There is no C. Just A) and B). Trust me, the bar is really low.

Take 'Extra Cinnamon Guy'. Okay, he's easy on the eye but when it comes to chat-up lines and banter: must try harder.

Yes, I'm new at the café.

No, I don't bake the muffins myself.

Yep, they do look tasty.

And speaking of blokes, note to self: next time you fall for some random dick-wazzock, ask outright – are you married? And don't stop there, obvs. Are you married with kids and do you get a kick out of stringing women along for *two years*, especially women with what you'd call 'body-clock issues'? Just 'cos I *seem* worldly-wise doesn't make me anything of the kind. I'm thirty-five and I've had three proper boyfriends. Exhibit One fell in love with my so-called best friend. Number Two announced he was gay during a weekend in Marrakech then disappeared with a waiter. Hashtag Bastard #3 omitted to mention his WIFE AND TWO KIDS, which makes him not only a shit but the shittiest shit ever to come from Shit-world and leave a shitty trail of shite.

Better out than in, as Nan would say.

I'm not in a state because of Damian, aka Love Rat, aka Cockweasel (that scar is fading, thank God) but because The Thoughts keep coming and **OMG I COULD THROW SCALDING WATER ON THAT CUSTOMER RIGHT NOW!** (there you go, right on cue). There doesn't seem to be anything I can do to stop them happening whenever they like. Apparently, they have a name: Intrusive Thoughts. The CBT woman told me they're more common than you might think, a form of Obsessive Compulsive Disorder, and pretty much everyone has them at some point, but while she was speaking all I could think was, Cognitive Behavioural Therapy is bullshit and **WHAT IF I STABBED YOU IN THE EYE WITH YOUR PEN?**

Still, I completed the six-week course – part hope, part desperation. Because when you're an actress and The Thoughts keep coming while you're onstage in front of an audience or surrounded by cast and crew on a TV or film set and all you can think is **I'M GOING TO FLASH MY BOOBS!** you end up paralysed with anxiety and suffering the worst form of stage fright, something people dismiss as luvvie-speak for 'a bit nervous' but which makes it impossible for you to do the job you've spent your life training for and killing your career stone dead. It's not the same as Tourette's, BTW, that's a neuropsychiatric disorder that usually takes hold in childhood, whereas The Thoughts only started to become *really* intrusive when I hit my thirties.

Thank God people seem to like my voice. I'm okay in a little sound booth, just me with a producer on the other side of the glass working the widgets. A radio ad here, an audiobook there means I can still call myself a professional actress, but only just. Things might pick up when the full moon brings a grand cross with Jupiter, but lately even voice-over work seems to have dried up, which explains why I'm pulling double shifts at the New Dalston Café.

It's also why I entered the competition to be the Voice of London.

You know those tannoy announcements on the tube? *Mind the gap between the train and the platform edge. The next train to Cockfosters will arrive in two minutes.* That disembodied voice on the bus? *Seventy-three to Stoke Newington.* That could be me, assuming my voice hits the sweet spot with whoever dreamed up the competition on behalf of Silk FM and Transport for London. First prize: five thousand pounds and the chance to be the Voice of London. I'm guessing it would mean a few days in a small Soho studio, recording the announcements. I could handle that.

I think.

If I win (not gonna happen, I *never* win anything), and

assuming I can beat The Thoughts, maybe I'll finally pluck up courage to use the £5k to try my luck in Hollywood. Three months sofa-surfing should be enough to hook a decent agent and cash in on the demand for Brits. Assuming The Thoughts stop, of course, which is a big 'if'. I keep telling myself, 'think positive, Harriet' and 'fake it till you make it' and all that other self-help crap. Okay, here goes.

I'm visualizing it now. My name above the title.

Starring Harriet Brown ...

A suite at the Chateau Marmont ...

A star on Hollywood Boulevard ...

On the other hand, if I never get well enough to go to LA I can spend the rest of my life as a bag lady, riding the tube all day and listening to myself bossing commuters about.

Please allow passengers off the train before boarding.

Move down inside the carriage. Please use all available space.

See? That's typical. I'm always planning for when things *don't* work out. Probably because apart from a six-week stint on *EastEnders* and years of what-the-hell-was-*that*-all-about? fringe theatre,* the truth is I'm just another wannabe, still living with Mum and Dad and serving lattes with a smile that doesn't reach my eyes. And no bloke. At thirty-five. Ideal for someone who was six when she decided on names

---

* I forgot, last year I 'played' a dead body in *Midsomer Murders*. I was able to do it because it didn't involve any actual lines, just lying in a ditch, because, you know, corpse. Even then, every time the director called 'Action', The Thoughts kept coming: **I'M GOING TO START SINGING AND RUIN THE TAKE!**

for the sprogs she'd have with Mr Right. (Annie, Dot and Freddie.)

Meanwhile, Mum and Dad are on their once-in-a-lifetime cruise. Three months with no escape from each other. Bet they're fighting like rats in a sack.

Actually, it's their bickering I miss most – the way the house comes alive when we're all at home: me watching telly, Dad botching some DIY, Mum baking a cake. After they left, I managed two nights on my own then moved in with Nan in Walthamstow. She always makes me laugh. Last night, after her bedtime Baileys, she listened to me wanging on about Cockweasel, took out her teeth then said, 'The best way to get over a bloke is to get under a bloke.' I like her style. (Not sure about her dildo collection, but that's another story.)

RICHARD

Every family has secrets but ours has more than most. For instance, no one knows I'm on happy pills, and Tom has no idea why his mother took off for Goa, nor the slightest inkling about what she calls 'the stuff' and that's how it will stay.

Meanwhile, yours truly is keeping shtum about my depression. I can't risk the bosses at Silk FM thinking I'm anything other than the cheery soul I pretend to be between noon and 3 p.m., Monday to Friday.

If being a DJ was a daft way to make a living when I was nineteen, it's more so now. Still, it keeps me in Châteauneuf-du-Pape, even though my salary is half what it was in my heyday. Somehow, more niche radio stations and DJs equals more choice for listeners and advertisers but less £££ for the people behind the microphone. Unless you're on the A-list, which I can't help noticing I'm not.

Don't get me wrong, I'm not complaining. At the risk of sounding smug, the secret of professional contentment is simple: big fish, small pond. You get the kudos that comes with a modicum of celebrity (decent tables in restaurants, etc.) without the neurosis that seems to make the premier league behave like arseholes.

It's not a bad life. While most of London fights for a seat on the tube, I stroll through town, arriving at the studios around 10. Over coffee, my producer, Pam, and I scroll through the emails and select six problems submitted by listeners, one for each half hour of the show – anything from bereavements to broken hearts, from eating disorders to erectile dysfunction.

Or loneliness.

I've learned a lot about that subject this year. My shrink told me 'depression is anger with nowhere to go', so I told *her* where to go and now I'm saving enough money to buy a better class of vino.

After selecting the problems of the day, I make notes on sources of help and information – advice that has been known to rescue listeners from despair. According to letters I receive, it may even have saved a life or two. So it's a daft way to make a living but it does no harm – perhaps even a little good.

After prepping the *Dear Richard* emails, I leaf through the red tops, looking for showbiz gossip to sprinkle among the classics for which *The Richard Young Show* is known.

By rights, I should be on Radio 2 at this stage of the game. I'm too young to be working for what one snarky critic labelled 'Stairlift FM' but like all freelancers, I take what I can get. Besides, I've come to appreciate the likes of Frank

Sinatra, Ella Fitzgerald, Billie Holiday, Tony Bennett, Nina Simone et al. – giants whose talent will outlast even the best of today's so-called stars. Ed Sheeran? Adele? Gimme a break.

The session singers who recorded my jingles placed the emphasis on my last name (Richard *Young!*) which is why I chose a single-syllable surname when starting out. Let's face it, my real moniker was never going to catch on. Imagine the jingle.

Dick BROCKLEBANK!

I ditched the 'Dick', reverted to 'Richard' then toyed with other surnames.

Richard KNIGHT!

Richard PRINCE!

Richard LOVE!

Richard *Young!* won when Bonnie said she liked it. 'Young by name, young by nature.'

So that was that.

I'm not sure when I became 'the Agony Uncle of the Airwaves' but I suppose the nickname gives a USP to distinguish me from my fellow DJs, most of whom are little more than the human equivalent of a jukebox.

Even real talents such as Chris Evans pale alongside true originals like the late great Kenny Everett and, in his own daffy way, the indefatigable Tony Blackburn. Me, I'm halfway down the B-list and happy to muddle through to the final curtain. (Speaking of which, I promise not to have 'My Way' at my send-off. It's the most requested song at funerals. What is *wrong* with people?)

Assuming my ratings stay healthy, I'll soldier on till I drop at the mic. Welcome to the life of the DJ. Zero security and you're only as good as your last RAJAR figures.

As for what the doctor calls my 'low mood', losing my wife to a yoga teacher does little to boost serotonin levels. I haven't told Tom about his mother's affair and I doubt she's had the guts. Apparently, he's 'too sensitive'. Hmm ... He certainly behaves like a snowflake. He also dresses down, even at work, like Mark Zuckerberg without the billions. And if he says 'like' one more time ...

I know I haven't been fair on the boy – ignoring calls and emails, pretending to be out when the doorbell rings – but he's twenty-five, it's not my job to put a gloss on the world. Besides, going off the radar is more honest than pretending things are hunky-dory when they're not.

As for the rest of our so-called family, Bonnie's parents are no longer with us, neither is my mother, and it goes without saying that confiding in my father is out of the question. More anon, as they say.

I spend a lot of time hanging around the Silk FM studios, so I'm seldom alone for long, which is a blessing. The flat can seem very empty, the atmosphere as cheery as a launderette on a rainy Sunday night. Tom suggested a pet but I'm allergic to cats and dogs are too needy.

(I can hear Bonnie now. 'Pot meet kettle.')

If you believe her, I've never had a talent for friendship, one of my many shortcomings. Maybe she's right. It's not that I don't have ways of killing time. There's usually a PR bash in the evening – a book launch or a screening, some-where to scoff canapés so I needn't resort to the microwave every night – but I don't mind admitting: I miss having someone to do *nothing* with. As for women, I'm resigned to being invisible to the opposite sex. Unfairly, it happens to men later than women – around forty in my case – but it comes to us all and surely it's better to resign oneself to the inevitable than turn into one of those tragic Peter Pans, flirt-ing for England and trying to catch any passing eye in the hope of an ego boost.

(Incidentally, anything you want to know about ready meals, I'm your man. My favourite is Marks and Spencer's Scottish Lochmuir oak-smoked salmon topped with Pacific-fresh king prawns. I also have a soft spot for their moussaka: intricate layers of tender minced lamb, sliced potatoes and roasted auber-gines with a creamy béchamel sauce. I might write a book: *Ready Meals and Other Staging Posts on the Road to Hell*.)

I suppose there's a slim chance that Bonnie might come to her senses. Until then, there's *The Richard Young Show* to keep me from navel-gazing, plus a ton of extracurricular activities, like sifting through entries to the Voice of London compe-tition. Over the years, I've talent-spotted several successful wannabes, plucking their DJ demos from the slush pile, so when Transport for London asked if I'd judge the shortlist of entrants it seemed like what Tom would call a no-brainer.

Few people understand the importance of a voice. Its timbre – its character – is as unique as any fingerprint. Reactions to a voice can determine the course of a life: jobs you get, friends you make, people you fall for. When I met Bonnie she said mine sounded like 'honey on hot buttered toast'. God knows what she'd compare it to now. A worn-out Brillo pad?

Think about it. The voice you want to hear reading a bedtime story is different from the one you want whispering sweet nothings, and worlds apart from the voice you need ordering you to fasten your seatbelt and prepare for turbulence.

So far, my favourite Voice of London entry comes from an out-of-work actress who's making ends meet as a barista in a Dalston café. She sounds classy yet classless, calm yet authoritative, clever but not smart-arse. There's a husky quality to her voice that I find enticing. Apparently, her dream is to make the Hollywood big-time so she can buy her Nan a rose-covered cottage in the country.

No promises, my lovely, but if you're half as nice as you sound, you're very nice indeed. I'll put you at the top of the pile.

TOM

So before the shit hit the proverbial – before the con-man, the stolen diamonds and the skeleton in the family closet that made me re-think everything I knew – life was trundling along as you might expect for a twenty-five-year-old hack renting a one-bedroom flat in hipster central, aka vibrant, noisy, scruffy Dalston, spiritual home of sourdough, beards and bikes. Okay, my father was a DJ and I'd grown up in a posh part of London so maybe it wasn't the most normal upbringing but there was nothing to prepare me for the bombshell that would rock my world.

Looking back, it's weird how easily I came to accept everything that happened – how quickly it became the new normal. If I'd known then what I know now, would I have behaved the same? Would I have allowed myself to fall for an older woman with beautiful green eyes and a gorgeous voice? Who can say? I dabbled in philosophy at uni (a bid to impress girls) and as Kierkegaard said, 'Life can only be understood backwards but it must be lived forwards' and WTF is the use of that?

There was no time to ponder the mysteries of existence, however, because I was broke. I worked out that if I cut out my daily cappuccino I could save sixty quid a month – that's £750 per year. On the other hand, I wouldn't have the chance to talk to the woman in the New Dalston Café. I was chuffed when I realized Harriet no longer had to ask my name, she simply scrawled it on the cup when I sauntered in and started to banter.

If only it were that simple. I've never 'sauntered' in my life. I'm a loper. It's what tall people do – we lope. And when it came to 'bantz' I was no natural. The moment the alarm went off I'd start thinking about what I'd say to her but at the crucial moment, my head would fill with white noise and I'd blurt the first thing that came into my head. This morning was typical.

'Hi, Tom.' She flashed a smile over a freckled shoulder while setting a cup under the Gaggia. 'How's tricks?'

'So far, so good,' I said. Then came the brain-freeze. I couldn't stop myself spouting nonsense. 'But it's only eight o'clock so, like, anything could happen.'

I forgot the compliment I'd been honing since daybreak – the one about her voice sounding like music and her long, lustrous hair reminding me of polished conkers – so I had no choice but to go with the flow.

'Such as?' she said, smiling over her shoulder. (*That smile. I can't even.*)

'Sorry?' I said.

'You said "anything could happen". Like?'

I should have shut up but the idiot who controls my mouth decided this was the ideal moment to keep digging.

'Like a big ...' I tailed off. Harriet arched an eyebrow, still smiling as she frothed the milk. I carried on, hurtling towards disaster. 'Like a big ... truck crashing through the window and wiping us all out. Blood everywhere. Broken limbs. Maybe a decapitation.'

Her smile faltered. The woman behind me put a hand to her neck, as though feeling the truck's impact.

'Riiiiight,' said Harriet, drawing out the word.

You'd think I'd have the sense to shut up. Nope.

'Do you know what a palindrome is?' I said.

Her smile faltered. I was mansplaining.

'Let's see, could a palindrome be ... a word or phrase that reads the same backwards as forwards?'

I nodded.

'Like "madam",' I said.

'Or "kayak",' said Harriet.

'Kayak. Better than "madam". Much better.'

'Thanks, Tom.'

The smile had disappeared.

'Sorry,' I said. 'I don't mean to sound patronizing. It's just ...'

She finished frothing my cappuccino then set the cup on the counter and held my gaze.

'Just what?'

'I was wondering if you knew the waitress's palindrome.'

'No.'

I cleared my throat.

'"Stressed? No tips? Spit on desserts".'

'Very clever.'

She picked up the shaker, sprinkled cinnamon on the froth then snapped a lid onto my cup. 'Have a good day,' she said. 'And watch out for idiots driving those big trucks.'

'You too,' I said, making sure to include the woman behind me as my idiocy soared to Olympic heights. 'Let's hope we make it through the day without being decapitated.'

Harriet held up the card reader. I tapped my Visa and fled.

Outside, heading for the bus stop, I silently berated myself. I know how it looks but I'm not always a knob. I hold down a job, I survived uni without making a total idiot of myself, and I've been lucky enough to go out with some brilliant women. Five, if you want to know. Not that I'm counting. Well, obviously, I *am* counting but you know what I mean. I'm not sure what the definition of 'player' is but I'll never be one because I'm allergic to one-night-stands. I also remember one of the few pieces of advice my father gave me.

'When it comes to women, these are the priorities: kind, clever, funny, gorgeous – in that order.'

I can't pretend I always follow his edict – I'm twenty-five, FFS, there are nights when gorgeous seems like the most important thing – but he was right in principle. And the more I saw of the girl with green eyes, the more I thought she ticked all four boxes – and in the right order.

Dad was still off the radar, ignoring my calls and emails. But while I was outside the café, waiting for the bus and

21

sipping my coffee, I glimpsed his face on a poster for Silk FM. The ad was on a bus heading for Hampstead. I suddenly remembered an outing when I was a kid. He dragged me to the Hampstead Observatory: a big white dome on top of the hill; a giant telescope manned by blokes in bobble hats, queuing up to peer through the lens.

Before I could change my mind, I'd walked back into the café. Harriet was busy with a customer, a fit-looking bloke with a beard and backpack. She was laughing at something he said and I felt a powerful urge to punch him. They were talking about the London Marathon.

'You look *so* fit,' said the hipster. 'Are you running this year?'

Harriet shook her head, unleashing a cascade of curls.

'If God had meant us to run he would never have given us sofas.'

Beardie laughed. My urge to hit him reached new heights. I had an image of them kissing and felt a physical pain in my gut. After more lame banter he paid for his coffee and left. I positioned myself in Harriet's eye-line and took a deep breath.

'Me again,' I said. 'I think you're very cool. I only come in because I want an excuse to talk to you but I can't afford overpriced coffee every day. If you say no, I, like, totally get it, but is there any chance you might be free on Saturday night, and could you be arsed to come to Hampstead Observatory and look at Saturn? Well, not just Saturn, obviously – there are other planets – but Saturn is cool.'

Saturn is cool. FFS!

The silence seemed to last an age. She broke it with the worst sentence ever.

'You've got froth on your nose.'

My hand jerked to my face. I wiped the froth away then turned to leave, hoping the ground would open up and swallow me alive.

'Tom?'

I turned. She was smiling.

'Yes, I can be arsed.'

So that's that.

We're on for Saturday.

(Incidentally, I don't usually offer unsolicited advice but if I *did* it might include: don't take your cat to the vet on the day of a date. If she claws your face while you're putting her in the carrier you'll show up with a plaster across the bridge of your nose, which will make you look like a dick. Not just a dick – a dick's dick.)

HARRIET

I'd rather have gone to the pub. Not that I need to drink myself into oblivion because Cockweasel turned out to be *married with kids* (I'm *so* over Damian, as you can tell) but after a week of double shifts I'd have preferred a log fire and a cheeky bottle of red. Still, it's not every day a nice-looking bloke invites you to go star gazing and like Nan says – try everything once except incest, folk dancing and bin juice.

It turns out Hampstead Observatory is a ten-minute walk from the tube. The dome is near Whitestone Pond, set back from the road, almost hidden from view. It was a chilly evening in late October. A dozen nerd-wazzocks in anoraks were milling around the dome, taking turns to peer through the telescope. No sign of Extra Cinnamon Guy. For a moment, I wondered if I'd got the wrong date but then I saw him hurrying up the hill, waving. As he drew closer, I saw an Elastoplast on his face.

'What happened to your nose?'

'Let's just say my cat hates the vet.'

A cat. Tick.

Tattoo. Tick.

No aftershave. Double tick.

Especially after You-Know-Who, the one I'm not mentioning.

'What's your cat's name?'

'Nelson.'

'As in Horatio?'

'As in Mandela.'

Hmm. Bit too earnest for me?

'What's wrong with him?'

'He had a fight with the cat next door. And he's a she.'

'With a name like Nelson?'

'She was a rescue. They told me *she* was a *he* but she wouldn't let me pick her up for weeks so I couldn't take her for a check-up. By the time she trusted me enough I'd settled on Nelson. I can hardly change it now. Plus I don't want to saddle her with gender identity issues. She's been through enough.'

Sense of humour. Tick.

'How did you choose her?'

'I asked for the oldest cat, the one no one wanted to adopt.'

'Sweet.'

'Tell that to Nelson. She bites the hand that feeds – literally.'

'Maybe she needs a cat shrink.'

'Not on my salary.'

'What do you do?'

'Don't ask.'

'Why not?'

'Because I was going to get rich and famous writing musicals but ended up writing articles about double glazing.' He moved on swiftly, changing the subject. 'As for Nelson, I can hardly afford her elk meat let alone a shrink.'

'You feed elk meat to your cat?'

He nodded.

'Imported from Sweden. She won't eat anything else. Not even tuna unless it's fishmonger-fresh.'

'What kind of man won't give sushi-grade tuna to his cat? I'm not sure I should have come.'

'Pity. Saturn's gorgeous.'

He smiled and caught my eye. I thought he was going to say something cheesy like, 'so are you' but the moment passed. I followed his gaze to the skies. He pointed to a speck of light then told me waaaaaay more than I needed to know about Saturn. It's the sixth planet from the sun, apparently, the second largest in the solar system.

'There are nine rings.'

'Made of what?' I asked.

'Ice particles. And rocky debris and dust.'

'Space-dust? The stuff that fizzes on your tongue?'

He nodded, deadpan.

'They dig it out of space-dust mines then transport it from Saturn.'

Not scared to be silly. Tick.

I let him rattle on about astronomy, enjoying his enthusiasm. I like it when people talk about their passion.

'What sign are you?' I said.

'Rabies.'

A sceptic. Never mind. Most people are.

'I'm guessing you're Libran,' I said.

He arched an eyebrow.

'Nice trick.'

'I'm Aquarius. Highly intuitive. Also curious and prone to addiction.'

'Ri-ight.'

He didn't ask follow-up questions so I let the subject drop and made an effort to quell The Thoughts that leapt into my mind. **I'M GOING TO STRIP IN FRONT OF THESE MEN THEN HAVE SEX WITH ALL OF THEM!**

Luckily, the CBT woman told me sex can be a big part of intrusive thoughts, also weird ideas about religion, e.g., **WHAT IF I'M JESUS COME BACK TO EARTH AS A WOMAN?** But sexual identity is a common subject too, e.g., on my way here I thought **I WISH I HAD A STRAP-ON SO I COULD FUCK THAT WOMAN ON THE ESCALATOR** even though I haven't had a crush on another female since Chloe Mills wore spray-on black jeans in the school production of *Grease*. Some sufferers have horrible thoughts about harming children or being attracted to them but it doesn't mean they're baby-killers or paedophiles, it's just part of 'Pure OCD', also known as Pure O. With 'ordinary' OCD, people have compulsions and rituals, like washing their hands a zillion times, or not stepping on cracks in the pavement. With Pure O, instead of battling intrusive thoughts with actions, people like me try to minimize the stress by performing repetitive mental rituals, like counting down from a hundred to one before getting into a lift. It's usually a hidden disorder, so hard to treat, and some people go years without seeking help. So thank you for trying, CBT lady, but I'm no better than I was and the idea of telling Tom about it, or anyone else – even Nan – is a non-starter **AND MAKES ME WANT TO PUSH PEOPLE UNDER A TRAIN!**

Avoiding Tom's eye, I counted silently and slowly from ten down to one, composed myself then made a determined effort to shift my focus to the gaggle of astronomers. They wore fleeces, knitted hats and gloves.

'Do we get a go on the telescope or only if we have a woolly hat?' I said.

We joined the queue. Trying to keep my mind busy, I began to talk about how, in astrology, Saturn is the planet of concentration, tenacity and ambition.

'When it moves into your sign it brings success. So next year is going to be busy for me.'

'In the café?' said Tom.

'No, I'm an actress. The café pays the bills.'

'I know the feeling,' he said. 'The day-job's keeping me going till my musical opens on Broadway and I'm a Tony-award-winning millionaire.'

'What could possibly go wrong?'

'I know, right?'

'Is it a big cast, like *Hamilton* or *Les Misérables*?'

He shook his head.

'It's a six-hander about dysfunctional families. It's called "They Fuck You Up".'

'From the Larkin poem?'

He seemed pleased I'd got the reference but I was glad he didn't make a big deal out of my knowing a bit of poetry. Cockweasel used to take the piss, as if a girl from Walthamstow had no business knowing anything except dog racing and jellied eels.

'Would I have seen you in anything?' said Tom.

My least favourite question, especially since The Thoughts put paid to me going to auditions.

'Doubt it. Unless you watch *EastEnders*.'

'Are you in it now?'

'No, I was the love interest for one of the regulars a couple of years ago. They gave me a character arc. Six weeks.'

He was about to ask another question when one of the bobble hats told us it was our turn on the telescope.

To be honest, five minutes was enough. Don't get me wrong, I loved the rings and learning that Saturn is named after the Roman god of agriculture, but when it comes to freezing my arse off, a little goes a long way.

Luckily, Tom felt the same, or maybe he was being polite, because it wasn't long before he told me he'd booked a restaurant – two, in fact – and did I prefer sushi or Italian? When I picked option B, he phoned the Japanese place to cancel, so he's A) organized and B) knows how to behave like a gent, unlike some fuck-trumpets I could mention.

Tick, tick, tick.

The restaurant was full of Saturday night couples. Two well-groomed guys sat at the next table, negotiating the end of their relationship and arguing over which of them would get custody of the tropical fish. All very Hampstead.

Tom said he'd grown up nearby (posh boy!) but now lives in Dalston, which is why he keeps coming into the café. His mum owned a minicab company but it went bust when Uber took over the world so she's on a yoga sabbatical to 'find herself' in Goa. I said I loved yoga and had been meaning to go backpacking in India but never found the right travelling companion.

'Why not go alone?' said Tom.

'Not my style.'

'I've been loads of places on my own,' he said. 'America, Vietnam, Cambodia. I'm a bit of a loner.'

'As in, "the shooter was a loner and loved his mum deeply"?'

He smiled.

'As in, I like doing stuff on my own.'

'No, you don't,' I said.

'Sorry?'

'People say they like it because it sounds cool but they're kidding themselves. An experience is only worth having if it's shared.'

'I must remember that.'

I thought I'd pissed him off but he was still smiling. I'd almost forgotten the plaster on his nose. We talked families. His mum was a workaholic till she discovered yoga. His granddad, 'Gorgeous' George, sounded like what Nan would call a ladies' man. As for his father, Tom hardly mentioned him, except to say their relationship was 'tricky'. All through school and uni, nothing was good enough.

'I'd get an A and he'd say, "What's wrong with A-plus?"' A muscle tightened in his jaw. 'Sometimes he'd hardly speak to me for months. Once, he ignored Mum for a whole year.'

'Seriously?'

'Not a word.'

'What's she like?'

'Complicated. Bipolar.'

'Manic depression?'

He shook his head.

'That's what they used to call it. Now it's "bipolar disorder". She's fine till she forgets her meds. Then things get out of hand.'

'Such as?'

He thought for a moment. 'She once turned up at sports day with, like, a hundred ice creams, one for every kid.'

'I bet you were popular.'

'Yes, till she stripped off and insisted on taking part in the egg and spoon race. She tried to convince everyone else to get naked, too. The teachers bundled her into the staff room and phoned Dad. I think she took an overdose that night – she went off in an ambulance – but they never talked about it . . . at least, not to me.' He sighed. 'There are tons of examples of her having an "episode" but Naked Sports Day is the one I remember best.'

Understands mental health issues. Tick.

'How come they've lasted?' I said.

He shrugged.

'They live pretty separate lives. I'm not sure we were ever a family or just people under the same roof. Plus I think Dad probably . . .' He tailed off, running a finger around the rim of his wine glass.

'Probably what?'

'Had affairs. They argued a lot when I was young.'

'About other women?'

A shrug.

'I don't know for sure, but he's a good-looking dude and loves women so I wouldn't be surprised.'

'My dad's a pussycat,' I said, then wished I hadn't. It sounded like showing off. I stopped myself from telling him about the night Dad phoned Cockweasel and threatened to tell his wife about me unless he stopped texting and left me the fuck alone. Long story short, I calmed Dad down. No sense making a bad situation worse, IMHO, and the less Wifey knew the better. Not that I'm trying to keep the door open or anything.

All in all, it was a nice evening – just what I needed. I offered to pay my way, obvs, but Tom wouldn't hear of it.

Tick.

'I'll get the next one,' I said.

'It's a deal.'

So, the million-pound question: do I fancy him? Yep. He's my type, and best of all, he knows how to listen. As for the age difference, would anyone raise the issue of a bloke fancying a woman ten years his junior? No, so let's not even. Pity I'm not up for romance at the moment. I'm over Cockweasel but there's no need to prove it by sleeping with some random. Like Nan says: a bit of time on my own will do me good. (Just last week, she asked if I thought *she* should go on Tinder. I was like, no way! She's seventy-five, all those dick pics would finish her off.)

It was only as I clocked the Silk FM poster on the bus home that I remembered I hadn't mentioned the email from one of their DJs. A bloke called Richard Young. Seems I've been longlisted for the Voice of London thingamajig. I'll tell Tom next time I see him – assuming there *is* a next time. I'll check the forecast for Aquarius and see what's on the horizon.

RICHARD

Old saying: one of the best feelings in the world is to do a good deed anonymously and have it discovered by accident. Well, let's see if putting Harriet Brown on the Voice of London longlist turns out to be a good deed. If not, I'll keep shtum about having cast the deciding vote. (The Transport for London marketing people were more enthusiastic about a Streatham woman who works in a call centre but I turned the charm up to eleven and talked them round.)

Sometimes I try to work out how people *look* based on how they sound on the radio then check Google Images to see if I'm right. I'm seldom wide of the mark and was spot on in the case of two of the twelve finalists. The TfL PR woman brought them into the studios for what she called 'a mingle', so we could get their measure. Quality of voice aside, were they people who could, in PR-speak, be 'ambassadors for London's transport network'? Whatever *that* means.

By the time they arrived, I'd narrowed the field to three front-runners and checked them out online. They were younger than typical Silk FM listeners, who are chiefly ABC1 baby boomers with a taste for crooners and a fondness for the good old days (as if they ever existed). What with Spotify, Alexa, podcasts and all the other alternatives just a click away it's a miracle radio survives but somehow we dinosaurs soldier on.

Samira Khan from Croydon was as vivacious as she sounded, exactly matching the image in my mind's eye. Likewise Acton's Andy Smith: short, round and smiley. The one who surprised me was Harriet Brown from Walthamstow. Having been impressed by her entry (she read a Shakespeare sonnet, a bold choice) I'd visualized a plump woman with short blonde hair. How wrong can you be? It turns out that Harriet is slim with long brown hair and a lovely smile that put me in mind of Julia Roberts. She's in her mid-thirties, an actress–slash–singer working double shifts in a café while waiting for her career to take off.

Not to be the voice of doom but how many performers get a break after thirty? Yet Harriet Brown is still plugging away, hoping for the role that will see her name in lights, so she can say, 'Told you so!'

As per the arrangement with the TfL PR, I recorded brief interviews with all twelve contenders. The plan was to give listeners a chance to judge their personalities as well as their voices then open the premium-rate phone-in vote, which rakes in a ton of cash for Silk FM.

Posing for photos, I made sure to stand next to Harriet. I only just managed to stop myself asking the name of her perfume.

After the photographer left, the PR woman swore all the contestants to secrecy, reminding them it was vital to keep quiet about being longlisted until the official campaign launch next week. I lingered longer than planned, making small talk, but it was Harriet I was drawn to, probably because of her lack of bullshit. Unlike the other contenders, she didn't pretend to be a regular listener. In fact, she apologized for not recognizing my name.

'I only found out about the competition through a poster on the bus.'

'No need to apologize,' I said. 'It's just a matter of time before we welcome you to the Silk FM family. Ol' Blue Eyes gets everyone in the end. Well, everyone with a soul.'

Turned out the only Sinatra song she knew properly was 'My Way'. Can you believe it? The worst thing he ever recorded. I told her she should check out 'One For My Baby' the second she got home. I'm not sure why I happened to mention that particular song – maybe it suited my mood – but she surprised me by whisking out her iPhone and finding it on Spotify. There followed a peculiar scene: me, Harriet Brown and the other finalists standing in the Silk FM boardroom, sipping cheap white wine while listening to one of the most melancholy songs ever recorded.

I could see she liked it. Roly-poly Andy Smith started to make jokes, just as that blissful piano intro crept in ('Music to slash your wrists by,' he quipped) and she shushed him, which was brave. Then she insisted on listening to all four minutes and twenty-four seconds in respectful silence.

She was clearly moved by the lyrics. She may even have welled up. Perhaps she was feeling a bit raw, like me, or maybe she's just one of those people whose emotions are too close to the surface. Stealing a glance in her direction, I definitely felt a connection. As if I'd known her for years.

Odd.

Very odd indeed.

'You're my kind of girl,' I told her as the song ended, then immediately regretted calling her a 'girl'. Very non-PC. Before I knew it, I was fretting about sounding like a lecher. I found myself looking into her eyes (green, soulful) and wondering if a fifteen-year age-gap is really such a big deal and whether I should invite her out for a drink.

Luckily, I told myself to stop being an idiot. Number one, I'm married (well, technically). Number two, I'm too old for her, even assuming she's single. Number three, I've never been good at chatting up women. It's one thing sounding like a smoothie on the radio, quite another being a ladies' man in real life.

I knew Bonnie would tell me off for thinking this way.

'Women don't like smooth, they like *real*.'

Then again, my own wife would hardly be offering me dating advice. Or would she? Given the circumstances, perhaps it's the least she could do.

It was raining so I took a taxi home. (God knows why I keep the Jag; I hardly use it.) The flat seemed chillier than usual, emptier too. Sitting at the oak table, I looked around the kitchen. The granite worktops, the range cooker, the butler's sink, the recessed lighting subtly illuminating cupboards filled with Anthropologie tableware, the Rothko prints – all chosen by Bonnie in happier times. Taking a supper tray into the book-lined sitting room, I sat in my favourite Charles Eames chair and watched a couple of *Seinfeld*s while polishing off a bottle of Merlot and toying with an M&S *champignons en croute* (mushrooms in a sherry and spinach sauce wrapped in flaky puff pastry).

Only as I was brushing my teeth did I notice anything odd. The loo seat was raised. I'd learned long ago never to leave it up for fear of triggering a spat with Bonnie.

'Will you please *remember to put the seat down?'*

'Or you could put it down when you use the loo. I'm a man, I *need it raised.'*

'It looks better down.'

'It's a loo seat. Who cares what it looks like?'

'I bloody do!'

Trivial, I know, but the point is, leaving the seat down was the norm around here, which meant there were two possibilities: either I'd forgotten (highly unlikely) or someone had been in the flat.

I had a shrewd idea who. Time to change the locks.

GEORGE

I'd never call my son stupid but only someone afflicted by hopeless naïveté would leave a key under the mat, especially in London. You never knew who might get a copy made so they can pop in for a pit stop while you're playing records and talking *merde* on the radio.

Since my return from Palm Springs I'd been immersed in a new 'project'. Her name was Imelda Shine. She was eighty, like me, but smelt of money, a fragrance that always has a rejuvenating effect, shaving off years, sometimes decades. (Some 'ladies who lunch' prefer a younger gentleman; others are happier with a man their own vintage – someone who remembers rationing and the Coronation.)

I'd first met Imelda in Monte Carlo. She was mourning the loss of her billionaire husband (big in oil, I gather) and making a magnificent job of it, selflessly spending long hours at the roulette table. It wasn't so much her svelte figure that caught my eye as the insouciance with which she took losses in her stride: tens of thousands lost on a spin of the wheel were met with a shrug. An impressive display of sangfroid. My kind of gal.

The widow Shine was one of those people for whom summer is a verb, as in, 'I summer in Positano'. Our first tête-a-tête, in a hilariously expensive harbour-side restaurant, was memorable for the way she ordered three Dover sole: one for herself, the other two expertly filleted by a white-gloved waiter for the benefit of four stray cats. She was amused by my spectacles – *actual* rose-tinted glasses – and I was delighted by everything she said. Dinner led to coffee in her suite at the Hôtel de Paris, then breakfast, and the rest, as they say, is history.

On her annual return to London, at the end of September, Imelda invariably took up residence in her suite at the Savoy. This year, she invited me to move in for what she called 'fun and frolics in the last chance saloon'. Despite being born and bred in an insalubrious part of London, my favourite words have always been 'room service' so it seemed churlish to decline, especially since she refused to allow me to put my hand in my pocket for anything except a little blue pill. (*Merci*, Pfizer; may your share price rise as reliably as my honourable member.)

As Blanche DuBois didn't say, I've always depended on the kindness of strangers' widows. Some people, my son included, disapprove, but I like to think I provide a service as essential to the wellbeing of my benefactresses as the phalanx of doormen, chauffeurs and concierges who cater to their every whim; the legions of hairdressers, manicurists and dress designers who send them into the world feeling good about themselves; and the battalions of cruise ship's captains, waiters and maîtres d' whose unctuous smiles reassure them that their arrival is the highlight of the year.

Years ago, Richard accused me of having no conscience. When I insisted that nothing in my career had caused me to lose a minute's sleep he informed me that I was a sociopath, something I found laughable.

But when I committed a transgression that even I had to admit was beyond the pale (don't worry, all will be revealed) I was forced to take an unflinching look at myself and didn't like what I saw. In a moment of weakness, I'd recently drunk-emailed Richard at Silk FM, hoping to elicit some kind of response, whilst knowing he'd ignore me, as he had for twenty years. I remember thinking how much simpler everything would have been were I a Catholic. A spot of mumbo-jumbo, a wafer on the tongue and I'd have been off the hook for all eternity.

Still, as Lady Macbeth nearly says, 'What's done is done and cannot be undone,' and there's nothing to be gained by looking in life's rear-view mirror. For me, the only way is to keep moving forward, like a shark, and dedicate myself to pulling off one last job, the Big One – an adventure that would finally allow me to put my feet up and dispense with those little blue pills once and for all.

Which is why I'd told Imelda I was off to South America, 'doing some hush-hush scouting for an old pal in the mining industry'. My four-week no-show in London served two purposes. As everyone knows, absence makes the heart grow fonder so it's only sensible to create an artificial scarcity of oneself. The clandestine nature of my supposed trip also set the scene for the ruse that was to come. Imelda, of course, had no idea that my 'travels' would take me no further than Rochester House in Camden, where my old mucker, Paddy, kindly provided a bolthole anytime I needed a place to lay my *chapeau*. I'd have preferred somewhere more salubrious but the truth is, without the generosity of the widow Shine and her ilk I don't have two brass farthings to rub together. The state pension barely keeps me in Grecian 2000.

Now, after a month of lying low, I was 'back in town' and looking forward to 'the big one'.

(So, apparently, was Mrs Shine. Boom-tish. I'm here all week.)

TOM

Bad day at the office. The new editor, Colin, emailed asking for a 'road map of your work-in-progress and your focus going forward'. Mate, just ask for an update, like an actual human. I know I should find another job. This one pays a pittance and the work makes me want to cut off my typing fingers, but finding the courage to quit isn't easy.

As a rule, I'm, like, conscientious to a fault and never late for work, or anything else. Two, maybe three times in my whole life. I can't bear to keep people waiting. I knew a girl at uni. She was studying psychology and told me I was neurotic about punctuality because my dad froze me out as a kid and was a stickler for timekeeping. Apparently, I'd learned not to anger him in a bid to win his approval. My goody-two-shoes behaviour was rooted in a deep-seated fear of abandonment, blah blah blah. I told her, 'He's a difficult sod but he'd never abandon me.'

'You're missing the point,' she said. 'He already did. Everything you do – passing exams, phoning regularly, letting him win at tennis – it's about one thing: trying to get your father to love you.'

At the time it sounded not only stupid but also pathetic. Still, her words have stayed with me – the way things do when a nerve is touched – and I wonder if she had a point. Maybe I try to be a halfway decent son because I'm hoping he'll finally take notice. Maybe that's why I'm trying to write a musical. It's logical, when you think about it. I grew up around a man who loves music but seldom showed affection. If I can write songs he likes, maybe he'll like me, too. Could it be that simple?

I kept my head down all morning and drafted articles on prospects for self-cleaning glass and the boom in aluminium composites and foiled PVCU caused by householders deciding to improve rather than move, and please kill me now. The *Double Glazing Monthly* office is open-plan – five women, Colin and me. Mostly, we rub along okay, except when the pressure is on and he turns into the boss from hell. Then we all start googling job ads and I fantasize about quitting and working for Deliveroo while working on the musical full time. I'm no Stephen Sondheim or Lin-Manuel Miranda but I *am* doing my best to be a one-man-band – writing the music, lyrics and book myself. Sometimes I wish I had a collaborator – I'd be more productive with someone spurring me on – but for now I'm trying to be Andrew Lloyd-Webber, Tim Minchin and Richard Stilgoe, all rolled into one.

If you're thinking, 'Who is Richard Stilgoe?' you've

nailed the fate of the unsung heroes of musical theatre. He wrote the librettos for *Starlight Express* and *The Phantom of the Opera* but all the kudos went to Andrew Lloyds-Bank. Nevertheless, Stilgoe made a fortune, donating huge earnings from *Starlight Express* to a village in India. So far, my own feeble attempts at philanthropy extend no further than the teetering pile of *Big Issues* in my manky bathroom, but I'm only twenty-five, so there's time to save the world – if only I didn't have to spend my life churning out copy on double-sodding-glazing.

At midday I snuck into the toilet and listened to the opening of the old man's show. He seemed to be alive and kicking. One less thing to worry about. For some reason, my mind wandered to all the things Mum had taught me – the everyday life-lessons a father might teach his son. Tying shoelaces. Crossing the road. Riding a bike. How to swim. How to use a knife and fork. Chopsticks. Tying a tie. A bow-tie. How to shave. There's a movie cliché that always makes me wince: a boy watches his dad shaving then copies him, covering his face with foam and pretending to shave his 'bristles'. Not in our house. I learned by watching Mum shave her legs.

After lunch, I proofread a double-page spread on product certification in the PVCU window and doorframe market, resisting the urge to stab my eyeballs with a fork. Finally, I pinged my 'road map' into Colin's inbox before clearing off on the dot of 5.30 while he was in a meeting with the organizers of the Glass Industry Awards Dinner, to be held at the Basildon Marriott.

I hadn't planned on going to the New Dalston Café but the prospect of solitary spag bol followed by a fruitless evening working on *They F**k You Up* filled me with gloom so I took a chance on Harriet being at work – and she was.

The café was empty, the muffins all gone. She seemed pleased to see me, gave me a latte on the house then carried on cleaning up. I offered to mop the floor but she laughed, said it was specialist work and I'd only mess it up. (God, I love how she laughs.) While she mopped, she told me there might be good news on the work front but that she'd been sworn to secrecy. Something to do with some kind of voice-over about London but it sounded like more than just an ad. I asked her to keep me posted. She said she would, which I took as a good omen.

She also said yes to a drink so I waited while she closed up then helped to pull down the shutters. It began to drizzle. I fished an umbrella from my backpack.

'What are you, ninety?' she said. 'It's only rain.'

But she didn't object when I sheltered her under the brolly. We made our way along the traffic-choked high street to a basement bar where they serve the finest cocktails Dalston has to offer and play jazz from the forties and fifties.

Settling at a corner table, she asked if I was a jazz fan. I told her I'd had a bellyful growing up but the classics were hard to beat. She asked about my childhood but the waiter arrived to take our order (mojito for her, negroni for me) and the moment passed.

Besides, I was more interested in talking about Harriet. Her father owns two greengrocers in Bow; her mum is a social worker and midwife. Both worked long hours while she was growing up so she's close to her widowed grandmother. Now in her seventies, it was Nancy, aka Nan, who gave young Harriet tea after school, supervised homework and encouraged her to apply to drama school. She still works part-time as a dinner lady. They live near each other in Walthamstow and Harriet's staying at her house while her parents are on a cruise.

'What does your family think of you being an actress?'

She looped a strand of hair behind her ear. I love the way she does that.

'Nan's cool about it,' she said, 'but Mum and Dad think I'm nuts. They take the mickey out of the way I speak.'

'Why?'

'They say I'm posh. Compared to them I suppose I am.' She sipped her drink and grinned. 'Not as posh as you, though.'

'I'm not remotely posh.'

'Says Mr Belsize Park. And "remotely" is a posh word.'

'You're confusing me with my father. Belsize Park is his manor, not mine.'

The grin widened. 'Nice use of "manor", posh boy. What meal do you eat in the middle of the day?'

'Lunch.'

'Nan eats dinner, which is what you eat in the evening, right?'

'Or supper,' I said.

'What's the difference?'

'Dinner is eaten with other people – friends or guests, not just family. At a dining table. Supper you eat at the kitchen table.'

'With guests or family?'

'Either. Then it's "kitchen supper".'

'What's it called if you eat on your own?'

'Pot Noodle.'

She laughed.

'Why do we make everything so complicated?' I drew breath to respond but she answered her own question. 'Because we're English and messed-up.' She took another sip of her drink. 'I ironed out my accent before I went to drama school. It wasn't a posh one. They took ordinary kids, like me.'

There's nothing ordinary about you . . .

Another drink and I might have said it but I held back. You'd have been proud of me.

'I started lessons when I was nine,' she said. 'After school and Saturdays. Bloody loved it.'

She reeled off names of famous alumni of the theatre school, including Amy Whitehouse, a Spice Girl and an actress who appears in the sort of Sunday evening dramas Mum loved before she became obsessed with yoga and started going out every night.

'When I'm famous I'll go back to the school and teach kids like me,' she said, swirling ice around her glass. 'I'll give them an endowment. "The Harriet Brown Award for Most Promising Newcomer".'

I gave an encouraging nod. A half-forgotten line of poetry

floated into my mind, one of Dad's favourites. 'Ah, but a man's reach should exceed his grasp or what's a heaven for?' Don't worry, I know better than to spout Browning on a date. But there was no denying it – she was definitely giving me all the feels.

We started talking about how weird it was that neither of us was checking our phones every five seconds or posting pictures of our drinks. Turned out she hates social media as much as I do – well, almost.

'It's for old people,' I said.

She raised an eyebrow, amused rather than offended.

'Like me?'

I felt my cheeks burn.

'That's not what I meant. I was just . . .'

She reached out and put a hand on my arm.

'I'm kidding. Relax.'

I sipped my drink, playing for time.

'What's your number one ambition?' I said.

She shrugged.

'Do good work, stay solvent. That's all any actress wants.'

The waiter was hovering, on the verge of trying to blag us into ordering another round but at a tenner a pop the answer was 'no'.

'Feel like something to eat?' I said. 'My spag bol could teach Jamie Oliver a thing or two.'

'I'm vegetarian,' said Harriet.

'I'll do veggie lasagne. Ricotta, courgette, mozzarella, mushrooms.'

She downed the last of her cocktail and let me down with a smile.

'I don't think so.'

I tried not to feel crushed.

'Okay, no problem.'

'Ask me another time?'

Result!

Feeling the adrenaline surge, I remembered the opening scene in my musical: a young couple on a riverside picnic, still at the starry-eyed phase of romance. A sideways glance, a quickening of the pulse.

This is how it begins . . .

I left a decent tip and we walked up the rickety staircase, back to the real world. I stood aside, letting her go first.

'Thank you, kind sir.'

Outside, the drizzle was heavier but there was now a glamour to the rain-slicked streets. The neon lights were brighter, the colours sharper. Harriet turned up her collar.

'Thanks for the drink.'

I handed her the umbrella.

'Pretend you're ninety.'

Smiling, she hesitated before taking it and walking away. Then she stopped, walked back and planted a kiss on my cheek.

''Night, Extra Cinnamon Guy.'

She turned and hurried away, leaving behind a trace of perfume and a surge of desire. I watched her round the corner then strolled home, enjoying the feeling of the rain on my face. Earlier, the air had been cold and dank, now it felt crisp and clear, and the world was a shining, golden palace and I was winning at life. As I turned the key in the door, I realized I was humming an old Nat King Cole song, one I must have heard on Dad's show. 'When I Fall in Love'.

HARRIET

I was having fun till he mentioned spag bol, Cockweasel's favourite. Silly how something like that can crash my mood, especially as I hardly think about you-know-who any more. It's weeks since I found out about Wifey. You have to feel sorry for her. Not only is she married to a lying shit-pouch but her name is Candida and who names a kid after a yeast infection?

Damian (aka Cockweasel) always said he preferred home cooking to eating out. I thought he was just a typical Leo but now I realize he was not only a cheapskate, he didn't want to risk being seen in public. Sometimes, usually just after we'd had sex, he'd murmur in my ear. 'We're in our own bubble, babe. You and me against the world.'

No, 'babe'. Turns out it's you and *her* against the world. She's got herself a handsome maxillofacial surgeon (me neither – it's part dentist, part plastic surgeon) and I've a hole where my heart used to be.

Truth is, it's shaken my confidence, which was already

pretty fragile. Not just my faith in men (that's been rocky ever since Mum caught the Saturday girl giving Dad a blow job in the store room) but in myself. If I can be so wrong about a person maybe I'm wrong about everything. Maybe I'll never get rid of The Thoughts or find a decent bloke. (Would it have killed him to say those three little words, just once?) As for wasting two years of prime fertility, don't get me started or I'll end up banging on about Annie, Dot and Freddie who, even though they have yet to be born, are my only hope of making my mark in this world.

Maybe The Thoughts are God's way of telling me I'm wasting my time trying to be an actress. Maybe I should get a proper job. What if I'm one of those wannabes who keeps ignoring reality, plugging away till menopause then jacking it in and re-training as a yoga teacher – like the world needs more of *those*.

Actually, I love yoga. As well as CBT I've tried pretty much everything to get rid of The Thoughts – from herbal remedies like kava and chamomile to nutraceuticals (me neither) like magnesium and inositol; from beta blockers to breathing-control apps. If they do the trick for other people, whoopsie-do, but what works best for me is yoga. Mum and I go to a studio opposite the park in Stoke Newington. It's a fair old hike but we have tea in the café afterwards and look at the deer in the enclosure. 'A bit of girl-time,' Mum calls it. 'Exercise and cake. Perfect combo.'

Last time we talked about my so-called love life. She gave me the body-clock lecture – *again* – and I got pissed off.

Especially when she trotted out that rubbish statistic – the one about women who aren't married by thirty growing warts and being burned at the stake. FFS, how many times? Kids, yes. Husband, meh.

So I had an audition yesterday, the first for ages. I'd hardly slept and was tempted to back out but my agent would have been pissed off so I made myself go through with it, even though The Thoughts were threatening to get out of hand like **I'M A WORTHLESS, TALENTLESS FRAUD AND NO ONE LIKES ME AND THE MOMENT I GET ONSTAGE I'M GOING TO WET MYSELF!**

The job was in Guildford, a production of *Macbeth*. I wasn't up for a big part, just one of the three witches, but by the time I got to the theatre I was sweating buckets and must have looked as if I was coming down with flu. I sat in a stuffy little room with two other actresses. (Yes, I know some people use 'actor' for both sexes, but it's always sounded a bit daft to me so I stick to 'actress'.) Anyway, they were chatting away and trying to include me but I answered in monosyllables and couldn't stop shivering so they gave up. They went first, called by the director's assistant, Michael. I went to the loo, twice, but couldn't stop The Thoughts so by the time he came back for me I was a wreck. Silently repeating my mantra ('fake it till you make it'), I forced myself to walk onstage and peer out into the auditorium. The director consulted her clipboard and smiled.

'Harriet Brown, is it?'

'Yes.'

I'M GOING TO WET MYSELF!

She asked a couple of banal questions, designed to settle my nerves, but I couldn't tell you what I said in response because **THE THOUGHTS THE THOUGHTS THE FUCKING THOUGHTS.**

'Thanks for coming,' she said. 'Ready when you are.'

I cleared my throat and took a breath. What I *should* have said was, 'When shall we three meet again, in thunder lightning or in rain?' What I *actually* said was:

'Um ... Er ...'

I'M GOING TO PISS MY PANTS!

The director raised an eyebrow.

'Sorry,' I said. 'Um ...'

She looked down at her clipboard.

'You're reading for the witch, right?'

'Yes ...'

BUT I'M GOING TO WET MYSELF, OR MAYBE WORSE ...

'Okay, Harriet. No pressure. In your own time.'

Which is when I said it.

'I'm sorry ... I just can't ...'

I walked offstage and ran out of the theatre and all the way to the station and waited for a train then a tube and made it back to Nan's and told her I was fine, just tired, and shut myself in the spare room, flung myself on the bed and sobbed into my pillow for an hour.

*

I saw a documentary about people like me. One bloke stabbed himself in the head, trying to stop the voices. Another jumped off a motorway bridge. FFS!

Later that same day, I tried to get hold of my agent, to apologize. Didn't go well.

'Hi, it's Harriet calling for Graham.'

'Sorry, who?'

'Harriet Brown. I'm a client?'

'Oh, right, sorry.'

'Who am I talking to?' I said.

'Sasha. Graham's new executive assistant. Sorry, I'm still familiarizing myself with his list.'

'No problem. Is he there?'

'Oh. I thought he'd, like, told everyone? He went to Colombia this morning.'

'Colombia?'

'He's getting married? To Pablo.'

'Oh.'

'Exciting, right? *Love* Cartagena.'

'Did he mention anything about me before he went?'

'In what way?'

'An audition? For *Macbeth* in Guildford? Or any voice-over work?'

'He didn't say anything but I'll ask him to give you a call when he's back.'

'How long is he away?'

'A month. Honeymoon all over South America.'

'Great. I'm very happy for him.'

'Totally. And don't worry, he checks in all the time.'

'Good to know.'

I asked her to tell him about the Voice of London competition. She didn't sound impressed. But it was the way she ended the conversation that made my heart sink.

'Sorry, would you mind repeating your name?'

NO PROBLEM, RIGHT AFTER I COME TO THE OFFICE AND SET FIRE TO YOUR HAIR!

Nan's not feeling great. She had a fall while I was working at the café. Nothing too serious but I could see she was going to be a bit wobbly for the next couple of days. Mum and Dad Skyped from the ship. They're in Malaysia. Next stop: Hong Kong then Vietnam then God knows where. I told Mum I'm watering her plants but have started kipping in Nan's spare room, in case she needs me in the night. She's old-school; there's no way she'd call an ambulance just for a fall.

'Wouldn't want to put them to all that bother, darlin'. Anyway, I forget the number.'

'What number, Nan?'

'Nine-nine-nine.'

'That *is* the number.'

'What is?'

'The number – if you need an ambulance.'

'Who does?'

'Who does what?'

'Need an ambulance.'

'Not me, but you might.'

'Says who?'

'Never mind, Nan. Fancy a film?'

'Now you're talking. *Psycho*?'

As for Tom, he seems old-school in his own way. Nice manners. Opens doors. Lends you his brolly. I bet he'd drape his jacket over your shoulders if you were cold. And not only is he a good listener, he laughs at my jokes, which makes a change from the piss-wizard. Seems lots of men feel threatened by potty-mouthed, funny women. God knows why. You'd think laughs would be a priority when deciding, 'Is this the person I want to watch staring at their phone for the rest of my life?' Which is another tick for Tom: he never fiddles with his mobile when he's with me, not once. On the other hand, you'd have to be *seriously* loved-up to marry someone with a surname like Brocklebank. I can imagine Dad's wedding speech.

Congratulations Mr and Mrs Bottle-bank . . .

Okay, I know I sound like a love-struck kid, and no, I'm not practising signing my married name but I've always had a fast-forward button in my head when it comes to blokes. Can't help it. I have a tendency to skip ahead to see what might be around the corner. Or who. (Would Tom say 'whom'? Must check.)

If he shows up again, that's cool, but I'm not bothered. Staying at Nan's means I'm not lonely. Plus, I've plenty of stuff to think about, like should I try and find a new agent or would that just be rearranging deckchairs on the *Titanic*? Above all, how am I going to stop The Thoughts from sabotaging my career, not to mention the rest of my life? That's the shit thing about being single – no one to chew things over with. Nan's great but career advice isn't her thing, especially showbiz. She thinks it's all premieres with Bradley Cooper but the reality is more panto with Bradley Wiggins – if you're lucky.

To her way of thinking, I hit the big-time when I played a dead barmaid in *Midsomer Murders*. Six hours in a ditch while proper actors got to do actual acting with *actual dialogue*. The bluebottle wrangler kept bringing more and more flies. Six thousand bluebottles. Hundreds of maggots. Who says show-biz isn't glamorous?

At least it was something for the CV. Right now, there's sod all else on the horizon except frothing cappuccinos for hipsters who can't be arsed to make eye contact.

But then, just when you think it's all doom and gloom, along comes something that makes you shout 'plot twist!' and feel one of those bursts of optimism that keeps you dreaming of Hollywood long after any sensible person would have given up.

I'd left my phone in my jeans so it wasn't till I got back to Nan's that I found the email from Richard Young, the DJ at Silk FM. I'm sworn to secrecy but I've made the Voice of London shortlist! Apparently I mustn't tell a soul until the winner is announced so obviously I told Nan straightaway. She was chuffed, even though she didn't really understand what it meant.

'So ... you'll be a station announcer? "Next train to Clapham Junction platform eleven" – all that malarkey?'

'Not exactly, Nan, no.'

Sitting in her cosy kitchen, I explained that if I win it would mean recording the announcements for all the buses and tubes.

'It's a voice-over job. Probably take a few days to record all the variations. Just me and a producer in a studio, like recording an ad, which I can handle without freaking out.'

'Oh. So not really a proper job.'

'Depends what you mean by "proper".'

'One you go to, Monday to Friday. With wages.'

'No, not like that.'

'Oh, well – never mind.'

'You don't sound too happy.'

'If you're happy, darlin', I'm happy. Just don't give up the day-job.'

I hate to admit it but she's right. Still, it looks like I might be in with a chance. It was only when I re-read the email that I noticed Richard's PS. *Congratulations! May I take you to lunch to celebrate?*

He's given me his personal email address. Isn't that nice?

RICHARD

Oh, for heaven's sake, where's the harm in lunch?

Harriet's email was polite but made it clear she couldn't take time off during the week. I'd planned on leaving it there but something got into me, possibly the third glass of prosecco at the publishing party for a book on super-yachts. In the last two weeks, I've endured PR bashes for a computer game (never play them), a slasher film (asleep after ten minutes) and the launch of a new 3-D printer (can barely work the microwave). Why I go to these things I have no idea.

When I got back to the flat, I popped something in the oven, opened a decent bottle of red and sat in darkness. I must have dozed off because next thing I knew, the slow-cooked lamb shanks with honey-roasted root vegetables were burned to a crisp. I chucked them and ate some baked beans straight from the tin. Then I dragged myself to the laptop and tried to read the news but couldn't concentrate.

Flicking through emails (mostly Viagra spam) I re-read Harriet's reply, then pinged her a line suggesting lunch on

Saturday. (I mean, what's the difference between lunch on a weekday and lunch on a weekend? Lunch is lunch, right?)

To be precise, I suggested *brunch*. More casual than lunch and it seems to be what young people prefer (not that Harriet is young, exactly, just younger than me). Everywhere you go on a weekend, smug couples are queuing for Bloody Marys and Eggs Benedict, as though they'd invented the concept of brunch whereas some of us have been scoffing pancakes with bacon and maple syrup ever since we were knee-high to the proverbial.

I didn't hear back straightaway, which was fine, but when I woke up the following morning, still half-dressed, I found I'd not only finished the bottle of Merlot but made serious inroads into a second. Which is when I started to get antsy. Strictly speaking, I'm not supposed to drink while I'm on these pills. Had I over-stepped the mark with Harriet Brown? Been 'inappropriate'? (God, how I hate that word.)

I hurried to the laptop to check the email I'd sent the night before. It seemed harmless enough.

Let me know if brunch on Saturday suits you. The Wolseley does the best Eggs Benedict. I'll book for midday on the off-chance you're free.

Too keen? Perhaps, but it had been ages since I'd invited a woman to . . .

. . . To what exactly? This wasn't a date, it was a work thing. Well, work-*related*. But did it pass the 'inner voice' test, i.e., could I claim it on expenses without troubling my conscience?

Not really.

So ... did that make it a date? Maybe, maybe not. Either way, I was over-thinking the whole thing and behaving like a teenager with a crush on the girl next door.

I took my pills and showered, then got dressed without looking at my mobile to see if there was a reply from Harriet. Emerging from the flat, I sucked in the soggy autumnal air and donned my Ray-Bans, even though the skies were leaden and grey. It had rained overnight, leaving the air tangy and fresh. Taking my usual route into town, I kicked through sodden leaves in Regent's Park and considered the dire state of my social life and marriage. *Solvitur ambulando*, as Diogenes said. *It is solved by walking*.

The circumstances surrounding Tom's arrival had had many lasting ill-effects, not least sending me into my shell. But Bonnie hadn't been in touch for months. Did I miss her? Sometimes, especially on a Saturday morning with the weekend ahead and only white space in the diary. Would she come back? Possibly – she had before, more than once. Could I forgive her – yet again? The jury was out. Meanwhile, the prospect of a leisurely brunch with the dark-haired, green-eyed actress put a spring in my step – assuming she would accept the invitation. I strolled through Mayfair and Soho, determined that my mobile would remain in my pocket, the voicemail resolutely unchecked.

On the dot of 10 a.m., I arrived at the Shaftesbury Avenue

studios, mustered a cheery hello for Jools on reception then had coffee with my producer, Pam. She's a nice woman and good at her job but says things like 'two more sleeps before Crimbo' and 'I can't wait for my holibobs', which makes me want to kill her. Five minutes into the meeting, she asked if I was okay.

'Fine, thanks. Why?'

'You don't seem your usual self.'

'Who am I? Tutankhamen?'

She smiled.

'Seriously, Richard, are you okay?'

I tried to sound more confident than I felt. 'Never better. Unless you know something I don't.'

We moved on to the Agony Uncle emails. She was resist-ant to including two on depression (we'd tackled the topic last week) but I stuck to my guns. 'You wouldn't believe how many people are affected.'

Scrolling through the listeners' emails I stopped at the sight of one signed 'George B'.

Dear Richard, I'm estranged from my son. I did something unforgivable many years ago and he's never let me forget it. Do you believe in second chances? My son doesn't. I'm in the autumn of my years and winter is approaching. Is there anything I can do to make him see sense before it's too late?

'He can fuck right off,' I said to no one in particular. I deleted the email. Pam seemed startled by the vehemence in my tone. She leaned forward.

'Is there anything you'd like to talk about?'

'How about super-yachts?' I said.

'Super-yachts?'

'I went to a party last night. I know a lot about super-yachts.'

'I wasn't thinking of super-yachts.'

'What, then?'

She took a breath.

'Never mind. As long as you're okay.'

'Hunky-dory, thanks for asking.'

We talked for another few minutes then wrapped things up. Trying to put 'George B's email out of my mind I spent a desultory half-hour flicking through the tabloids, looking for showbiz titbits to read on the air. It wasn't until eleven that I escaped to the loo and allowed myself to scroll through my iPhone with what I admit was feigned insouciance.

Still nothing from Harriet Brown.

Zilch, nada, nichts, rien, zip.

Not a peep.

Which was fine.

Absolutely fine.

I slipped the phone into my pocket, stared into the middle distance and took a breath. Time for a reality check.

Why was I in a state of suspended animation over a woman I'd met only once?

More importantly, why was I hiding in the lavatory, feeling on the verge of a panic attack? It couldn't be the medication. I'd been on the same pills for months.

I considered the possibilities. Was it that I hadn't heard from Tom for a while? The boy seemed to have given up on me. If so, I could hardly blame him. I'd made no attempt to return his calls. He wasn't to know I was low.

In that moment, hiding in the loo, I felt horribly alone. My son was a stranger. My wife was on a beach in Goa, or maybe having life-affirming sex with her lover. And here was I, spirits nose-diving, stomach churning with anxiety. Staring at the door, I had one of those rare bursts of clarity that take me by surprise.

I'm on my own. Me, myself and I.

Bonnie would say it's my own fault, at least as far as Tom is concerned. And I'd have to agree. As for me driving her into the arms of someone else, it's not so simple. True, I've let friendships peter out. Men do. We're lazy, content to let our wives run our homes and everything else, from booking holidays and dentists' appointments to remembering birthdays and buying presents.

Mea culpa, mea maxima culpa.

As for the wider family, since Bonnie's parents died it's been just the three of us: me, her and Tom. Unless you count 'Gorgeous' George, which I don't. As his email confirmed, he's not dead (more's the pity), just dead to me. My mother, on the other hand, is long gone and well out of it. I know 'this too shall pass', and it's not as if I'm actively contemplating launching myself off Beachy Head, but oh, won't it be peaceful when the whole shebang is done and dusted?

I was ruminating along these lines, sinking deeper and

deeper into despair, when I heard footsteps outside the cubicle. A male voice, one of the production assistants. His name's Luke. He's about twelve. Isn't everyone nowadays?

'Richard?'

I said nothing.

'Pam sent me to say you're on air in two minutes.'

Christ! How long had I been hiding?

'On my way,' I said.

I flushed the loo. He sounded relieved.

'Okay, I'll tell her.'

I waited till I heard him leave then emerged from the cubicle and washed my hands. I stared at my reflection. No wonder Pam had asked if I was okay. The overhead lighting didn't help but I looked as if I'd spent the night in a skip. I'd missed a spot shaving, my shirt was crumpled, my hair was like a mad professor's and there were dark circles under my bloodshot, rheumy eyes. We're not talking bags, we're talking suitcases. Nine months shy of my fiftieth birthday I was staring at the face of a raddled old soak, someone who might sell you a copy of *The Big Issue*. I made a mental note to book an appointment at the spa in Knightsbridge. Facial, manicure, haircut. The Full Monty. And then it happened.

I walked into the corridor and strode towards the studio and my phone pinged.

An email from Harriet Brown.

Sorry for slow response. Saturday should be fine. Okay if I confirm tomorrow? Where is The Wolseley?

A surge of relief flooded my body. Feeling ten feet tall and lighter than air, I pushed open the studio door, donned my headphones and sat at the mic. On the other side of the glass, I could see Pam, her expression a mixture of bewilderment and relief. Waiting for the newsreader to finish, I felt more cheerful than I had for days – no, *weeks*. A burden lifted. The world was a sunnier place.

The news ended. I tapped the screen and played the opening jingle.

'The Richard Young Show!'

Switching on the mic, I addressed hundreds of thousands of Londoners, burbling my customary blend of cheerful nonsense while my mind replayed Harriet's words over and over and over . . .

Saturday should be fine.

As I introduced the first love song of the day, another voice – my own – was playing inside my head, responding to her question:

'Okay if I confirm tomorrow?'

You bet! Yes, oui, si, tak, jawohl and yee-hah!

From despair to elation because of an email from a woman I barely knew.

Uh-oh.

TOM

In a weird display of workplace sadism, Colin insisted on drag-
ging out the Friday editorial meeting – 'our A-team catch-up'
as he likes to call it. As the clock ticked towards five-thirty, the
six of us were marooned in the strip-lit boardroom, grinding
through the agenda. I found myself concentrating on an elaborate doodle on my notepad. At one point, Colin leaned over.

'Who's Harriet?'

'Sorry?'

'Your doodle. "Harriet". New love interest?'

'Nope.'

I left it at that and stifled a yawn. Colin blinked at me.

'Are we boring you, Tom?'

'Yep.' It slipped out before I knew what I was saying.
'Look, it's, like, five-thirty on a Friday.'

'And?'

'Mate, I want to go home. We all do.'

Cue stunned silence. Mercifully, Priti (graphic designer,
total sweetheart) saved the day by saying she had to take her

daughter to the dentist. Colin grudgingly brought the meeting to a close and released us into the wild.

And wild it was: torrential rain and winds howling around the Embankment and adding to the rush-hour misery. I left my bike in the rack and squeezed onto a bus. By the time I made it to Dalston it was almost seven o'clock. I ran the final few yards to the café, arriving out of breath only to discover Harriet had called first thing to say she wasn't coming in.

'Is she okay?' I asked her stand-in, a bearded hipster with a bad case of halitosis. He mumbled something about a family emergency. I fought the urge to tell him he could use a mint. Outside, sheltering in the doorway, I sent her a text.

At café. R U OK?

My mobile rang immediately. The sight of her name on the screen quickened my pulse.

'Nan had a fall. She won't go to hospital.'

'Is there anything I can do?'

'Have you got a helicopter?'

'It's being serviced.'

'Just my luck.'

'Seriously, can I do anything?'

'I managed to get the doctor out. He bandaged her up, gave her some painkillers.'

'What about food?'

She lowered her voice to a conspiratorial whisper.

'Sardines on toast. Nan's Friday treat. Followed by *Nightmare on Elm Street*. We're living the dream.'

I took a pen from my pocket.

'What's her address?'

'Why?'

'Just answer the question.'

Forty-five minutes later, soaked to the bone, I stood outside a neat two-up-two-down in a quiet Walthamstow street and rang the bell. Harriet appeared at the door, her eyes widening in surprise. I raised a Tesco bag.

'Veggie lasagne. All the ingredients. Just call me the fourth emergency service.'

She mustered half a smile.

'I can't cook.'

'No problem. This is a job for a professional.'

Another hesitation. She called up the staircase.

'Nan? Is it all right if a wet bloke cooks us supper?'

A voice from upstairs.

'Is he tall, dark and handsome?'

Harriet looked me up and down.

'Will two out of three do?'

'Ask if he likes sardines.'

The smile broadened to a grin.

'He can do better than that.'

The thing about coming from my background – walking on eggshells for fear of triggering Mum's bipolar disorder or upsetting Dad – is it makes you, like, hyper-vigilant, braced for an outburst of temper or loony-tunes behaviour, and always eager to please, sometimes *too* eager. But if cooking for someone's grandma isn't tantamount to a declaration of love, I don't know what is.

71

The kitchen was small and cosy. Fresh flowers on the pine dresser. A hand-embroidered tablecloth. Good quality pans, the kind designed to last a lifetime. Nancy remained upstairs, yelling out where to find things and how to operate the ancient oven. Harriet opened the wine I'd brought and sat on a stool, watching as I chopped onions, carrots and peppers.

'I lied,' she said, chewing on a thumbnail.

'About what?'

'Not being able to cook.'

'It's okay,' I said. 'I'm happy to do it.'

'I feel bad about lying. It's just . . .' She tailed off.

'Just what?'

'There was a bloke. I used to cook for him. But he turned out to be a total twat-sack.'

'In what way?'

She cocked her head to one side. I loved how she did that. It was all I could do not to kiss her.

'Maybe another time,' she said.

Trying to ignore the galloping of my heart, I turned my attention back to cooking, prepping the ricotta, spinach and eggs and making the white sauce.

'Are you a vegetarian, too?' said Harriet.

I managed a nod.

'Nothing with a face, right?'

A lie, but what the heck. She set a tray for her grandmother then laid the table. The kitchen smelled of home cooking. The house was warm and snug. A haven. Nancy called from upstairs. 'Is your gentleman caller behaving himself?'

'So far, Nan.'

'Never mind. The night is young.'

Their banter continued while I set the lasagne to bake. Harriet took a glass of wine up to Nancy but it was rejected in favour of a schooner of Baileys. When the meal was ready Harriet carried the tray up to the bedroom. Sipping my wine, I walked into the sitting room.

Like the kitchen, the walls were lined with photos: Harriet – gorgeous, green-eyed Harriet – laughing with her Nan and her parents. Holidays, birthdays, Christmases, picnics – everything that makes up family life. There were a couple of her and her mum, doing yoga. Taking stock, I felt a lurch in my stomach. When it came to happy families the Brocklebanks were a disaster. Forget picnics and parties – rifts and feuds were our thing.

I went back through to the kitchen and was grating a block of Parmesan as Harriet took her place at the table. Before she could start eating, Nancy yelled again.

'I think I'll watch another film. *Texas Chainsaw Massacre*. Loud. So I won't be able to hear you. In case you get up to hanky-panky.'

'We're having dinner, Nan, same as you.'

'I hope he's not touching my sardines.'

'No one's touching your sardines, Nan.'

Upstairs, the TV began to blare. Harriet and I exchanged a smile then began to eat, lapsing into silence. There was something unnerving – too intimate – about sitting at a kitchen table, like a long-established couple having supper at the end of a tiring week. I started to worry. Maybe we didn't have anything to say to each other ... Maybe I shouldn't have come ... Outside, the rain lashed the windows. Harriet pushed the food around her plate. I could sense her groping for something to say. I blurted the first thing that came into my head.

'Not much chance of seeing Saturn tonight.'

'Nope.'

More silence. More chewing. A sip of wine.

'Maybe I shouldn't have turned up on your doorstep.'

'No, it's fine.'

'A bit stalker-y?'

'Well, now you mention it ...' She smiled to show she was kidding. 'I had some good news,' she said. 'But it's supposed to be a secret.'

'So why mention it?'

'Because I'm excited. It means I might be able to go to Hollywood.'

My stomach gave a lurch.

'For how long?'

'Maybe forever. If I can stop the thoughts.'

'What thoughts?'

She looked away.

'Never mind.'

'Hollywood would be cool,' I said but my voice must have lacked conviction.

'You don't sound too happy about it,' she said.

'Why wouldn't I be happy? Whatever it is, it sounds great.'

The truth was, I was taken aback by the strength of my reaction. I'd only met her a few times yet it felt like the universe was playing one of its bad jokes. I was brought back to earth by the sound of Nancy yelling from upstairs. 'What's this food?'

I called towards the staircase.

'It's vegetarian lasagne.'

There was a pause.

'Who's that?'

'It's Tom,' said Harriet. 'I told you he was cooking dinner.'

'Tom who?'

'Tom Brocklebank.'

'What's he doing here?'

'He cooked your lasagne.'

'It's Friday. I have sardines on Friday. Everyone knows that.'

Harriet rolled her eyes and carried on eating.

The rest of the evening went okay, despite the hollow sensation that was gripping my stomach, a feeling no amount of alcohol seemed to ease. But the wine had loosened me up enough to find myself staring longingly in the direction of Harriet's graceful neck. I managed to keep my eyes from straying towards the tantalizing curve of her breasts, but it wasn't easy. Being close to her was driving me crazy. Resisting the temptation to stroke her arm, to raise her hand to my lips, I tried to focus as we discussed my musical and Harriet's ambitions – how she'd done some theatre in her twenties and had good reviews. They'd given her a sense that she might be on the right track so she'd pegged away.

Now, if she could just overcome a bout of what she called 'mega stage fright', it looked as if she might be moving into a position to take a crack at the big-time, the break she'd been waiting for. In Hollywood. Six thousand miles away. I couldn't shake a sense of impending doom.

'What's the matter?' said Harriet.

'Nothing. Been a long week.'

She didn't press the point. I could hardly tell the truth. A couple of cocktails, one kiss, and I was acting like a love-struck teen. Apparently it's not uncommon for women to meet a bloke and start projecting years ahead but I seemed to be doing it too. *Fuck's sake, mate, get a grip.*

'Do you like cats?' I said.

'Love 'em. Why?'

'I'm going to the Cat Café tomorrow lunchtime. In Shoreditch. They do tea and cakes and the cats wander around, or sleep on your lap.'

'Sounds great,' said Harriet. She wiped her mouth on her napkin. 'As long as Nan's okay, the answer's yes.'

'To what?'

'You *are* going to invite me?'

'Yes.'

'Good.'

My spirits lifted. Perhaps the Hollywood plan wouldn't come to anything, after all. Maybe the stage fright would persist. But . . . then she'd be crushed. A lifelong ambition would have come to nothing. She'd become disappointed and bitter . . .

My thoughts were running away with themselves. She was saying something.

'Wait ... Tomorrow? Saturday?'

'Yes.'

'Sorry. Got a lunch date.'

The world stopped turning. I managed a smile.

'Never mind. Just a thought.'

'I'd cancel it but it's to do with ... the secret thing.'

'Understood.'

I stood up. Time to go. My face felt hot. I couldn't wait to get out. Harriet didn't seem to notice my eagerness to leave.

'Any idea where The Wolseley is?' she said.

'Piccadilly. It's the sort of place my dad takes people he's trying to impress.'

'What does he do?'

I was about to tell her but Nancy yelled from upstairs. 'I could do with a cuppa to take away the taste of that muck.'

Harriet pulled an apologetic face.

'Well, *I* liked it.'

'No problem.'

I grabbed my coat and headed for the door.

'Have fun at the Cat Café,' said Harriet. 'Maybe another time?'

'Maybe,' I said, trying not to sound brusque. 'Enjoy The Wolseley.'

I walked out into the teeming rain. Head down, hands in pockets, heart in boots. I was halfway down the street when I heard a voice.

'Wait!'

I turned to see Harriet running after me, sheltering under my umbrella. She was smiling. 'You forgot this.'

I held the brolly over her head, shielding her from the rain. I held her gaze. Then I took her in my arms and kissed her. It was the best kind of kiss: soft, tender, filled with promise. I could have stood there all night but she pulled away.

'Hold the brolly still,' she said. 'I've got rain running down my neck.'

'Me too. I don't care.'

She grinned. 'Idiot.'

We kissed again. For all I knew the rain may have turned into a monsoon or ceased altogether. I didn't care about weather, or anything else, and neither, it seemed, did Harriet Brown.

GEORGE

Just after eleven o'clock on Saturday morning I emerged from my fifth appointment at the Kentish Town tanning salon sporting a skin tone somewhere between pine and teak, as befits a man who is supposed to have spent a month in Peru.

Paddy was already in the pub, sitting at his usual corner table and scanning the *Racing Post*. A swift half later, we repaired to the jeweller's on the corner of the high street. I asked to see a pair of sunflower stud earrings – white gold with diamonds – priced at £3,995. While Paddy distracted the jeweller, I performed a sleight of hand he'd taught me more years ago than I care to remember, surreptitiously pocketing the earrings and leaving the jeweller with a pair identical to the real thing in almost every way except value. The man will probably never notice and neither will his customers so no harm done.

Bidding *au revoir* to Paddy, I took a bus to Old Bond Street, sauntering into one of Imelda Shine's favourite stores where I sweet-talked a sales assistant out of a small gift box and an Asprey bag. In my experience, packaging is an essential part of any gift.

Walking along Piccadilly, I stopped in my tracks. On the other side of the road, Richard was getting out of a taxi, looking silly in a fedora hat. He didn't see me. I watched as he paid the driver and greeted the doorman outside The Wolseley restaurant then hurried inside. Although tempted to peer through the window to find out with whom my son was lunching I swerved and headed for Green Park tube station. His social life was of no interest to me. Besides, I had other *poissons* to fry.

HARRIET

Wow.

The Wolseley.

I mean, *wow*. Seriously.

From the moment you walk in you feel like royalty, only more glam and less stuffy. The friendly staff. The huge, high-ceilinged room leading to the bar. The hubbub of people doing deals, swapping gossip, being *in the swim*. The sense of being in the hands of professionals who know exactly what they're doing and will do whatever it takes to make you feel not just welcome but . . .

Okay, I'm going OTT, but only because I need you to understand how my mind was blown. And that's before the GQ-handsome maître d' in the charcoal grey suit whisked me to a table where the DJ was waiting. Mr GQ held my chair as Richard Young **OH MY GOD YOU'RE GORGEOUS** rose to greet me. I wasn't sure whether to go for an air-kiss or a handshake but Richard solved the dilemma by extending a hand.

'Lovely to meet you,' he said. 'Thank you so much for coming.'

Like I was doing *him* a favour. Classy, right? A twinkle-eyed silver fox. Posh black suit, cream shirt, big smile.

'Would you like a drink? Bloody Mary? Glass of champagne?'

I BET YOU LOOK GOOD NAKED!

I tried to silence The Thoughts and sound sophisticated.

'Why have tomato juice when you can have bubbles?'

'Why indeed?' Smiling, he turned to the man in the suit. 'A bottle, please, Max. The Veuve Clicquot.'

The maître d' nodded, settled me into my chair then glided away. **GREAT ARSE!** I smoothed a hand over the starched tablecloth and spent the next few minutes making small talk while trying not to show how overawed I was by my surroundings. It's not that I never eat out (I love a cheeky Nando's) but I'd only once been to a place like this and that was *the* most famous restaurant in London, The Ivy. My first agent took me to celebrate a TV contract then ruined everything by making a pass. I said no, he dropped me and the job never happened. Finish the well-known saying: *there's no business like . . .*

A waiter arrived. A menu appeared. The champagne was uncorked, a glass poured, a toast proposed.

'Congratulations on making the Voice of London shortlist.'

Richard raised his glass and smiled.

'Cheers.'

We clinked glasses and drank. (By the way, if anyone tells you there's no difference between champagne and prosecco they're crazy.)

Richard turned out to be charming but not smarmy. As I watched his lips move **I BET YOU'RE A GOOD KISSER** he recommended the Eggs Benedict with a side of caviar and another of chips. I asked for the veggie version, Eggs Royale with smoked salmon. (Okay, not strictly veggie but this was a special occasion and sometimes fishaterian is okay.) I thought he was joking about the caviar but he wasn't. I've only ever had lumpfish but I followed his suggestion and OMG! If this is how the other half lives where do I sign up?

'I'm thinking of becoming a vegetarian,' he said.

We talked animal welfare for a while, and how he was careful to eat only free-range chicken and eggs. To tell you the truth, nice though he was, I had trouble concentrating at first – my mind kept wandering to being with Tom last night, kissing in the rain like something out of *La La Land* (except he's no Ryan Gosling but then who is?). But the way he put up with Nan's nonsense? What a Mr Nice Guy. His lasagne wasn't bad either. I'd managed to scoff it without thinking about Cockweasel once. (Well, a couple of times but that's an improvement. Perhaps things are finally looking up.)

It was a while before I could focus properly on what I was eating. The grub was delicious, the surroundings made me feel relaxed, something I hadn't felt for a long time. I even used the right knife and fork without making a twat of myself **WHAT IF I SPIT FOOD ALL OVER RICHARD?**

Maybe it was the champagne but I couldn't stop thinking how nice-looking he was and how much I liked his voice. Well groomed, too. Hair: newly trimmed. Skin: moisturized. Nails: manicured. I wondered if he might be gay but he mentioned a wife and son so I'm guessing not and **HE'S PROBABLY GREAT IN BED.**

I'd done my best to scrub up. In the hairdresser's at nine. Proper make-up, too. Nan said my skirt was too short and my heels too high but I told her it was the twenty-first century and women are allowed to wear whatever we like. I don't think I'd made the effort *just* for Richard – despite all The Thoughts, it never seriously entered my head that we might become more than friends – but maybe I'm kidding myself, even now.

He dabbed his mouth with his napkin. His eyes twinkled.

'So, Harriet Brown, are you in love?'

The question came out of the blue and maybe the bubbly was going to my head but I didn't mind.

'No,' I said. 'Footloose and fancy free.'

'Do you like being single?'

I shrugged.

'Sometimes. Like now, if I was in a relationship I wouldn't be having lunch with a famous DJ. I'd be pushing a trolley round Aldi or putting on a wash.' I took another sip of champagne and could feel a nice buzz starting to settle in.

'What about you?' I said. 'Are you in love?'

'I'm married.' He leaned back in his chair. 'My wife's having a midlife crisis. She's gone away with someone.'

'Another bloke?'

He cleared his throat and looked away.

'Another woman.'

'Oh. Not being funny but you don't seem heartbroken.'

'Well, I'm not jumping for joy.'

'So you're still in love with her?'

He considered the question before answering.

'We've been together a long time. Love changes.'

'Really? How?'

He sipped his drink.

'People talk about being "madly in love", don't they?' he said. 'And with good reason. All those pheromones fusing the brain, getting in the way of rational thought. We go mad – literally. But that can't last forever – a couple of years at most, long enough to guarantee the survival of the species. Nature's way of ensuring "the heir and the spare". Then things calm down. And that's when love – the real deal – either takes hold, in which case people stand a chance of living happily ever after, or things fizzle out and they move on.'

Was he mansplaining? Being cynical? It didn't feel like either.

'Will your wife come back?'

'I don't know.'

'Do you want her to?'

'Good question.'

I searched his eyes and suddenly the alcohol seemed to be doing all the talking.

'Well, if you ask me, she's a lucky woman.'

He leaned forward, raising his eyebrows in surprise.

'If I didn't know better,' he said, 'I'd think you were flirting with me.'

Was I? After snogging Tom? Was I what Nan would call a slapper or was I simply enjoying attention from two blokes who didn't seem like total snot-bubbles?

'What star sign are you?' I said.

'Leo.'

'The king of the zodiac.'

He gave an indulgent smile.

'What about you?'

'Aquarius.'

'Does that mean we can be friends?'

'I hope so,' I said.

I didn't tell him what it *really* meant: that Leo and Aquarius make a great match, especially between the sheets, something I'd learned from Cockweasel. I could feel my cheeks burn at the memory and **OH FUCK I'M GOING TO LEAN ACROSS THE TABLE RIGHT NOW AND KISS YOU.**

Thank God my phone beeped.

'Sorry,' I said. 'I can't turn it off in case it's Nan. She's not well and I'm the only one around.'

'No problem. Go ahead.'

I checked the text. It was from Tom at the Cat Café – a photo of a black moggy wrapped around a tea cosy, soaking up the teapot's warmth. I scanned his message.

Think I've reached peak cat.

I showed the photo to Richard.

'Adorable,' he said. He peered at the text — the sender's name above the photo. 'My son's called Tom,' he said.

'Mind if I reply?'

'Not in the least.'

I tapped out a few words (*kidnap cat, leave big tip*) then sent the message and put the phone on the table.

'Where were we?'

He leaned forward and held my gaze.

'I asked if you were flirting with me.'

My phone beeped again.

'Sorry.'

He blinked.

'Go ahead. Might be grandma.'

But it wasn't, it was Tom again.

How's The Wolseley?

I pecked out a reply.

I'm moving in.

His answer was instant.

And the company?

I replied again.

Smooth.

'This "Tom" seems very persistent,' said Richard.

When I looked up he was smiling but I could see he was making an effort not to be pissed off. I switched the phone to silent and put it away.

'Sorry,' I said. 'No more texts.'

I stuck to my word, even though I could feel the phone vibrating in my pocket. After a decent interval, I excused myself, went to the toilet and checked none of the calls were from Nan. Nope – all pictures of cats at the Cat Café. I texted Tom, telling him to stop it because he was making me into the kind of rude arse-clown I hate. I got back to the table just as Mr GQ arrived with the bill. It was clear that Richard was a regular, asking after the bloke's knee op and taking a genuine interest in the response. Maybe it's something to do with all the crap jobs I've had (office cleaner was the worst), but the way people treat restaurant staff tells me a lot and Richard passed the test. Easy-going, friendly without being patronizing, excellent eye contact.

Tick, tick, tick.

'Can we go halves?' I said.

He smiled and shook his head.

'My treat. To congratulate you on making the Voice of London shortlist.'

Which is when I said it. Maybe it was the alcohol or maybe I just fancied him but let's face it, what came out of my mouth could have been a lot worse than what I actually said, which was:

'Is that the only reason?'

His face grew serious. He leaned closer.

'Since you ask, I was wondering . . .' He tailed off.

'Yes?'

He looked into my eyes.

'How you're planning to spend the rest of the afternoon.'

There was no mistaking what he had in mind.

Life boils down to a few key decisions. This felt like one of

them. I could feel my pulse quickening, my heart pounding.
I drew breath to reply ...

... and my phone rang. I'd forgotten that I'd turned it
back on. Nan's name flashed on-screen.

'Sorry. I need to take this.'

I stood up and walked towards the door, holding the
phone to my ear.

'You okay, Nan?'

'I can't find the TV thingamabob.'

'You mean, the remote? It was on your bedside table.'

'Who put it there?'

'You did. Have a look. Is it there?'

A pause.

'It's by the bed,' she said. 'Was there something else?'

'Sorry?'

'Why did you call me?'

**FUCK'S SAKE, NAN, I'M ABOUT TO HAVE SEX
IN A POSH RESTAURANT TOILET!**

'*You* called *me*,' I said.

'What for?'

I sighed.

'I'll be home soon.'

'Don't hurry on my account.'

By the time I got back to the table Richard had paid the
bill. He was tapping a finger on his coffee cup. Tap, tap, tap.

'Sorry,' I said. 'That was Nan.'

'Is she okay?'

'A bit confused.'

He leaned back, studying my face.

'I think the moment has passed, don't you?'

I played dumb.

'What moment?'

And that's when he said it – the thing I'd always remember.

'If I were two hundred years younger, Harriet Brown, you'd be in a lot of trouble.'

Mr GQ arrived, clutching a hat. **FUCK, NOT A FEDORA, THEY MAKE MEN LOOK LIKE KNOBS.**

'Your taxi's here, Mr Young.'

'Thanks,' said Richard. He smiled at me. 'I ordered a cab, while you were on the phone.'

'Oh,' I said, doing my best not to sound deflated. But he was right: the moment had gone. He slipped a banknote **FIFTY FUCKING QUID!** into the waiter's hand then got to his feet. I followed him to the door.

'Now I feel bad,' I said.

'Ill?'

I shook my head.

'Like I was a rubbish guest.'

'It's been lovely,' he said. 'Maybe that's the problem.'

He ushered me outside, into the street. The fresh air made me giddy. He looped his arm through mine, guiding me towards the taxi.

'You're going to be a star, Harriet. I feel it in my bones.'

I shook my head.

'I've left it too late.'

'Nonsense.'

The doorman greeted Richard with a smile, receiving a tenner for his pains.

'Just tell the driver your address,' said Richard.

'But it's your taxi.'

'I like to walk. The cab's on account.'

I opened my mouth to protest but he placed a gentle finger on my lips.

'Mustn't keep grandma waiting.'

His smile was warm but his tone brooked no opposition. I climbed into the taxi.

'Thank you,' I said. 'I had a lovely time.'

'I'll look for your name in lights.'

He started to walk away.

'Richard?'

He turned.

'Could we go for a quick drive? Around the block?'

He smiled, climbed into the cab and told the man to drive around Hyde Park Corner. As the taxi headed along Piccadilly, I took his face in my hands, leaned forwards and brushed my lips against his.

You know that sweet spot when the alcohol is working its magic, making you tipsy but not shit-faced, and you're kissing someone you really like, for the first time? That pretty much describes the next couple of minutes. Our kissing was hesitant at first, then more passionate. Before I knew it, we were back on Piccadilly, pulling to a halt opposite The Wolseley. I was the first to break the clinch.

'So,' Richard said. 'Where to now?'

I traced a finger along his cheek.

'Lovely brunch,' I said. 'Lovely bloke.'

LET'S GO BACK TO THE RESTAURANT FOR A QUICKIE IN THE LOO.

FUCK'S SAKE, HARRIET, GET A GRIP!

I let him out then gave the driver Nan's address and was driven away. As I craned my neck to look out of the rear window, Richard was watching, lighting a cigarette. The taxi turned a corner. He disappeared from view. I leaned back and closed my eyes, feeling my heart thumping in my chest.

Tick, tick, tick.

RICHARD

If it weren't for all that kissing I might have found it easier to put her out of my mind. Evolutionary science offers several explanations for the kiss. It allows women to get close enough to detect the scent of men whose immunity-coding gene differs from their own. Mixing genes enhances a child's immune system, giving a better chance of survival. And our old friend dopamine, the feel-good neurotransmitter, is boosted by new experiences, which explains why a first kiss can feel so good.

Knowing this makes not the slightest difference – not when you're on the receiving end of a kiss from a beautiful woman only slightly tipsy on champagne and in complete control of her faculties.

Brunch was going well until we were interrupted by texts from some idiot in a café full of cats. His name was Tom and that's all I know. Harriet didn't volunteer more information and I didn't ask.

Our conversation confirmed she was single, so was I out

of line when I began to flirt? I didn't think so and judging by her reaction nor did she. Setting aside the age gap, when it came to banter, eye contact and body language, the lovely Harriet Brown gave as good as she got. If we hadn't been interrupted by poor old Grandma who knows how the afternoon might have turned out? A room at The Ritz? Or back to Belsize Park? As it was, I watched her taxi pull away then headed for home, walking along Piccadilly with a spring in my step and a song on my lips. 'You Make Me Feel So Young' by Ol' Blue Eyes himself – who else?

I hadn't felt so cheerful for ages. And if I had to pretend to be a vegetarian for a while, so be it. At the same time, I felt uneasy, as if I'd crossed a line. But what line? There's no rule about DJs fraternizing with listeners. In any case, Harriet wasn't a Silk FM fan, she'd simply read about the competition and submitted an entry that had made the shortlist. Should I have given her my private email address? Should I have invited her to brunch?

Why not? She was in her thirties not some teenybopper (do they still have those?). Yet something wasn't right.

Back home, I slowly climbed the staircase and put my key in the front door. I asked myself a question: would she have made the final three if I hadn't lobbied the TfL executives on her behalf? Answer: probably not. They'd preferred another entrant but I'd argued for Harriet. Her husky voice was classy yet classless, mellifluous yet commanding, calm yet authoritative. Above all, it had a quality that somehow made it the perfect voice for London. I hadn't seen her in the flesh until the photo call so there was no way my preference could have been dismissed as lechery (which is bad, obviously) or even lust, which even in these PC-blighted times is normal and experienced by men *and* women and whatever other genders they have these days. Thank God for that.

All the same, my antennae were twitching, sending warning signals. In the current climate, if the tabloids got a sniff of anything registering on the Harvey Weinsteinometer, no matter how unfairly, I could find myself being buffeted by a social media storm faster than you could say 'MeToo'.

All of which was going through my mind as two things happened, both equally disturbing. The first was the onset of a creeping suspicion that someone had moved my laptop from one side of the kitchen table to the other. The second was the arrival of an email from Bonnie, telling me she wanted a divorce.

The first matter was simple. I'd been procrastinating but it was definitely time to call a locksmith. That was as much as I could think about the intrusion for now. I knew who the intruder was, of course – George, my so-called father – but doing anything other than making the flat impregnable would risk opening a Pandora's box I'd sealed years ago. The contents remained toxic.

The second matter, Bonnie's email, was more complicated. She'd been gone a long time but in my heart of hearts I must have believed she'd come back and that normal service would be resumed as soon as she'd got it (whatever 'it' was) out of her system. Denial is part of being human. God knows how people get through the day without it. But there comes a time when life catches up with you.

Despite what Tom may think, I've never been one for affairs. Like drugs, adultery is a form of adventure for the unadventurous. Nevertheless, it seems that I'm the one stuck in Belsize Park while Bonnie is having an affair at the Blue Moon Retreat in Goa, so what do I know about anything?

I poured a large glass of wine and sat at the table, staring at the blister pack of happy pills. *Not to be consumed with alcohol.* Easier said than done, pal. Try having a midlife crisis. Try losing your wife to a yoga teacher with buns of steel *and a vagina.* Try alienating your son through no fault of his own.

Try falling for a woman fifteen years younger than you.

And there it was – the thought that snapped me out of my spiral of self-pity. *Was* I falling for Harriet?

As if on cue, an email pinged into my inbox. As if she could read my mind. As if we had a connection. Spirits lifting, I took a breath and clicked the email.

> Dear Richard, thanks for brunch and sending me home in such style. Sorry about all the cat texts and Nan. But it's just as well she phoned . . . don't you think? 😊
> H xxx

I felt a surge of optimism, a sense that she was fishing. And there was a smiley emoji and three *xxx*! One was mere punctuation. Two showed affection without being over-the-top. But *three!*

I downed the wine in two gulps. Refilling the glass, I paced around the kitchen, my mind racing, blood thudding in my ears. That irritating saying came to mind. *No fool like an old fool.* I sent it packing, to languish alongside *Not to be consumed with alcohol.* Then I sat at the table and re-read Harriet's message, focusing on the last sentence.

It's just as well she phoned . . . don't you think?

Was she fishing? Yes. The giveaway was the 'don't you think?' But most of all it was the ellipsis.

I typed a single word.

No.

I hesitated, finger poised over the keyboard. Then I pressed 'send' and stared into the middle distance before forcing myself to come back to earth. I re-read the message from my wife.

Dear R, I've been doing a lot of thinking and have come to the conclusion that there's only one way forward: divorce.

I can't pretend it came as a surprise. Not after twenty-two years. Did I still love Bonnie? The answer was probably yes – but more out of habit than any grand passion.

I never cease to be amazed by couples who stick it out through the Steradent years, hip replacements and flagging libidos, all the way to the final curtain. Bottom line: we all change. The dreamboat you fell in love with decades ago is not the same person today and nor are you. If we're lucky, we adjust to whoever our spouse turns into and vice versa. If that's the case, maybe we'll make it to the rose-covered cottage. Most aren't so lucky. Too many of us won't admit we no longer even *like* the person we're stuck with. We're too cowardly to concede defeat so we wait till we fall off the perch. That wasn't Bonnie's plan. Good for her.

Just as she'd become Bonnie 2.0, I seemed to be morphing into Richard 2.0. She was right. It was time to move on to the next chapter. And let's face it, the fallout would be easier to handle with someone new waiting in the wings.

GEORGE

Old joke: what's the difference between a gigolo and a lawyer?

Answer: a gigolo only screws one person at a time.

I've never been called a gigolo (well, not to my face) but if that's what I am then *c'est la vie*. Better and more honest than being a lawyer. I like to think of myself as someone who discreetly helps to make the world a better place for a discerning type of lady. As for 'con artist', that's not a description I accept. There's nothing admirable about con men (although with Captain CombOver making it as far as the Oval Office, the limitations of their 'profession' may require a re-think). Bottom line: a con-man takes all he can but gives nothing back, a modus operandi that has never been my style. I've given plenty of myself over the years, thanks to those little blue pills, and there have been few complaints, even when *l'affaire* has run its course and the time has come to move on. But however you care to describe my curriculum vitae, it's safe to say that Richard does not approve.

Sometimes I let myself into his flat and just sit there. Not when he's at home, obviously, but at lunchtime, when he's out at 'work'. I tend not to listen to his programme. All those crooners' *chansons d'amour* remind me of the career I might have had had things turned out differently. I'm not complaining. Life in the fast lane has treated me well so I'm nowhere near ready for life in the bus lane.

I've never been a family man but on my last clandestine visit to Richard's flat I found myself leafing through his diary and making a note of Tom's address. Not that the lad has expressed the slightest desire to see me but you never know when a family connection might prove useful. On the other hand, given the circumstances, perhaps it's wisest to let this particular sleeping dog lie.

Today was the big day – my reunion lunch with Imelda Shine. Dinner was too run-of-the-mill; a lunchtime assignation seemed a more appropriate forum in which to 'casually' put forward a business proposition. Besides, it was her birthday – what better gift than the opportunity to invest in a sure thing?

I insisted on meeting somewhere other than her usual haunt, the Savoy, and booked a table at Le Caprice. This was no time to be availing myself of her generosity (she insisted on paying for all our outings); this was a moment to demonstrate my independence if only by picking up the tab for lunch. My turf, my game, my rules of engagement. There was the birthday *cadeau*, too, of course – the earrings from, er, Asprey . . .

A loan from Paddy had allowed me to make this

lunchtime gesture. Stake money, he called it. The old sod may have gone legit but he's still got an eye on the main chance. And, like me, he remains hopeful of pulling off the big one before it's too late.

Alighting from her chauffeur-driven Bentley, Imelda was impeccably groomed, as usual, her blonde bob perfectly coiffed, her slim figure clad in a navy blue Chanel suit rounded off with a pair of impossibly high-heeled shoes, which she swore were as comfortable as slippers.

'Never choose comfort over style,' said the now eighty-one-year-old as I murmured compliments while settling her into a booth.

'You look ravishing,' I said. *'Bon anniversaire.'*

'Don't remind me. Being old is nothing to celebrate.'

'It beats the alternative,' I said. 'Dom Perignon?'

'I suppose so.'

The earrings went down well. We ordered without consulting the menu. I've noticed how the rich automatically assume any restaurant will be able to provide whichever dish takes their fancy regardless of whether or not it's on the menu. Miraculously, they're never disappointed. On this occasion, our order couldn't have been simpler: Dover sole for the lady, steak tartare for me. The champagne arrived. She took a sip then peered at my face.

'You look burned to a crisp. How was Peru?'

I felt a flicker of relief. My sunbed tan had clearly passed muster. (I'm not daft enough to use a spray; the smell is a dead giveaway.)

'Well, since you ask . . .'

I waxed lyrical about my canoe trip along the River Santiago, Peru's last frontier for illegal gold mining. I'd spent a lot of time on Paddy's iPad, getting the hang of Google and was confident that my descriptions sounded convincing. Unsurprisingly, the question of the legality of these gold mines didn't raise a flicker of concern from Mrs Shine. She was, let's remember, the widow of a man who had made his billions in the oil industry; scruples and ethics were low on her list of priorities. And like all wealthy people, when it came to money there was no such thing as enough.

She listened as I told her about mining prospects in the Madre de Dios, in the south of the country, and how my dear old pal Carlos knew a good thing when he saw it. Then, troublingly, she stifled a yawn as I warmed to my theme and outlined how a small investment in Carlos's latest venture would likely see a return of at least thirty per cent within a year.

'How small?'

I gave a nonchalant shrug.

'A million. He's not letting anyone in for less. Too much aggravation.'

I drew breath to elaborate but she swallowed a mouthful of sole and held up a hand.

'Do I treat you like an idiot, George?'

'Never,' I said mildly.

'In which case, do me the courtesy of returning the compliment. Does our arrangement suit you?'

I nodded, trying to ignore the uneasy feeling in my stomach.

'Then let's enjoy lunch and perhaps a little afternoon delight at the hotel. But please – no more about "Peruvian gold" or unicorns at the end of the rainbow.'

So that was that. I knew her well enough to be sure there was nothing to be gained by pressing the point, not even later, during the pillow talk that would follow our 'afternoon delight'. All that painstaking research, those days lying low at Rochester House, those uncomfortable hours in the wretched tanning salon – all *pour rien*. It was time to admit defeat. As lunch progressed, with Imelda droning on about her plans to visit Palm Springs at Christmas, my mind wandered to the Napoleonic strategy: *reculer pour mieux sauter*, otherwise known as making a strategic retreat before renewing an advance. There was no point in renewing my efforts to interest this particular prospect in Carlos and his gold mine. Moreover, despite a good innings of eighteen months, if my days as her paramour were now numbered I had no one to blame but myself. Everything had been fine so long as I'd never actually *asked* for anything but now I'd blown it. Being a die-hard republican, the widow Shine had never been impressed by my 'Lord Buckingham' shtick, not even in the early days. And when the truth had come out (she'd stumbled on my real passport during a trip to Mustique) she'd never seemed bothered that I had posed as a member of the aristocracy, merely amused.

Let's make a deal, Georgie-Boy: no bullshit, just fun.

103

Which is what our time together had been – fun. Now I'd poisoned the goose that had laid so many golden eggs. Soon, she would punish me by finding a replacement. They always do. *C'est la vie.*

Still, if life gives you lemons, make a gin and tonic. As I finished my steak tartare I resolved to undertake what film directors call a 'slow fade' from the scene, making a strategic retreat to Rochester House. I didn't buy Paddy's weary mantra: 'as one door closes another one shuts'. Even at eighty there was hope. Sooner or later, the next merry widow would appear, bringing a new opportunity to pull off the big one. It was just a question of biding my time.

Needless to say, I had no way of knowing just how swiftly the next prospect would appear, or how a woman I had yet to meet would change my world. And wake a pack of sleeping dogs.

TOM

The Cat Café wasn't as much fun as I'd expected, not even with one of the feline residents taking to my lap while I ate a plate of sandwiches and drank a mug of tea. The sense of let-down was my own fault. I'd set myself up for disappointment by looking forward to sharing the experience with Harriet. As a rule, I enjoy doing stuff alone, especially at weekends. Galleries, walks, movies, markets, street food, gigs ... When a man is tired of London ... etc. And if ever I *do* feel lonely, it's usually a prelude to getting down to work on *They F**k You Up*.

That's the weird thing about being creative. To write lyrics or compose music you need to spend time alone so you'd think it's a lonely life – but nope. When it's going well – those occasions when you're, like, in the zone and the words are flowing and the music's whirling inside your head – that's when your mind is filled with the characters you're creating, worlds you're conjuring from nowhere. It's the one time it's impossible to feel lonely. At least, that's how I remember it. It's been a while.

I pitched the show to a producer at a networking event, a bloke called Paul Mendoza. He's produced a string of musicals in the provinces but is still looking for The One – his *Cats* or *Follies* or *Matilda*. We got on like the proverbial and he told me to send him my libretto-in-progress and demos of three songs, so I did. Didn't hear a word.

Maybe it's because I was feeling down (and pretty loved-up) that I started texting those cat photos to Harriet. Maybe I was jealous, too. Did her Wolseley brunch have anything to do with her Big Secret? Were plans for a Hollywood trip more advanced than she let on? Maybe some big-shot American director was schmoozing her, whispering dollar signs in her ear. Maybe he ordered champagne. Maybe they went back to his hotel and . . .

. . . *Perfect!* A snog with a woman you barely know and you're jealous of an imaginary bloke pouring imaginary champagne.

All the same, there was no denying the presence of the green-eyed monster. Which meant two things. I was falling in love. And I was in trouble.

I've been in trouble lots of times, in love hardly ever. The first girl to fill my stomach with butterflies was Carol Dixon from Sullivan Primary School in Parson's Green. She was nine, I was eight-and-three-quarters, which makes her my first older woman. (Mum's theory: men spend the first half of their lives looking for an older woman, the second yearning for a younger model.)

Apart from Carol, almost no one had made my head

swim and my heart lift, not seriously, till I was much older. I'd had crushes, of course, but it wasn't till uni that I fell in love. I'm not talking about hormones messing up your head but the full enchilada. Her name was Michelle. And maybe Dad isn't a total waste of space because when it comes to love maybe his mantra about priorities is right: 'kind, clever, funny, beautiful – in that order'. That was Michelle all over. Year one: we dated. Year two: we shared a flat. Year three: she broke my heart by dumping me for an estate agent. (I know!) I didn't ask anyone out for, like, a year. There have been others, of course, but no one made me feel like Michelle. Not till now. And now there's Harriet Brown.

So when she texted just before seven on Saturday evening I felt like a kid on the first day of the summer holidays.

Don't suppose you feel like company? xxx

I played it cool as long as I could (thirty-nine minutes) before texting back.

Am working but Nelson would love to meet u. Especially if u pick up a curry

Her response was immediate.

Tell Nelson I'm on way. Address?

I replied then launched a frenzied bout of clearing up. It's only an IKEA-furnished studio flat on the second floor above a launderette but it's amazing how much mess one bloke can make if he doesn't have many visitors. I took the world's quickest shower and managed to stub my toe on the loo. I shoved the bathroom mess into the laundry basket, stacked the dishwasher and made the bed. Then I un-made it, changed the sheets and made it again. I sniffed my armpits then took a second shower and dressed in proper clothes – okay, jeans and T-shirt, but still.

Nelson was nowhere to be seen. I hoped she'd return in time to assume her position in the basket underneath my keyboard.

It was like an hour before Harriet arrived. I'd had time to nip to the off licence for a six-pack of Stella then go back for a bottle of red in case she turned out to be one of those oddballs who drinks wine with curry. I even had the gall to pinch a few flowers from my neighbour's window box and stick them in a glass on the bookcase. Then I sat at the table and carefully arranged the iPad and notebooks that contained my so-called work-in-progress.

Five minutes later, the buzzer went. I counted to ten before letting her in, keenly aware of the blood thudding in my ears. I listened to her climb the stairs. She wore a leather jacket with skinny-fit jeans and Chelsea boots. She brandished the takeaway.

'Dinner is served.'

I moved in for a kiss but she swerved and we ended up with an awkward brushing of lips (mine) to cheek (hers). Bemused, I ushered her towards the kitchen. Our kisses in the rain seemed to have been forgotten. I swallowed a pang of disappointment then busied myself with plates and glasses. She looked around.

'Nice place. Hope I gave you time to tidy up?'

'Just about. How's Nancy?'

'Drinking Baileys and watching *The Exorcist*.' She nodded towards the cat bowl. 'Where's Nelson?'

I gestured towards the cat flap that led to the balcony and the rooftops beyond.

'Out with friends.'

She ran a finger over the Yamaha's keyboard. 'How's the musical going?'

'Slowly.'

She squinted at my notebooks. The pages were a mess: doodles, scribbles, crossings-out, half-baked ideas for lyrics.

'"Boy Meets Girl"?'

'The opening song,' I said.

She flipped through the pages.

'"Honeymoon Blues"?'

'Second song.'

'"Once More With Feeling"?'

'A duet.'

'About?'

'Pretending you're still loved-up even though you know the relationship is over. It closes Act One. Well, it will if I ever finish it.'

'What's stopping you?'

I shrugged. 'Life.'

'Don't be glib. I'm interested.'

I started opening the cartons of food and spooning out rice and vegetable curry.

'I write all day at work. It's boring bollocks about double

glazing but it's still writing. When I get home my brain's, like, fried.'

'So get up early, work on the musical before you go to the office.'

She crunched on a poppadom. We opened cans of lager, sat down and started to eat. And the weird thing? It felt like the last time we'd had supper together, at her Nan's house. It felt like we'd been doing this for years.

Later, she asked me to play one of the songs so I sat at the keyboard and picked out the opening notes of 'Boy Meets Girl'. She held up a hand.

'Wait. Set the scene.'

I cleared my throat.

'Act One, Scene One: a prison.'

She frowned.

'I thought it was a show about dysfunctional families.'

'It is. The prison is a metaphor for the way we're all captives of our upbringing. The boy's Raphael, his visitor's Jessica. They're in their twenties, from rival crime families.'

'And they're in love?'

'Not yet. They've never met but hate each other anyway. She thinks his father murdered hers.'

'Did he?'

'Wait and see.'

'Why is she visiting him?'

'To let him know that he'll pay a price for what he did.'

'Sounds dark.'

'The best musicals are dark. *Chicago, Les Mis, Cabaret* . . .'

'I know. I'm an actress.' She nodded towards the keyboard. 'Play it again, Sam.'

'You know, Humphrey Bogart didn't actually . . .'

'. . . say, "Play it *again*, Sam." I know *Casablanca* by heart, Tom. Just let me hear the song.'

'You're not expecting me to sing?'

'You hum. I'll read the lyrics.'

So I played the first verse. Harriet listened intently, absorbing the song's rhythm. I played it again as she hummed along, half-singing, half-reciting the lyrics in time with the music.

Boy meets girl
In a room
Tensions high
Pulses racing
Girl meets boy
Threatens doom
Time goes by
He is pacing

She raised a hand. I stopped playing.

'"He is pacing"?'

'Yes.'

'In prison?'

'Why not?'

'I assume they're in a visitor's room?'

111

'Exactly.'

'How come he's walking around?'

'It's theatre. They can't sit still, talking. People will die of boredom.'

She thought for a moment.

'They've never met, right?'

'Right.'

'So instead of "he is pacing" how about, "finally facing"? As in, meeting for the first time?'

She was right: it was better.

'Let me think about it.'

She shrugged.

'Either it's better or it's not.'

'I like it,' I said. 'It's in. Thanks.'

'No problem.'

She ran a finger down the page and frowned.

'"Threatens doom"? Seriously?'

'Are you going to do this all evening?'

'Not if you're going to be a hyper-sensitive fuck-trumpet.'

I managed to keep my smile in place.

'It's cool,' I said. 'Tell me what you think.'

And she did. As the evening wore on, we worked our way through the four songs I'd completed, or so I'd thought. There was no doubt: Harriet's ideas improved two of them – not musically, that wasn't her forte, but she had a knack for sniffing out a duff lyric and coming up with an alternative that was spot on.

After my early defensiveness, I made myself relax and took

her suggestions on board. I managed to convince myself my original lyrics were rough drafts, placeholders awaiting the real thing. As we warmed up, Harriet began to sing the lyrics rather than recite them. Her voice was lovely, especially when she sang the part of Roxanne, the female lead. Clear, mellifluous, perfect pitch.

Just after eleven-thirty the man downstairs sent a text telling us to 'pack in the racket'.

'I should go,' said Harriet. She grabbed her jacket. I reached for my wallet.

'Go halves on the curry?'

She shook her head. 'Cook for me sometime.'

'It's a deal.'

A peck on the cheek. She held my gaze.

'Don't give up, Tom. It's good.'

Then she was gone.

And that was that.

Despite the meal, my stomach felt hollow. Had I been friend-zoned? Nothing in her manner had encouraged me to make a move or given any sign that she remembered our kissing marathon in the rain. She'd been friendly and shown interest in the musical but that was it.

I cleared the table then opened another beer. For the first time in ages I was energized, eager to work. Settling at the keyboard, I plugged in the headphones so as not to disturb the neighbour. I started scribbling ideas for a new song called 'Better Together', fooling around with a basic chord progression and a simple melody: a C-chord, followed by a D-chord, with an F-minor to mix things up, fitting the melody alongside the chords and coming up with a tune that was optimistic without being too jaunty.

Next time I checked, it was 2 a.m. and Nelson was coming in through the cat flap. I spooned food into her bowl but she wasn't interested. She climbed into her basket underneath the Yamaha and settled down for the night. Perhaps she was being fed elsewhere. I wouldn't put it past her. Cats can be fickle. Especially females.

HARRIET

Today was the first time I heard myself on the radio – the *real* me, that is, doing something other than a voice-over. A text from Richard told me when to tune in.

Listen at 12.15. R x

I snuck into the café's loo and downloaded the Silk FM app. He was on-air, talking about the Voice of London competition.

'... *so here's the second person on our shortlist of three: meet actress and barista Harriet Brown from Walthamstow* ...'

He played thirty seconds of our interview – the bit where he'd asked what I like most about travelling by bus. Sitting on the loo, I winced at the sound of myself wittering on about the view from the top deck of the night bus from Walthamstow to Trafalgar Square. Then Richard was back.

'... *So that's finalist number two, Harriet Brown. If you think she should be the new Voice of London text 97902 to the following number* ...'

He played clips from the other finalists' interviews: Samira

Khan first, then Andy Smith. I reckoned it would all come down to whether or not the judges thought commuters wanted a woman herding them around on tubes and buses. If so, Samira was probably more suitable – more London. But if people wanted a bloke both of us were sunk.

Back at the Gaggia, I made three cappuccinos and two lattes, operating on autopilot while thinking back to our encounter outside The Wolseley. True, the champagne had gone to my head but had I been drunk? Nope. So why had I kissed Richard – a proper long snog in the taxi – when a peck on the cheek would have done? Yes, he was nice-looking and flirty but he was also married, not to mention fifteen years older. I like maturity in a man, so age wasn't the issue – but what about his wife? He'd said she was having an affair. Did that make him fair game? Or did he make a habit of taking women to posh restaurants then hitting on them? That might explain why his wife had run off with someone else.

I was unclear about his situation but sure about one thing: no more married blokes. Not after Cockweasel.

Speaking of Damian, I may have behaved like a love-struck twat-nozzle, but the ride was worth the fall. Not only was he tall, dark and handsome, he was a maxillofacial surgeon. One day he might be doing dental implants or cosmetic surgery on someone injured in a car crash, the next he might fly to Africa to give free reconstructive surgery to poor people who've had cancer. He's part dentist, part plastic surgeon, part Superman. He's also gorgeous and a demon in the sack.

His father was another story: a career criminal, said to have been involved in the Mayfair safe deposit robbery, and to have been the only one who got away with his ill-gotten gains. His name was Jack Vance and Damian didn't like talking about him, which was disappointing but no surprise. I'd often wondered if Jack's 'profession' had helped set Damian on the straight and narrow, making him determined to do good in the world, if only to make up for his old man's criminal career.

As for Tom, I might never have taken that curry over to his place if it hadn't been for an email pinging in as soon as the taxi dropped me back at Nan's. At first, my mood soared at the sight of my agent's name. Emailing on a Saturday. Interrupting his honeymoon in South America. This had to be big. How wrong can you be?

Dear Harriet,

I heard how things went with the *Macbeth* director then Sasha gave me your message about the Voice of London competition. I've been thinking for some time that we're not the right fit for each other and this confirms my view. If you win the contest you will always be known as the 'bus and tube girl', not helpful for an actor, especially one suffering from the longest bout of stage fright known to mankind. I wish you every success in your career and in finding new representation.

Shit.

FUCK YOU, INTRUSIVE THOUGHTS!

I felt like crying but managed to pull myself together and took Nan a cuppa. She was still in bed.

'Nice lunch?'

'Fine, thanks.'

'So why the long face?'

'I've been dumped by my agent.'

'Oh. I thought it was something serious. Any Hobnobs?'

Not long ago I'd have been straight on the phone to Cockweasel, angling for consolation and hoping he might finally say those three little words. But those days were gone. Even so, I felt an urge to hear his voice.

It'll be okay, babe . . . Everything will be okay . . .

Phoning was out of the question, obvs. But would a text be so terrible? It was weeks since I'd found out about Wifey and chucked him. Not a peep since. And I'd been *so* good, sticking to Nan's advice.

Cold turkey, sweetheart – the only way.

I made myself a cuppa and sat at the kitchen table, chewing on a hangnail while staring at my phone. Next thing I knew, it was dark and I'd not only sent Damian a 'poor ickle me' text, I'd been on tenterhooks waiting for a reply for *two hours*, which makes me A) pathetic B) an arse-womble and C) did I mention pathetic?

Confession time: obviously I hadn't deleted his number. Plus I was still reading his horoscope every day. We've all been there, right?

Right?

Nan was in bed, watching *The Omen*. I lay down next to her, glad of the company. She paused the DVD and fixed me with one of her looks.

'Do I need to remind you?' she said.

'About?'

'The best way to get over a bloke ...'

I finished the sentence for her.

'... is to get *under* a bloke.'

'So what are you waiting for?'

Which is when I decided to text Tom.

Don't suppose you feel like company? xxx

I regretted it as soon as I pressed send. Not because I don't like him – I do – but I wasn't in the mood for sex, no matter what Nan had to say. It was ages before he replied. He asked me to pick up a curry but by the time I got to his place I was feeling even sorrier for myself and had lost my appetite.

When I arrived, he moved in for a kiss. I acted like we'd never had that snog in the rain. I steered the conversation to his musical – and that's when the evening started to take off. His tunes were good – *really* good. I suggested a few changes to the lyrics, which he pretended to like.

His flat's nice. A bachelor pad, all IKEA stuff but cosy. What with the flowers on the table, the cat and his liking for musicals, if I hadn't known better I'd have thought he was gay.

I left before midnight. If he'd been hoping I'd stay, well, as Nan says, 'if wishes were horses then beggars would ride'.

On Sunday morning I took her breakfast in bed – a bacon

butty with HP sauce – then borrowed her Micra and drove to Mum and Dad's to water the plants and **IF I SWERVE ONTO THE PAVEMENT I COULD CRASH INTO THAT TREE**. The house was cold so I climbed into bed and stayed there all day, necking Heinz tomato soup and watching YouTube. I was tempted to text Tom again, to keep things ticking over, but managed to resist despite a feeling of rising panic and a tsunami of Thoughts.

I'VE LOST MY AGENT AND MY CAREER'S IN THE CRAPPER AND I'M GOING TO DIE ALONE IN A BEDSIT ABOVE A KEBAB SHOP. EVEN IF I HAD KIDS I'D BE A CRAP MUM BECAUSE ALL I CAN THINK ABOUT IS STANDING ON THE ROOF OF A HIGH RISE AND DROPPING MY BABY AND WATCHING HIM SPLATTER ON THE GROUND AND WHEN AM I GOING TO GET GOOD AT ADULTING?!

Eventually, I managed to pull myself together and get on with what passes for my life, but there's no doubt that The Thoughts are getting worse, not better.

As for hiding in the café loo and catching myself on the radio, the whole thing felt like a weird out of body experience, like I was listening to someone else. Nan phoned to say she'd voted for me twenty-five times. Bless.

It turns out the Voice of London result will be announced at the end of the week. I had an email from Richard's producer, Pam, asking me to come in on Friday lunchtime, along with the others on the shortlist. I said I'd be at work and could I do it by phone. She sounded pissed off and ended the call abruptly. Then Richard phoned while I was on the bus home.

'You should come into the studio.'

'Why? Have I won?'

'I don't know,' he said. 'The listeners are still voting.'

'Are you saying I'm in the lead?'

Pause.

'I'm just saying come in.'

OMFG! Better pull a sickie!

RICHARD

So I had the locks changed then I sent Tom a text.

He's back. Don't give him money.

Five hours later, he replied.

OK.

That was all. I can't blame him. Not after I'd frozen him out for a year. As for Bonnie, I should have seen the divorce coming but was it weird that I was already starting to adjust to the prospect of a life after marriage? I knew she'd been unhappy but things weren't helped by her business going under. I also knew she was dreading turning fifty. The midlife crisis takes many forms. In her case, it's an addiction to yoga and falling for a (younger) woman. Maybe the same goes for me, minus the yoga.

Namaste.

Thirty-second clips of the three Voice of London finalists had been airing all week, one per hour, on rotation. The idea was proving a hit with listeners, with tens of thousands texting votes for their favourite at a pound a pop. Last time

I checked, the vote was a nail-biter, practically a tie for first place. Pam refused to tell me the name of the front-runner.

'You need to sound as surprised as everyone else.'

Transport for London had booked a studio for the winner to record the announcements for the transport network, a task scheduled to take three days.

Mind the closing doors.

Northern line to Morden.

Please move down inside the carriage.

Walking into town on that fateful Friday, I had a rare sense of wellbeing. Nothing to do with the antidepressants, I was actually *happy*. At first, I admonished myself. My wife wanted a divorce, my relationship with my son was a disaster and who knew what chaos 'Gorgeous' George was about to unleash? What was there to be happy about?

I knew the answer, of course. Like the man said, 'to be happy we need something to do, someone to love and something to hope for'. For once, I had all three. Okay, maybe I wasn't *in love* with Harriet – not the full-blown can't-live-without-you down-on-bended-knee – but I was smitten.

No, more than smitten. *Enchanted*.

Touch wood, I've been lucky with my health – admitted to hospital just once, for appendicitis, and that's pretty much it. On the rare occasions I fall ill I tend not to mess around. Norovirus twice. Flu three times – the real McCoy not just a heavy cold. Oh, and a rogue oyster almost saw me off during a holiday in Corsica. It's the same with matters of the heart. When I fall, I fall big.

I wasn't kidding myself that Harriet felt the same way. I felt sure *she* wasn't kicking through leaves in the park, unable to think of anything except those soft, tender kisses in the taxi, her brain fused by a cocktail of hormones and fizzing with every glorious cliché in the Great American Songbook, from 'You Make Me Feel So Young' to 'Bewitched, Bothered and Bewildered'. But she *had* kissed me.

Her rivals, Samira Khan and Andy Smith, arrived at the studios at the same time. Harriet was late, to Pam's obvious irritation. I pretended not to mind her cutting it fine but my stomach clenched every time the door opened. The Transport for London PR arrived half an hour before the show began, accompanied by their Head of Marketing. We made small talk over coffee and pastries. As the clock ticked towards midday I assembled my clutch of emails and notes then made my way to studio B. It was only as I sat at the mic that I saw Pam through the glass giving a thumbs-up: Harriet was here.

The news came to an end. I tapped the screen and played the jingle.

The Richard Young SHOW!

I introduced the first song of the day ('Every Time We Say Goodbye') then took off my headphones as Pam ushered in the three finalists and settled them at the guest mics. She handed me the envelope containing the winner's name, prompting nervous laughter from the three contenders. I was careful not to show favouritism but I'd already chatted to Andy and Samira, so I asked Harriet if she was feeling okay.

'Terrified.' She looked it, too. 'How many people are listening?'

'Try not to think about it,' I said. 'Just picture one person and talk to them.'

She nodded.

'Okay, I'll talk to Nan but I'll probably babble nonsense. I always do when I get nervous.'

She poured water from the cooler, handing paper cups to her fellow finalists.

Andy made a toast. 'Cheers. May the best man win.'

Samira gave a thin-lipped smile.

'Or woman.'

The song ended and we were live on air. Switching on the mic, I introduced the guests in alphabetical order.

'Harriet Brown, Samira Khan, Andy Smith – thank you for coming in. And this is it – the moment of truth. We're about to find out which of you will be the new Voice of London, heard every day by millions of commuters on buses, trains and tubes all over the capital. There's a cash prize of five thousand pounds for the winner and a thousand each for the runners-up.'

Harriet took me by surprise, leaning in to her mic.

'Sorry I was late, Richard. The bus broke down. Funny, really. Today of all days.'

I glanced into the control room, seeking out the PR woman. She was smiling. Harriet continued.

'By the way, your listeners should know something: you're taller than you sound on the radio.'

I laughed, thrown by the *non sequitur*.

'How tall do I sound?'

'Five-foot-two. Your nose sounds bigger too – massive, in fact – but it's totally normal. Weird.'

Andy and Samira exchanged a glance. Were they supposed to join in?

'I'll take that as a compliment,' I said before turning to Andy. 'Andy Smith, tell us why you'd like to be the Voice of London.'

His answer was on the banal side – something about it being an honour to have been born in the best city in the world – but his voice was rich and deep, it compelled you to pay attention. I posed the same question to Samira. She responded in her lilting tone with an over-rehearsed response about how public transport in the world's greatest city deserved a distinctive voice reflecting London's diverse population.

'Finally, Harriet Brown – why would you like to be the Voice of London?'

She smiled.

'Okay, it's confession time: the truth is, I like bossing people about. If I win I can ride the buses all day, and the tube, watching people do as I say.'

I smiled back.

'Are you a control freak?'

'So my last boyfriend said. Maybe that's why I'm single.'

She held my gaze. Was this flirty banter or anxious chatter?

The three of us carried on talking for a few more minutes then I flourished the envelope.

'We've had thousands of votes from all over London and we're about to find out who they've chosen to be . . . the new voice of London.'

A tap on the screen produced a drum-roll. I opened the envelope.

'In third place . . .' I paused, allowing the tension to build. 'In third place . . . Samira Khan.' Another tap on the screen triggered canned applause. 'In second place . . . Andy Smith . . . Which means the winner – and the new Voice of London is . . . Harriet Brown!'

There was a split-second of disbelief then her smile lit up her lovely face. And lo! – it was a wonder to behold.

HARRIET

OMG!
  I won!

TOM

He's back. Don't give him money.

That's all the text said. After a year of silence. I took a while to calm down then responded with a terse 'OK'. It was all I could muster. Just after midday, I took my phone into the loo at work and listened to Silk FM to see how Dad was sounding. He was chatting to some guests, something about a competition to be the new voice spouting travel info on buses and tubes. I was on the verge of switching off when I heard a name that made my heart leap in my chest.

' . . . *Finally, Harriet Brown — why would you like to be the Voice of London?*'

It felt as if my brain was blowing a fuse. My mind did cartwheels, settling on the obvious explanation. Just a coincidence . . .

Then I heard her voice.

'*Okay, confession time: I like bossing people about. If I win I can ride the tube all day, watching people do as I say.*'

'*Are you a control freak?*'

'*So my last boyfriend said. Maybe that's why I'm single.*'

I sat on the toilet seat.

So many questions.

Did she *know* he was my father?

If so, why hadn't she told me?

Could this *really* be a coincidence or was something weird going on?

I glared at my phone, as if staring hard would make sense of what I was hearing. My father was saying something.

'*We've had thousands of votes from all over London and we're about to find out who they've chosen to be . . . the new voice of London.*'

A drum roll . . .

An envelope being ripped open . . .

'*In third place . . .*' He paused. ' *. . . Samira Khan.*'

Canned applause.

'*In second place . . . Andy Smith . . . Which means the winner – and the new Transport for London Voice of London is . . . Harriet Brown!*'

I carried on listening but I couldn't tell you what was said.

Dad?

And Harriet?

On the radio?

Bantering like old pals?

Not bantering, *flirting*.

Was this actually happening? FML!

Back in the office, I tried to concentrate on finishing

the copy for a piece about self–cleaning glass but my mind seemed to have shut down. I walked into the kitchen. Waiting for the kettle to boil, I composed a text to Harriet. I tried to appear calm.

Heard u on radio. Congrats! Why didn't u say u knew my dad?

I pressed 'send' then took a deep breath, bracing myself for her reply. Colin walked in and gave me a sideways look.

'You okay, mate?'

'Fine. Why?'

'You look weird.'

'Define "weird".'

'White. Pasty. If you're coming down with something do us all a favour and go home before everyone catches it.'

I didn't need telling twice.

'Great advice,' I said. 'Cheers.'

In case he had second thoughts, I was out on the street in, like, less than a minute. Before mounting my bike, I checked my mobile. No response from Harriet.

As I began to weave my way through the rush–hour traffic, a song was playing inside my head. 'Eleanor Rigby' by the Beatles. However hard I tried, I couldn't shake the tune. It took a moment to work out the connection – a magazine article I'd read about coincidences. Apparently Paul McCartney chose the name Eleanor after working with Eleanor Bron during the filming of *Help!* The name Rigby came from a sign above a wine merchant's, Rigby and Evans. In the 1980s an old gravestone was discovered in the cemetery of St Peter's Parish Church in Woolton, Liverpool, which is where Paul first met John Lennon at a 1957 summer fete. The name on the headstone was, you've guessed it, Eleanor Rigby.

Then there's the fact that the grave of the first British soldier to die in the First World War is just seven yards from that of the last Brit to die in the same war. Totally unplanned. Just coincidence. There are tons more and they prove nothing, of course, except what we all already know: coincidences happen *every day*. Nothing weird or supernatural going on, they're just part of life.

All the same, what the actual fuck!?

It wasn't until I was halfway home that I felt the phone vibrate. I took the call but carried on cycling. Harriet got straight to the point.

'You're kidding, right?'

'About what?'

'Richard, of course. He's your *father*?'

'Has been for as long as I can remember.' A feeble attempt at keeping things light. 'Are you still at the studio?'

'No, I'm on the bus, going home. But I don't get it – you have different surnames.'

'Dad changed his when he became a DJ. No one was going to hire a guy with a name like Dick Brocklebank.'

'Oh my God . . . this is so weird.'

I pulled up at a red light.

'Why didn't you mention the TfL competition?'

'I did,' she said. 'The other night, in the café.'

A memory stirred.

'You said something about a London voice-over.'

'The Voice of London – exactly.'

'Okay . . . But you didn't say what it involved. Or that it was *on the radio.*'

'Is that what's pissing you off? That you found out *on the radio?*'

'Who says I'm pissed off?'

'Sounds that way. This is weird for me too, you know.'

The light turned green. I pedalled on.

'I'm still trying to take it all in,' I said.

'Meaning what?'

Meaning, I'm in love with you so it's a total mind-fuck finding out that you know my father and weirder still hearing you flirt with him on the radio.

'Oh, shit!' said Harriet. 'I missed my stop.'

I heard the ting of the bell then the sound of her footsteps clattering down the bus staircase.

'How long have you known him?' I said.

'Not long. A week, ten days.'

Which is when I was struck by the thought that made me jam on my brakes so hard I nearly flipped over the handlebars. Shaken, I climbed off the bike and dragged it onto the pavement.

'Was he the one who took you to The Wolseley?'

'Yes.'

'Ri–ight.'

'What does "ri–ight" mean?'

It means that's the sort of place he takes women he fancies. It

133

means I'm jealous of my own father. It means my brain is going to burst into flames.

'Nothing,' I said. 'I'm just trying to wrap my head around this.'

'Me too,' said Harriet.

'So you admit it's weird.'

'Of course it's weird.'

I said nothing for a moment. Trying to gather my thoughts. To say something normal.

'Good news about the competition though. Congratulations.'

'Thanks.'

There didn't seem to be much left to say but I wasn't ready to hang up.

'So, do you . . . ?' I tailed off.

'Do I what?'

'Feel like celebrating?'

'Um . . .'

'What does "um" mean?'

She sounded sheepish.

'I said I'd have a drink with him.'

'Let me guess – at The Wolseley?'

'No,' she said quietly. 'He invited me to his flat.'

HARRIET

Father and son?

Christ on a bike with fuck off sauce and fuck off sprinkles!

I was on the bus when Tom told me. Missed my stop. Even now, I can't see a resemblance but then I don't look like Mum or Dad so what did that prove?

Had I missed something? I remember Tom not wanting to talk about his father except to say they weren't on speaking terms and their relationship was 'tricky'. How had he put it? *Sometimes he wouldn't speak to me for months on end. Once, he virtually ignored me and Mum for a year.*

I'd assumed he was exaggerating but maybe not.

I also remember Richard mentioning a son called Tom.

Like there aren't ten billion Toms.

But that's it. Okay, so it was the mother of all coincidences but that's all it was – a fluke.

Still, what was I supposed to do about it? Tom had sounded seriously pissed off and who knew what Richard would say. Would they laugh it off? Maybe compare notes? Would they find out that I'd snogged them both?

It could have been worse. I could have slept with Tom. Or Richard. Or both of them. Just as well I hadn't taken Nan's advice.

But A) I hadn't done anything wrong and B) I genuinely liked them, both of them. Not just liked but *really* liked. Good company, fun, clever, kind, easy on the eye. If you'd met some of the knob-wazzocks I've known you'd understand. Blokes like these are few and far between. I've kissed more than my share of human arse-wipes so if I'd been lucky enough to finally meet a pair of princes I wasn't going to just wave them goodbye, not without a *seriously* good reason.

I knew I'd see Richard next week. Transport for London had booked a studio at Silk FM to do the recording – assuming the café gave me time off. But I didn't want to spoil stuff with Tom. He's *soooo* lovely. We were having a laugh working on the musical. Felt like we were making real progress, too. So all in all, maybe it was a case of Keep Calm and Carry On. Yes, this was a weird, messed-up situation but that's all it was.

(Okay – it was *really* weird. But at least it took my mind off Cockweasel.)

On second thoughts, I wondered if I should cancel the drink with Richard. I didn't want to annoy him but like Nan says, 'When a man invites you over for no reason, there's a reason'.

I dialled his number and pictured my name flashing up. He answered immediately. Sounded like he was smiling.

'Hello – is this the new Voice of London?'
'Yes,' I said. 'But I can't make tonight. Sorry.'
He sounded crestfallen.
'Is everything all right?'
'Kinda,' I said.
'Do you want to tell me about it?'
So I took a deep breath.
Then I told him.

RICHARD

As *l'enfant terrible* of tennis John McEnroe used to say, you cannot be serious!

Harriet and Tom?

My Tom?

Had someone put *all* the crazy pills in *all* the water?

Reeling, I sat on the bed, trying to make sense of what was happening. Should I have known? Had I missed clues? The only thing that came to mind was the guy who'd sent her those photos from the Cat Café. How was I to know that *her* Tom was *my* Tom? The world is full of bloody Toms.

His text was short and to the point.

I'm coming to see you. It's about Harriet.

I contemplated turning off the lights and pretending I was out. Then I pulled myself together, took a shower and swallowed a couple of extra pills. (Yes, I know that's not how antidepressants work – they're not like painkillers – but *you* try keeping it together when someone lobs a grenade into your life.)

By the time the doorbell rang I'd regained my composure and reached a decision. I would refuse to bow out gracefully. If it *was* finally my turn to enjoy some long overdue happiness, maybe even a new love, then he'd have to put up with it. He wasn't a kid. Most importantly, Harriet wasn't just any woman.

I buzzed him inside then went into the kitchen and opened a bottle of Chablis. I stood facing the window as I heard him climbing the stairs. He closed the front door and entered the room. Our first face-to-face encounter in more than a year.

'You've put on weight,' he said.

My back still to him, I waved the corkscrew towards the microwave.

'It's the ready meals,' I said.

I picked up the M&S packet and read from the label. 'Succulent roast salmon with a horseradish herb crust?'

'Is that an invitation to dinner?'

I didn't mention I'd planned on sharing it with Harriet.

'Would you like it to be?'

'Christ, Dad, why do you always answer a question with a question?'

'I don't know, why do I?'

Someone with a stopwatch would have judged our truce to have lasted precisely twenty seconds. I handed him a glass of wine and tried to sound casual.

'Have you heard from her?' I said.

'You mean Mum?'

'Who else?'

'A few weeks ago. She sounded fine.'

'Still taking her medication?'

'I guess so,' he said. 'God knows how she gets it in Goa. Any sign of her coming home?'

I shook my head. There was no need for detail. Where would I begin? It seemed clear she'd said nothing about the divorce. He set his glass on the table.

'Okay,' he said. 'That's the "happy family" stuff out of the way. What are we going to do about Harriet?'

I managed half a smile. It was clear he'd been working up to this.

'Are you in love with her?' I said.

'Maybe.'

'There's no such thing as "maybe in love". You are or you aren't.'

He sat at the table and swirled his wine around the glass.

'Suppose I am,' he said. 'Does that get us anywhere?'

'It clarifies things.'

'Does it make a difference? To how you feel about her?'

I sat down and considered his question.

'I'm not sure what you mean.'

'Bullshit. I heard you on the radio. You're smitten.'

'Am I?'

He sighed.

'Try and give a direct answer, please. Do you have feelings for Harriet Brown?'

'"Have feelings",' I said. 'How quaint.'

'The answer is . . . ?'

I cleared my throat.

'If I do, would it be such a crime?'

'No,' said Tom. 'Oh, wait – make that "no, apart from the fact you're married and she's half your age".'

'She's thirty-five. Hardly Lolita. Correct me if I'm wrong but aren't you too young for her?'

'That's not the same.'

'Really? Or is Mr Holier-Than-Thou-Millennial being sexist?'

He sidestepped the question, posing his own.

'Does she know how you feel?'

I thought back to The Wolseley. Her eyes dancing as I'd made my play.

I was wondering how you're planning to spend the rest of the afternoon . . .

It hadn't been wishful thinking – she'd held my gaze and allowed a lazy smile to spread across her face. My intention had been clear and she'd responded with a twinkle-eyed grin. No PC nonsense, no embarrassment. We'd kissed in the taxi all the way around Hyde Park Corner. If her grandmother hadn't sent that SOS who knew how the afternoon might have turned out.

Tom tapped a finger on the table. A tic he'd had since he was a teenager.

'Simple question, Dad. Does Harriet know how you feel?'

'I believe she does.'

'Does she feel the same?'

I gripped the stem of my glass. 'You'd have to ask her.'

'Maybe I will.'

'Does she know how *you* feel?' I said.

'We haven't discussed it. It's just ... *there*. In the air. Unspoken. But *there*.'

'On both sides?'

'Yes.'

'I see,' I said.

Tom's smile didn't reach his eyes.

'I hate to be old-fashioned,' he said, 'but I'm young, free and single whereas you're middle-aged and married.' He leaned forward in his chair. '*To my mother.*'

I hesitated. Was this the moment for a heart-to-heart? Perhaps not. But in our family there's no such thing as a good moment so what the hell.

'Technically, you're right,' I said. 'I am married.'

'What does "technically" mean?'

'I take it your mother hasn't mentioned anything.'

'About?'

'Filing for divorce.'

He blinked twice in quick succession.

'Seriously?'

'It's not the sort of thing people joke about.'

He sat back in his chair and blew out his cheeks.

'Wow.'

'Good point, well made,' I said.

'It's hardly the shock of the century.'

'Really?' I said. 'It came as a surprise to me.'

142

'After the way you've behaved?'

'How have I behaved, Tom?'

'You know very well.'

'Do I?'

I was goading him, I admit.

'Did you seriously think Mum was going to put up with you for the rest of her life? After all those other women?'

So there it was. Never before had he put 'it' into words but I knew what he *thought* he knew. I also had a shrewd idea how he felt about it. Yet again, I was the villain of the piece. I stood up and looked out of the window. This was not the moment to talk about Bonnie. Once we started, who knew where things would end.

'Let's stick to Harriet,' I said. 'Do you intend to carry on seeing her?'

'Yes. Do you?'

'Absolutely.'

He gave me a pitying look.

'Because Mum wants a divorce?'

'No, because I met a woman who makes me happy.'

He stood up, suddenly agitated, jostling the table. His glass toppled over, spilling its contents.

'Fine,' he said. 'We both know where we stand.' He headed for the door then turned and fixed me with a stare.

'Are you sleeping with her?' he said.

'Are you?'

He rolled his eyes. 'May the best man win.'

Then he was gone.

I smoked three cigarettes in quick succession while staring at the spilled wine. Then I scraped the ready meal into the bin and took the bottle to bed.

At first, Tom's departure was a relief, not least because it gave me a sense of occupying the moral high ground. God knows why, when the opposite was the case. What kind of father cock-blocks his own son? As so often, the answer was more complicated than it might have seemed.

Within twenty minutes, my mood had plummeted from righteous indignation to despair – and not just because of the bombshell about Harriet. The truth was, I'd been worn down by shouldering the burden of our family's very own skeleton-in-the-closet. It was a twenty-year-old secret which, according to my ex-shrink, explained a lot about my reliance on pills, my aloofness towards Tom and my inability to show him the affection he had every right to expect. Had he stayed that night, things would have become heated. I might have blurted the truth about secrets that must stay buried. Secrets about Bonnie's 'adventures' during our marriage. About her tendency to fall for people of either sex. About the crippling insecurity that had given rise to her childlike inability to resist flattery, especially from older men.

Above all, I might have broken the *omertà* that had blighted three lives – mine, Bonnie's and Tom's – since his sixth birthday when a bombshell had destroyed all hope of normality let alone happy-ever-after.

Lying on the bed, staring at the ceiling, I reflected that had Tom not walked out I might have worked myself into a fury and blurted the truth about his mother's affair with my father – the devastating 'I–couldn't–help–myself–please–forgive–me' fling that had resulted in the birth of the boy I had done my imperfect best to think of as 'my' son.

TOM

It was a miracle I didn't punch him. I'm not even convinced he was serious about having fallen for Harriet, he just didn't want *me* to have her.

Well, okay, 'Daddy Dearest'. Game on.

Option one: love-bomb her. Flowers, candlelit meals, country walks and every other cliché in the WLTM-swipe-right–GSOH book.

Option two: take a 'softly softly' approach.

Yes.

Better.

Not because Harriet was immune to romance but because I didn't want to scare her off by coming on too strong. 'Keep it real' seemed the way to go. And let's face it, I may have had youth on my side but I couldn't compete with Dad when it came to flashing the cash and making grandiose romantic gestures. Harriet wouldn't have been human if she didn't like nice restaurants, glamorous holidays and the other perks of dating an older, richer dude. (I'd add 'wiser' but if he was so smart how come Mum wanted a divorce? She was, like, the best thing that had ever happened to him. If he lost her, he was a bigger fool than I thought.)

He was right about one thing: I was younger than Harriet. But since when had that counted as a negative? It's not as if I was some spotty adolescent.

Forget father versus son, this was metrosexual versus millennial, smug Belsize Park versus edgy Dalston, experience versus energy.

Of course, I knew women found Dad attractive. All my life, I'd seen their faces when he walked into a room, the warmth of their smiles as he showed genuine interest in what they had to say, the way he paid attention – *proper* attention – when they talked. No mansplaining, no hectoring, no patronizing put-downs. I was forced to admit it: his charm wasn't superficial, it was the real McCoy. Women liked him because he liked *them*. And despite the chilliness that had blighted our relationship, maybe I'd learned something from him. Perhaps I'd picked up a few ideas about how to capture a woman's heart. After all, I was my father's son.

HARRIET

Still stunned by the revelation about Tom and Richard, I started recording the Transport for London announcements just after nine o'clock on Monday morning. I was glad of the distraction. I'd done enough voice-overs not to be fazed by the studio process, and The Thoughts weren't coming thick and fast, threatening to sabotage everything, but that didn't mean I wasn't nervous. In the control room, on the other side of the glass, sat a barrel-chested technician, Sadiq. Next to him was Martyn, the TfL Marketing Manager.

There was no sign of Richard. I'd had no contact with him since cancelling our date. Maybe my nerves were more to do with the prospect of bumping into him in the corridors of Silk FM. I did my best to put him out of my mind. Fat chance.

Sitting in the soundproof booth, I swigged from my bottle of water, opened the file of bus routes and set to work. We kicked off with (surprise!) route number one. After testing the mic for level, and a bit of discussion about how to put a smile in my voice without sounding like I was actually cracking a joke, I started to work my way through the stops.

Route one – to Tottenham Court Road
Rotherhithe police station
Surrey Quays shopping centre
Surrey Quays station
Warndon Street
Corbetts Lane
Rotherhithe New Road
Lynton Road
Etc ... etc.

By the time we got to the final stops in the West End ...
Drury Lane
Tottenham Court Road

... I was sneaking a look ahead to check how many sodding bus routes there are in London. Answer: 722 – and counting.

With route one sorted, I got a thumbs-up from Martyn and moved on.

Route two – to Marylebone station ...

We took a break at 11.00, routes one to forty crossed off the list. Martyn seemed pleased we were on schedule. He treated himself to a Snickers from the vending machine while I nipped out for an espresso from Bar Italia.

I'd assumed Richard might have shown his face by now but there was no sign of him. Maybe he was deliberately keeping his distance. Given the bombshell that had just exploded, I can't pretend I wasn't apprehensive about seeing him but did my best to focus on the job at hand. After all, I was about to be the new Voice of London *and* being paid five thousand quid. I needed to do a decent job, not least because I'd be forced to listen to the sound of my own voice every time I boarded a bus or tube.

Back in the booth, I flicked through the routes, my spirits lifting at the sight of something more substantial than yet another bus route – something I could almost think of as a line of dialogue.

Revenue inspectors operate on this route. Please ensure you have touched in with your Oyster card, contactless payment card or mobile device.

Hardly Shakespeare but at least these were actual sentences, something to get my teeth into. I could bring some character definition to the lines. 'Authoritative but not authoritarian' – that was Martyn's watchword.

I'd spent a lot of the weekend doing yoga in the white-washed studio opposite the park in Stoke Newington, or slumped on Nan's sofa watching rubbish telly. Not a peep from Tom or Richard. Just as well. I was still having trouble wrapping my head around the coincidence that had brought these two men into my life. I'd no idea what they were thinking, or if they'd talked to each other. If so, would either of them speak to me again?

Over cod and chips on Saturday night, I told Nan what had happened. As usual, she saw the funny side.

'Take notes,' she said. 'It'll be good for your autobiography.'

I said I was relieved that I hadn't done the dirty deed with either of what she called my 'suitors'.

'If push came to shove,' she said, 'which would it be?'

Good question. Personality-wise, both ticked a lot of boxes: decent, clever, generous, kind. As for looks, Tom was definitely my type whereas Richard was more distinguished-looking. Older, of course, but in good shape for his age. Bottom line: I wouldn't kick either out of bed.

'This is better than *EastEnders*,' said Nan. 'So what are you going to do?'

The obvious answer was: do nothing. Let the whole thing fizzle out. Okay, so things had got a bit flirty and there had been a couple of snogs but that was it. Nothing to see here, move right along.

On the other hand, I'd made it to thirty-five without finding Mr Right. Was I seriously going to let two possible-maybes slip through my fingers?

I asked Nan for advice.

'You don't need advice, love. Just do the right thing.'

'Which is?'

'You'll know. When the time comes.'

'Great. Thanks, Nan.'

But once again, she was right. It was while I was brushing my teeth on Monday morning that I had a lightbulb moment. Like it or not, Richard was married. Okay, so Bonnie was having an affair, but that didn't change the bottom line. He had a wife, end of. So on the bus into town (when I wasn't

151

trying to pay attention to the recorded announcements) I finally decided what to do.

To tell the truth, if it hadn't been for the bombshell about Richard and Tom I'd probably have carried on seeing both of them until things sorted themselves out. Instead, I decided to tell Richard how grateful I was for everything he'd done for me, that I knew I'd been flirty over brunch (and while we were bantering on the radio) but that was as far as things would go and please could we just be mates.

It's not that I'd committed to zero-ing in on Tom, or that I definitely preferred him — it wasn't that simple — I just needed a clean slate, to see how, or if, things might pan out. The fact that Richard almost certainly didn't want more children — not at his stage of the game — may have played a part in my thinking. Annie, Dot and Freddie were still a possibility.

I knew he was on-air between noon and 3 p.m. but after lunch the TfL recording session started to fall behind schedule and Martyn kept cracking the whip until gone five-thirty when he announced he had a train to catch and made a speedy exit. I'd assumed that Richard would be long gone so was surprised to see him emerging from the boss's office and walking down the corridor. His expression gave nothing away.

'How's it going?' he said.

I tried to sound casual.

'Slowly but surely.' I cleared my throat. 'I'm sorry about cancelling Friday. Things got weird.'

He smiled.

'You can say that again. I had a visit from Tom.'

Oh.

'And?'

'Everything's fine,' he said. 'Nothing to worry about.'

I blinked, nonplussed. Should I leave it at that or launch into my spiel about wanting to be just good friends? Richard checked his watch.

'I don't suppose you've got time for that drink?' He saw my hesitation. 'Just a quick one. I've got news.'

I grabbed my coat and followed him out of the door, into Shaftesbury Avenue. The evening rush hour was at its height, traffic choking the Soho streets. Rain was starting to fall. I'd assumed we were going to a pub but after half a block he stopped in a doorway and pressed a buzzer. The door opened. He led me upstairs to a private members' club that occupied the entire building. Posh tuberose candles. Soft lighting. A hidden world. The receptionist was a stylish black woman, Eve, who could easily pass for a supermodel. Richard greeted her like an old friend and introduced me.

'Hi, Harriet,' she said. 'Welcome.'

Eve said we'd find a table in the Shaftesbury Room so we headed up another flight of stairs. The dimly lit bar was packed with people chatting and drinking or tapping at laptops. The restaurant was full. I'd put the average age at thirty. Richard stood out – the oldest by a mile.

'Glass of champagne?' he said, settling me at a corner table. I was tempted (who wouldn't be?) but this was not the moment to get sloshed so I asked for fizzy water. Richard smiled at the waiter who took our order then left.

'I'm glad Tom's cool about everything,' I said, without specifying what *everything* meant. But Richard didn't want to talk about his son.

'Don't worry about him,' he said, failing to mask a flicker of impatience. 'I need to talk to you about something else.'

'Oh?' I said.

'Can you keep a secret?'

'Try me.'

He leaned forward in his chair, keeping his voice low.

'I've had a couple of meetings with the programme controller, Jennifer. She asked if I'd be interested in taking over the breakfast show.'

I must have winced. Judging by his face it wasn't the reaction he was expecting.

'Have I said something wrong?' he said.

'No,' I said. 'But all those early mornings. What time would you need to get up?'

He shrugged. 'Half-four, maybe five. But that's not the point. It's a big deal to do a breakfast show. It's the flagship programme of any radio station and gets the biggest audience. If people listen first thing, they tend to stay tuned for the rest of the day. There's a lot riding on it.'

'So it's a promotion?'

'If you want to put it like that.'

Our drinks arrived: my water, Richard's wine. He made a point of looking the waiter in the eye.

'Thanks, Fredo.'

'Enjoy,' said the waiter, then he glided away.

I raised my glass in a toast. 'Congratulations.'

We clinked glasses and drank.

'Are you a morning person?' I said.

Richard shrugged. 'For the kind of money they'd pay me, you bet. But the other consideration is this: the show's over by nine a.m., which leaves the rest of the day free for additional work – or just having fun.'

'Sounds perfect.'

'I'm glad you think so,' he said. 'Because there's something else: the second banana. It's what they call a sidekick on radio and TV.'

'Like a double-act?'

He nodded. 'Some shows have a zoo format – three or four people in the studio or on outside broadcasts, bantering, supporting the main DJ. Most have a single presenter.' He leaned closer. 'Some stations team the presenter with a "second banana", someone to bounce off. He or she might do the traffic reports or weather, or both. They're every bit as important as the DJ, crucial to the success of the show.'

It was clear where this was heading but I stuck to nodding as he continued.

'Jennifer asked me how I'd like to play things – would I want to do it solo or would I prefer a "zoo" format or maybe a second banana? She's given me carte blanche.'

'And?'

He smiled and picked up his glass.

'I thought you and I had fun the other day, when we did the Voice of London thing in the studio. You ad-lib like a natural.'

I couldn't play dumb any longer, not without seeming like an idiot. I arched an eyebrow.

'Are you saying what I think you're saying?'

He nodded and smiled.

'There'd be an audition process, to show the bosses what you're made of. We've already identified the downside: the early starts can be a bitch. But let's not forget the upsides: a regular gig that pays well . . .' He paused for effect. '. . . and would leave the day free for whatever else comes your way. Jobs in theatre, film, TV, voice-overs . . .'

I could feel the blood thudding in my ears.

'Are you making me an offer I can't refuse?'

His smile turned into a grin.

'I'm asking if you'd be my second banana.'

RICHARD

The affair between my wife and my father took place twenty-six years ago and lasted less than a fortnight, coinciding with one of her 'episodes'. That's what Bonnie told me and I see no reason to disbelieve her. I never heard George's side of the story because I never gave him the opportunity to 'explain', because how could he?

The bottom line: the loathsome shit took advantage of a vulnerable woman at her lowest ebb. Bonnie is the kindest, smartest woman I know but she's suffered from catastrophically low self-esteem all her life – a legacy of her relationship with her own sorry excuse for a father. I won't go into gory details – it's her story not mine – but take my word for it: the sick bastard was lucky to be killed by a reversing lorry before I had a chance to wring his miserable neck.

So not surprisingly, life isn't easy for Bonnie. Never has been and never will be, whether she comes home or remains in the lotus position on a beach in Goa for the rest of her days. She's also lived with a diagnosis of bipolar disorder since she was fifteen, and whether that's down to nature or nurture is irrelevant – it just *is*. Naturally, I knew about it when I got down on one knee, at sunset on Waterloo Bridge, and popped the question all those years ago. Her eyes widened in surprise.

'I have an illness,' she said, as if I hadn't noticed. 'It's part of me.'

'I love all of you,' I said.

Cheesy? So sue me. It's how I felt.

In the years since, I've seen her stratospherically high and suicidally low. I've watched her order six £1,000 bottles of vintage champagne for a bar full of people then stand on a table and sing 'God Save The Queen'; I've sat vigil during nights when she's been unable to speak for weeping, or begged me for a razor blade so she can end it all. Thank God for modern meds, which keep her relatively 'chilled', at least most of the time.

My own dalliance with depression is nothing compared to the toll taken on Bonnie by her illness (because that's what it is: an illness). Call me old-fashioned but I intend to stand by her to the end, divorce or no divorce. I've never told anyone about her affairs for the simple reason that I love her. I know she loves me, too, in spite of everything.

It's not that I'm a henpecked pushover or a stickler for all that *till death us do part* wishful thinking, devised when life expectancy was thirty-five not eighty-five. No, it's just that I've always hoped she and I might make it to the rose-covered cottage together, against the odds – like battle-scarred soldiers limping home from a combat zone then collapsing under a shady tree, relieved and bound together by shared experience, good and bad.

At the time of their fling, I was working for an oldies' radio station – Strawberry Fields 94.9 FM. I presented the early-evening 'Seventies Sounds' show, from 6 to 9 p.m. on Monday to Friday, a regular commitment that allowed Bonnie and George to conduct their brief affair in the sure and certain knowledge that I was never going to show up unexpectedly. That's the thing about being married to a DJ: if you want to check his whereabouts just turn on the radio.

I only found out by accident, years later. It was Tom's sixth birthday, a day that coincided with one of Bonnie's low episodes. She was in bed, with the curtains closed. I stayed downstairs, supervising the boisterous party – a horde of six-year-olds booing 'Mister Bonkers', the so-called entertainer. In need of a cigarette break, I crept up to the landing. Passing the bedroom door, careful to avoid the creaky floorboard, I could hear Bonnie on the phone, talking to someone about how the guilt was unbearable. I can almost hear her now, whispering between sobs.

'I was ill … off my meds. You took advantage of me … Now I have to carry this secret for the rest of my life, and it's killing me.'

I went downstairs and waited for the call to end. Then I picked up the receiver and pressed 'redial'. My father answered. I've never spoken to him since.

Long story short: four days later (by which time Bonnie was back on an even keel), I told her what I'd overheard and asked, 'so what was the "secret"?' Which is when she broke down and told me: Tom was George's son, 'but only biologically speaking'.

Once the shock had worn off (which took a year, a year during which I'm ashamed to say I could hardly bring myself to speak to Tom, let alone his mother) there was no question of my leaving Bonnie or abandoning the boy she and my father had brought into the world – not least because of her two suicide bids. Triggered by guilt, one was an overdose, the other a botched attempt to slash her wrists. To call these desperate efforts 'emotional blackmail' is to over-simplify what happened, as well as to misunderstand mental illness, but if her behaviour *was* tactical, it worked. Rightly or wrongly, I'd found it impossible to stop myself withdrawing from Tom, almost to the point where he had no father, at least none worthy of the name. To risk depriving him of a mother too would have been unthinkable. So I stiffened my spine and Bonnie and I somehow managed to stay together – for better, for worse . . . blah, blah, blah.

A week after the bomb dropped, I discovered a series of sketches of her, hidden under the mattress. Drawn by George, they showed my wife in a variety of poses, naked. In a fit of blind rage, I dragged the mattress downstairs, onto the pavement, dumped the sketches on top and set fire to the lot. And they all lived unhappily ever after.

*

Harriet told me she needed to think about the job at Silk FM. In fact, she seemed scared by the prospect. Fair enough. It's a big commitment and a big decision. Was I trying to steal a march on Tom? Maybe. Would I have made the offer had I not been smitten? Perhaps not. But I was sure of one thing: Harriet was up to the task. I may be a fool when it comes to affairs of the heart but I had no intention of committing professional suicide. I told her not to take too long to decide. Once change is in the air at Silk FM things tend to move fast. And they did.

Within twenty-four hours of my conversation with Jennifer, the current breakfast show presenter (Chris, nice chap, lousy ratings) had been informed of what was diplomatically termed 'a reshuffle'. Which meant the cat was not only out of the bag but hissing and clawing. Hell hath no fury like a DJ saddled with the 2–6 a.m. graveyard shift.

On Tuesday evening, as soon as Harriet had finished her Voice of London recording session, I introduced her to Jennifer over a drink at the club on Shaftesbury Avenue.

'I gather Richard has told you what we're thinking.'

The 'we' was a good sign. I knew Jennifer had eavesdropped on Harriet's recording sessions.

'I'm flattered to be considered,' said Harriet.

Correct answer.

'He says you're an actress.'

'When I'm not frothing cappuccinos for Hackney hipsters.'

Jennifer smiled. The woman was ambition on legs and extremely smart. I could see her brain whirring, doing lightning calculations. Harriet was down on her luck. She wouldn't expect big money. And there was another plus. Piggy-backing on the Voice of London launch would provide a perfect publicity angle, ideal for cross-promotion. If a fraction of the capital's commuting millions tuned in to the breakfast show because they liked Harriet's voice on the buses and tubes, ratings would soar.

They chatted for a while. Harriet didn't bother to pretend she was a Silk FM fan, which was another clever move. In the radio business, Jennifer Ingham is famous for two things: her bullshit detector and her ability to sack people without losing sleep.

'Do you like the music we play?'

Harriet shrugged.

'The all-time greats. What's not to like?'

'Hardly your age group,' said Jennifer.

'Or yours,' said Harriet.

Another canny answer. They were the same age. They talked some more. On the surface, it was idle chit-chat but we all knew the game that was being played: two clever women sizing each other up.

Do I like you?

Can I trust you?

I barely said a word. First impressions are everything and Harriet was doing fine. I hadn't told her that Jennifer's brief from head office was to broaden the Silk FM demographic and cultivate a younger audience without alienating our existing listener base. At thirty-five, Harriet skewed a little young but still fitted the bill. I'd pitched her as old enough to sound like a grown-up but not so young as to annoy the baby boomers.

'Can you stay late tomorrow evening, after your TfL session?' said Jennifer. 'I'd like to put the two of you in a studio and see what happens.'

Harriet beamed.

'Can't wait.'

I didn't invite her to stay for another drink or risk anything that might be taken as an overture. Every instinct I had was telling me to play the long game. Meanwhile, there was no word from Tom, which came as a relief.

As things would turn out, he was merely biding his time and planning his own campaign but how was I to know?

Wednesday was Harriet's final day of recording the Voice of London announcements. I kept my distance from her studio but asked the technician, Sadiq, to let me know of any problems or signs of unprofessional behaviour. Three full days of reciting bus and tube routes was hardly hard labour (especially with a five grand fee) but would be a test of patience and resilience. She passed with no problem, taking suggestions with a smile and doing exactly as directed by Martyn. According to Sadiq, she was 'a total pro'.

The TfL Marketing Manager was full of praise, too, delighted to have accomplished his task on schedule and in good time for the new Voice of London's debut, which was imminent. All that remained was to programme the recordings into the system. (I didn't ask. Never been one for the technical side.)

Settling at the microphones in studio B, we started our first dry run on the dot of 7 p.m., acting as if we were doing a live breakfast show at the other end of the day. Pam supplied Harriet with traffic reports, horoscopes and weather updates and picked the playlist. Jennifer wanted to retain the 'agony uncle' element of the show so I'd selected a couple of emails from listeners. I considered letting Harriet see these in advance, so she could prepare her response, but decided against it. She needed to be up to the job or we'd both suffer a very public humiliation. Live radio is about dealing with the unexpected, the ability to ad-lib without making an arse of yourself (although that can work, too, as many of my peers demonstrate every day).

Jennifer and Pam took their seats in the control room, watching as Harriet sat at the guest mic. I operated the control panel, flicking up the two mic faders.

'Good morning from Silk FM,' I said. 'Welcome to the breakfast show. I'm Richard Young ...'

'... and I'm Harriet Brown. London's weather: looking mixed – a sunny start with a top temperature of nineteen centigrade and the possibility of showers this afternoon ...'

I did a time-check, cued the first track – Nat King Cole's 'Mona Lisa' – and we were off. And the weirdest thing? Even then – right from that very first link, when Harriet picked up from me mid-sentence, with no rehearsal – it felt like we'd been working together for years.

Things continued in the same vein, with Harriet back-announcing Nat King Cole and doing a time-check.

'Thank you for your emails to agony uncle Richard,' she said. 'It's great to be working with such a wise owl.'

I smiled. 'Flattery so early in the morning?'

'I don't want to embarrass you,' said Harriet, 'but I knew you were smart the first time I met you.'

'Only because I paid for lunch.'

'No, because you *listened*. Which makes you a rare bird. As my Nan says, "knowledge speaks but wisdom listens".'

'Sounds like a woman who knows a thing or two.'

'Guess who said it first.'

'Confucius?' I said. 'Oscar Wilde?'

'Jimi Hendrix.'

I was about to interject but she was in full flow.

'Do you know the difference between knowledge and wisdom, Richard?'

'No?'

'Knowledge is knowing a tomato is a fruit. Wisdom is knowing not to put it in fruit salad.' Without breaking her stride, she glanced up at the clock. 'And with the time at exactly six minutes past seven we go from the wisdom of the late, great Jimi Hendrix to Silk FM's own breakfast-time guru, Richard Young . . .'

Which was my cue to read the email.

'"Dear Richard," writes Janis from Finsbury Park, "I'm a single mum with three kids and two jobs. My boyfriend wants to move in but has no job and no income thanks to chronic back pain. He says he'll pay his way by being a house-husband and babysitter so I'll save on childcare. I love him to bits and the kids like him, too. Do I say yes?"' I turned to Harriet. 'Before I respond, what do you think?'

'Hmm. Tricky one, Janis,' said Harriet. 'I'd need to know more before offering serious advice, like how long have you been together and what's his history? If you're going to leave your kids with someone, you need to be a bazillion per cent sure who you're dealing with.'

'My thoughts exactly,' I said.

Which was true. Okay, hardly a tough test but I'd lobbed her the question with no warning and she'd responded off the cuff. Most importantly, she'd impressed the boss. I could tell by the look on Jennifer's face.

The rest of the hour continued in the same vein. Right from the start, Harriet seemed entirely at ease. By the time we hit eight o'clock she sounded like a complete natural. Warm, witty, relaxed – everything required of a sidekick. As the hour came to an end, Jennifer took me aside, to ask if I was happy.

'Very,' I said.

Even so, I was surprised by the speed of her decision. She called Harriet over.

'How would you feel if we offered you the job, starting two weeks on Monday?'

Harriet didn't miss a beat. 'Ecstatic.'

'Terrific. We'll talk money later.' Jennifer extended a handshake to seal the deal. 'We're kicking around ideas for the show over the weekend. Are you free?'

'I am now.'

'Good. It's a two-day brainstorm, figuring out a three-year strategy for Silk FM, with the focus on the new breakfast show. There'll be flip charts and blue-sky thinking courtesy of overpaid consultants who say things like "going forward" and "360-degree thinking".'

Harriet turned to me, grinning.

'Is this really happening?'

I could feel my pulse quicken as I returned her smile.

'Yes,' I said. 'It's happening.'

HARRIET

Not gonna lie, I was *totally* freaking out in that studio. The Thoughts were back with a vengeance and kept crashing over me like waves during a storm **I'M GOING TO SAY FUCK-FUCK-FUCKETY-FUCK IN FRONT OF THE BOSS AND RUIN EVERYTHING** but I managed to push them away and it must have gone okay or they wouldn't have offered me the job.

Thank God for Nan – *again*. If she hadn't given me one of her pep talks I'd have been sunk.

'You'll do fine, love. It's just sitting in a little studio, chatting, like one of your voice-over thingumabobs, yeah?'

'Yeah, sort of, Nan, but—'

She frowned and wagged a finger at me.

'No buts, Harriet. The point is, it's not in front of an audience, or other actors, and that's what makes you have a bit of a wobble.'

I loved that. *A bit of a wobble.* Try: full-scale meltdown that leaves me gasping for breath and on the verge of a panic attack. All the same, she had a point. It *was* a bit like doing a voice-over or an audiobook, just without a script.

But if I'm honest, taking the Silk FM gig was also a way of telling myself that I wasn't really a barista, I was still an actress – well, a performer – without spending more than a nanosecond facing up to the fact that the thought of *ever* setting foot onstage again filled me with sheer blind terror. Trouble is, I've been reading up on 'Pure' OCD and that's exactly what they say you shouldn't do – use avoidance strategies. You're supposed to *embrace* The Thoughts so they lose their power, not keep pushing them away to smoulder in the dark, gathering potency like psychological compost.

And as for the possibility of them taking over while I'm live on-air, with gazillions of people listening to me have a very public meltdown, well, I'm not even going there …

TOM

I wouldn't call it stalking but that doesn't make what I did right.

Harriet called on Saturday afternoon.

'They've offered me a job.'

'Who have?'

'Silk FM. I'm going to be your dad's sidekick. On the breakfast show.'

Fuck!

I knew it was his dream gig. By the sound of it, it was hers too. She had the grace to sound sheepish but I could tell she was excited.

'It all came together over dinner last night . . .'

Over *dinner* . . . ?

'. . . after we'd finished the dry run. Jennifer said they don't normally move so quickly – and she wasn't even thinking about a co-presenter till Richard mentioned it – but she wants to cash in on the publicity for the Voice of London launch in a couple of weeks, so it's all kick-bollock-scramble.'

I cleared my throat, playing for time. This was not how things were supposed to go. It seemed pretty obvious that my father was more smitten than I'd thought. He had every intention of winning and was prepared to play dirty.

'Congratulations,' I said.

I could hear the relief in her voice.

'You mean it?'

'Absolutely. Why wouldn't I?'

'Maybe because I'm going to be working with your father?'

I did my best to sound nonchalant.

'You'll be colleagues. Co-presenters. Does that mean we can't be friends?'

'Of course not,' she said.

'So what's the problem? It's a great gig and leaves time for other jobs.'

'So you're happy for me?'

'Of course.'

I was amazed by the ease with which the lie sprang to my lips. We moved on quickly, talking about how the Silk FM PR woman was liaising with Transport for London's marketing department to organize, like, press interviews and photo-calls for the coming week. I was slow on the uptake. Maybe I was in shock.

'Does this mean you've quit your job at the café?' I said.

'Of course.'

I took a breath.

'Dalston will miss you.'

It was the best I could do.

'What about you?' she said. I could hear the smile in her voice. She was giving me an opening but I sidestepped it.

'We should celebrate,' I said.

'Definitely.'

I had no weekend plans but needy is never a good look.

'How's next week?' I said.

'Completely crazy.'

'Okay,' I said. 'I'll pencil in Friday. If you can't make it let me know.'

I heard the doorbell.

'Gotta go,' said Harriet. 'He's here.'

My stomach gave a lurch.

'Who?'

'Your father. Jennifer said we need to sound like we've known each other forever so he's taking me out.'

I tried to sound casual.

'Somewhere nice?'

'Just my local. He suggested a restaurant but I wanted to meet on home ground, somewhere I can be myself, not worrying if I'm using the wrong knife and fork or if the thoughts are going to . . .'

She tailed off.

'What thoughts?' I said.

Her voice sounded small.

'Never mind.'

We talked for another couple of minutes but I don't remember what was said. The conversation ended and I gazed at my phone for, like, half an hour, then stared into the middle distance till the room grew dark.

When an email pinged in, I waited several minutes before checking my phone. If this was a message from Harriet I wasn't sure I wanted to know what she had to say. That's the thing about being smitten. Falling in love blows a fuse inside my head and makes me doubt myself. Love should come with a health warning, like cigarettes. *Love may cause inability to think clearly. Do not love while using heavy machinery. Love may lead to loss of appetite and sleep. Love may lead to poor judgement.*

I finally checked the email and saw it wasn't from Harriet. My first reaction was relief. Then I frowned. It was from someone called Paul Mendoza. His name was familiar but it took a moment before things fell into place.

The producer guy, the one at the networking event.

I'd sent him a couple of songs from the musical and here he was, popping into my inbox on a Saturday night and apologizing for not having replied sooner. My pulse-rate quickened as I read his message. I read it a second time, blinking in disbelief not just at the contents but at the timing too. Next thing I knew, I was on my bike, heading for Walthamstow.

HARRIET

Dad would *soooo* love Richard's car. It's a 1964 E-Type Jag, pillar box red. The word 'phallic' doesn't do it justice. A babe magnet but classy, too. Some middle-aged blokes, they get a classic motor and look like knobs. 'Boys and their toys' and all that. Not Richard. He loves his car but he's not precious about it and it's not pristine. Thank God. The number of times I've spilled coffee or smeared ketchup all over Nan's Micra.

'Never save anything for best,' he said as we pulled away from the kerb. 'It's a nice car but that's all it is – a car. For driving, not sitting in a museum.'

I could do without the personalized number-plate – too flash for my taste – but each to their own.

We could have walked – the pub's only a couple of streets away – but I could see he wanted to check out my reaction to his wheels. I didn't have to pretend. I was impressed.

'Do you know about cars?' I said.

He shrugged.

'I can change the oil and fix a flat tyre but that's about it.'
Tick.

Dad says a man's not a man unless he can light a fire, wire
a plug and mend a puncture. Oh, and carve a chicken and tie
a bow tie – not that I've ever seen him wear one. I'm not sure
what he'd make of Richard. It's not the age gap, more the
way he makes his living. I can hear Dad now.

'A bleedin' DJ? Not exactly a proper job, is it?'

Like they say, you can take the boy out of the East End
blah blah blah . . .

(All the same, Richard could definitely be considered a
DILF. That's a thing, right?)

He found a parking space outside the pub. Heads turned
as we went inside. A couple of lads laughed, taking the piss. I
was embarrassed but not about the car – it was Richard's hat
that made me want to roll my eyes. God, I hate fedoras. The
über-twat's hat of choice, IMHO. Still, I didn't know him
well enough to start criticizing the way he dresses. I once
told Cockweasel I hated him coming over in trackies and
trainers. 'It's disrespectful, like you don't think I'm worth
making an effort.' He told me he wore 'proper' clothes at
work so dressing down showed he was relaxed and I should
take it as a compliment. Then he saw my face so he apologized and promised to try harder. Next time I saw him he
turned up in triple denim and cowboy boots, taking the piss.
I should have known then.

Still, that was then, this is now. With the Silk FM job, the
Voice of London gig and two decent-looking blokes paying

a bit of attention, it was amazing how quickly things could turn around. At the same time, I knew everything could fall to pieces in an instant, especially if The Thoughts took over and/or I messed things up with Richard. So it felt like the pub was a test, a kind of audition. He hadn't mentioned our Hyde Park Corner snogathon and neither had I. It was our elephant in the room, flapping its ears and trumpeting, but if that's how he wanted to play things, fine by me.

He bought a pricey bottle of red and we settled at a table in the corner. We talked about the breakfast show for a while. He said the trick is to imagine I'm talking to one person.

'A mother getting the kids ready for school, say, or a man shaving. Think how they're feeling. Frazzled? Running late? Too much to do, too little time? Dreading the commute to work? They need a show that sets them up for the day. Music, news, weather and travel, yes – but they also need to feel the person on the radio is their friend, someone who knows what they're going through and can make them smile, which is where you come in.'

'I'm no comedian,' I said. 'Especially first thing in the morning.'

'Be yourself and the banter will come naturally.' He sipped his wine. 'Become your listener's friend and they'll stick with you for life.'

I like a man who knows what he's on about. Doesn't matter if it's beer or books, astronomy or architecture – there's something sexy about a bloke who knows his onions. (BTW: if you want to know where that phrase comes from,

Nan told me it was a bloke called S. G. Onions who made counterfeit coins to teach kids how to recognize the real thing. If they could tell the fake coin from the genuine article, it meant they 'knew their onions'. I don't believe a word but Nan swears it's true.)

I listened as Richard told me more about his hopes for the new show and what it had been like working at other radio stations and how he'd ended up at Silk FM, even though the music he has to play is for the Saga generation. Just as it was starting to feel like a monologue, he apologized for monopolizing the conversation and asked me about my family. So I told him about Mum and Dad's shops, how they'd spent years saving up for the cruise, and how I was staying with Nan while they were away.

'So you've never lived away from home?'

'I had a flat for a while,' I said, not mentioning that it was during the Cockweasel phase. 'But it got lonely so I moved back home.'

For the first hour, I was on my guard, hoping he wouldn't get flirty. By the time we ordered a second bottle there was no sign of anything leery so I started to relax.

'Tom says you have a tricky relationship,' I said.

Richard raised an eyebrow.

'I was wondering when his name would come up.'

'You have to admit, it's a weird situation.'

He nodded.

'I hope it won't be a problem.'

Which made two of us. I wasn't going to say anything to

jeopardize our professional relationship. Jennifer Ingham had phoned to talk money and I'd said 'yes' straightaway. To tell you the truth, it was a lot less than I was expecting but still pretty decent compared to what I was used to at the café. So here I was, drinking wine with my new colleague – a nice-looking bloke in a Paul Smith suit – and feeling good about things, which made a change from how I normally felt.

Bottom line: I'd waited years for a chance like this. Okay, so it wasn't a movie or Lady Macbeth at the National or the lead in a TV series, but it beat serving skinny lattes ten hours a day. Best of all, it would give me a steady income, a profile and maybe lead to other stuff. All I had to do was not mess up with Richard.

So when Tom walked in, my face must have been a picture. I could see Richard was surprised, too.

'Well, if it isn't the Boy Wonder.'

Tom pulled up a chair and sat down. His face was red, his brow sweaty, as if he'd been cycling for miles.

'Am I interrupting?'

'Of course not.' I hope I sounded genuine. The truth was, his showing up made me nervous. I felt as if I'd been caught out on an illicit rendezvous, which was absurd. 'How did you find us?'

'You said you were going to the pub. You can't miss Dad's car. Mum calls it a "midlife crisis on wheels".'

Richard gave a tight smile.

'Glass of wine?'

Tom ignored him, taking a swig from his water bottle.

'We need a chat,' he said, turning to me. 'We can't just pretend this is normal. I like you, Harriet – a lot. Dad likes you too and who can blame him? But the question is: what are we going to do about it?'

Talk about straight to the point. I'm not normally backwards in coming forwards but the question was directed at Richard so I waited for him to reply.

'Harriet and I are going to be colleagues,' he said. 'Who knows how things will turn out?'

Tom turned to me. 'Is that how you see it?'

I swallowed. It was time for some plain talking.

'Look, I really like you both,' I said. 'But the truth is, I'm still getting over someone. I'm excited about the Silk FM job and that's as far ahead as I want to look. I don't see why things should get complicated. We're all grown-ups.'

'O-kay,' said Tom. He sounded pissed off. 'Good to know where we stand.'

Richard leaned back in his chair. 'Well, this isn't at all awkward.'

Tom wiped his brow with the back of his hand.

'I had some news,' he said. 'About my musical. An email from a producer. He asked me to send some songs and he wants to see a showcase.'

'Cool,' I said. 'Anyone I might know?'

'His name's Paul Mendoza. He's done shows in the provinces and he's looking for a new production for the West End.'

'What's involved in a "showcase"?' said Richard.

'A one-off performance in a small venue,' said Tom. 'Maybe a room above a pub. It's so Paul can see if the show is worth investing in. It won't put my name in lights but it's a step in the right direction.'

'Brilliant,' I said. My grin was genuine. I love it when good things happen to good people. Tom returned my smile.

'I told him about you,' he said, leaning forward. 'I said I'd ask if you'd consider playing Roxanne.'

I blinked.

'You mean, the lead?'

He nodded.

'There's no dosh, I'm afraid, and there'll be weeks of rehearsals plus lots more work getting the show into shape, but the great thing is you can fit it around Silk FM. Plus you get to perform in front of a producer. Like an audition, only better. Who knows where it could lead?'

WHICH WAS *THE* MOST EXCITING OFFER – A *PROPER* ACTING JOB WITH BIG POTENTIAL – AND YET THERE WAS NO WAY I COULD SAY YES BECAUSE THE THOUGHTS THE THOUGHTS *THE FUCKING THOUGHTS!*

'Brilliant,' I said, trying to keep my voice from trembling. 'Count me in.'

'Cool,' said Tom. 'I'll drink to that.'

'I'll get you a glass,' said Richard. He got to his feet. I could see Tom was pissed off but my heart was hammering like crazy and I was having trouble focusing on what they were saying.

'You don't seem happy about my news, Dad.'

'Because it would be like congratulating you on buying a lottery ticket. Let's celebrate when you sign a contract.'

'Nice,' said Tom. 'Thanks a lot.'

His dad sighed, resumed his seat and ran his fingers through his hair and as I was watching the two of them, father and son, all I could think was **I JUST SAID YES TO SOMETHING *SOOO* SCARY AND I'M GOING TO HAVE A PANIC ATTACK AND WHY IS RICHARD STILL TALKING?**

But he showed no sign of stopping, leaning closer to Tom as he delivered a mini-lecture.

'Do you have any idea how hard it is to get a musical put on in a crappy little theatre in the arse end of nowhere, let alone the West End or Broadway? For every *Hamilton* or *West Side Story* there are a thousand flops.'

Tom responded with a quote that sounded like Shakespeare.

'"A man's reach should exceed his grasp or what's a heaven for?" Isn't that what you've always told me?'

Richard spread his hands in an expression of defeat.

'Good point, well made,' he said, getting to his feet. 'I'll fetch that glass.'

He left me alone with Tom and my heart was still hammering in my chest **BECAUSE FUCK IT, IT'S NO GOOD, I CAN'T GO THROUGH WITH IT BECAUSE THE THOUGHTS THE THOUGHTS *THE THOUGHTS* ...**

'Actually,' I said, trying to ignore my sweaty palms, 'I'm really sorry but I don't think I can.'

He smiled, not understanding.

181

'Sorry?'

'I can't play the lead. Or play anything for that matter.'

His brow creased into a frown.

'But you said . . .'

DON'T MAKE THIS HARDER THAN IT IS,
PLEASE.

'I know what I said, Tom. But I wouldn't want to let you down, so it's best if I say no. I'll still help out with lyrics and stuff, if you want me to, but I can't perform in your show.'

He opened his mouth to protest but I got there first.

'Please,' I said. 'No more questions.'

He sighed and shrugged his shoulders then lapsed into a puzzled silence. I took a gulp of wine to steady my nerves but couldn't shake the feeling I'd messed up *again* because of The Thoughts. Which is when my phone beeped with a text from Damian, aka Cockweasel. I'm ashamed to admit it but the sight of his name made my heart soar. There were just three words.

I miss you x

Fucking arse-biscuit!

TOM

I admit it, I was talking bollocks. I hadn't mentioned Harriet to Paul Mendoza. His email had said he'd attend a try-out of *They F**k You Up*, but only if I could pull it together before he set off on a forthcoming trip to America.

Still, as I cycled home from the pub, I congratulated myself on kiboshing Dad's bid to keep Harriet all to himself. Giving her the Silk FM job was a clever move, but there was no way I was going to give him a clear run.

As for why Harriet wouldn't star in the show, WTAF? Okay, so it was only a try-out but surely it was worth a shot, a chance to shine in front of a producer? Nope, she was adamant and there didn't seem any point in trying to talk her round. I'd no choice but to settle for a creative collaboration. The important thing now was to make sure she felt properly invested in the show. I'd happily give her the percentage she deserved, anything to make sure Dad couldn't monopolize her time.

It wasn't bloody-mindedness. There comes a time when

a bloke has to stand up for himself and that time was now. Plus, every man needs to beat his father at something – and maybe my 'something' was winning Harriet's heart. The more I thought about it, the more I saw of her, the more I felt sure she was Ms Right.

They say luck is when preparation meets opportunity. The truth was I was nowhere near ready to showcase *They F**k You Up*, with just four complete songs which had taken forever to write. I needed six more, *at least*, before I had anything approaching a proper show. But now I had a partner. And a plan.

RICHARD

Cheeky sod, waltzing into the pub like that. What was he up to? Trying to catch me holding hands with Harriet? To surprise us mid-snog, like drunken teenagers? Still, it took *cojones* to show up out of the blue, so I take my hat off to the lad: seven out of ten for chutzpah. (Speaking of hats, Harriet liked the fedora. I caught her looking at it out of the corner of her eye. I think she finds it stylish.)

Tom left shortly after she'd said 'yes' to helping write his, ahem, 'musical'. The one he's been working on since the dawn of time but which shows no sign of becoming a reality. Still, recruiting her was a canny move on his part, designed to neutralize my pre-emptive strike in signing her up for Silk FM. Whatever else the boy is, he's no fool. Under normal circumstances, I'd say 'the apple doesn't fall far from the tree' but let's face it, our family doesn't count as normal.

After Tom left, Harriet and I didn't stay long at the pub. She was distracted by a text – from her grandmother, or so she said. She dashed off a quick response, which was fine, but then her phone started pinging like a pinball machine. She began replying to message after bloody message. It wasn't long before I got fed up and suggested calling it a night. I pretended I had a dinner date; she pretended not to mind.

As I dropped her outside her Nan's house, we parted company with a quick peck on the cheek. I was careful not to say anything flirtatious. Play the long game – that's the thing. A less experienced bloke might have kicked up a fuss about her texting marathon but wasn't maturity the quality that gave me a crucial edge over Tom? He had youth on his side, and everything that goes with it. What could I offer? Some worldly wisdom and a few quid in the bank. Would it be enough to see off the competition? Time would tell.

For now, there was little point in pretending that maturity alone would make me irresistible, especially since I seemed to have developed some unfortunate tendencies, the kind that appear to be an inescapable part of the ageing process – and I'm not talking about physical decline. I play tennis, I walk a lot and I'm only forty-nine, so still a long way off being a grumpy old git (I hope!). However, the sight of people dropping litter makes me foam at the mouth, I can't stand music leaking from earphones, or the stench of Big Macs and fried chicken (who eats food by the bucket?). As for those idiots who narrowly miss bumping into you on the pavement because they're glued to their sodding iPhones – well, don't get me started.

Back home in Belsize Park, I put a tray of M&S lemon

sole goujons in the oven, opened a bottle of Pouilly Fuissé then sat in the Eames chair and watched two episodes of *Curb Your Enthusiasm* with just one thought in my head. *Softy softly catchee Harriet.*

HARRIET

The next few weeks were a blur. Richard was still doing his daily lunchtime show so we got together for more dry runs in the late afternoons, one every day, until sitting at a microphone and doing traffic reports, weather forecasts and blethering for England started to feel like second nature. I got a particular kick out of reading the horoscopes but I'm sure Richard is a sceptic, like Tom. Fair enough, but no one could deny that I was on a roll, which was in line with the forecasts for Aquarius, so they can both put that in their pipe and smoke it. There were trailers to record, too, to promote the new show. I re-tuned Nan's transistor from Radio 2 to Silk FM, so she could hear the clips of me and Richard doing our banter, giving listeners a taste of what to expect between 6 and 9 a.m. Monday to Friday.

'Is he being a gentleman?'

'So far, Nan.'

'He sounds like trouble to me.'

I told her not to worry: Richard was fun, friendly and

full of encouragement, but he was keeping things totally professional and showing no signs of being flirtatious. Our Piccadilly snog was ancient history, all the workplace boundaries seemed to be in place, and The Thoughts seemed to have receded, at least for now. Phew!

As for Tom, he was having a burst of creative energy that had prompted him to quit *Double Glazing Monthly* and kept him at home for days on end, living on pizza and working all hours. He FaceTimed me most days, playing me his latest songs and asking for my opinion. As with the first few I'd heard, the music was terrific (there was something Sondheim-esque about his melodies) but his lyrics needed work, which is where my strengths lie, so we made a good team. And he didn't press me on my decision not to perform in the show, which helped me feel like I'd made a good decision for once in my life.

I was genuinely excited about the prospects for *They F**k You Up* but with so much else happening I had to put it out of my mind or risk freaking out at all the stuff coming my way – especially the build-up to the Voice of London launch.

It's a funny thing – when change hits your life it feels like you're walking a tightrope, between skyscrapers. The only way to keep your nerve is to keep putting one foot in front of the other and never *ever* look down.

In the run-up to the big day, Transport for London's publicity department kept me busy doing interviews for local radio stations, websites and papers. The bosses at Silk FM weren't thrilled about me appearing on rivals, like Capital and Heart, but Richard managed to convince Jennifer Ingham that it was all good publicity for our new show, so I carried on regardless. After the first couple of days, I began to understand what it must be like to be one of those mega movie stars doing a publicity junket, with zillions of journalists wheeled in for fifteen-minute slots and asking the same questions over and over again and sometimes it got a bit stressful and **I WANTED TO BURST OUT LAUGHING AND STRIP NAKED** but mostly it was fine.

So what with one thing and another, I barely had time to think about Cockweasel. Okay, that's not strictly true. I thought about him a lot but was too busy to obsess over his texts and dissect every syllable, the way I used to before I discovered he was a total meat-muppet.

A married meat-muppet.

With kids.

I miss you x

That was the message that had kicked it off – the one he'd sent while I was in the pub with Richard. I'd fired off a quick response.

Tough!

He came back straightaway . . .

Don't be like that babe xxx

And before I knew it, we were texting like school kids on a sugar rush. He told me his dad had died so he was sad. I remembered him talking about his father – the famous bank robber – so I said I was sorry and hoped he was okay, which he took as a green light to send a bunch of messages about how depressed he was, even though Jack had left him a shedload of dosh. He even sent a photo of the Porsche he'd bought to cheer himself up.

Fancy a ride?

I didn't hesitate.

No.

Richard pretended not to mind all the texting but I could see he was annoyed, and who can blame him? After a while, he said he had a dinner date and dropped me back at Nan's. I sat on her sofa and carried on texting Cockweasel till he pissed me off by asking if he could come over 'for a chat'. I tapped out my reply.

No way!

I turned off my phone and went upstairs to watch *The Omen II* with Nan.

Honestly – blokes! They're like buses: you wait ages then three come along at once.

I didn't sleep the night before the Big Day. Not a wink. Mum and Dad sent a good luck email from Hong Kong and Nan insisted I wake her before leaving the house so I took her a cup of tea just before 5 a.m.

'Good luck, darlin'.'

'They don't say "good luck", Nan.'

'Who don't?'

'Showbiz people. They say "break a leg".'

'Tossers.'

I was halfway out of the door when her voice made me turn.

'Harriet?'

'Yes, Nan.'

'I'm proud of you. Your sod of a granddad would have been proud, too.'

'Thanks, Nan.'

She sipped her tea and frowned. 'You all right, love?'

'Fine, thanks. Just something in my eye.'

There was no traffic so the Uber to Shaftesbury Avenue took less than twenty minutes. Although I was nervous, sitting in the cab after being skint for so long felt good. The sun was rising and the streets were almost deserted, just a handful of early birds heading into tube stations or boarding buses. If everything was going according to plan, Transport for London would have switched the tannoy system to the new recordings. It was weird, thinking of my disembodied voice echoing along platforms around the network, from Morden to High Barnet, from Cockfosters to Heathrow. As we reached the West End I was tempted to dash into Oxford Circus station and listen to myself telling people to *please move right down inside the carriage*, but I was scared I'd be late getting to Silk FM so I put it off till later. It may not have been the bright lights of Broadway or the red carpet in Leicester Square but it was a big day in the life of Harriet Brown.

Richard was already in when I arrived, just after five-thirty, looking cool in one of his posh suits. He was talking to Pam. She'd brought flowers to wish me luck (bless!).

Jennifer was in early, too, her high heels clacking down the corridor as she arrived with coffee and muffins. Raising the latte to my lips, I spared a thought for whichever early-shift barista had frothed the milk and sprinkled the cinnamon. Then, sitting at the mic, heart galloping, I thought briefly of Tom and wondered if he was tuning in to my debut.

The clock ticked towards the top of the hour.

'Mobile off?' said Richard, donning his headphones.

I reached for my phone. It pinged with a text. From Cockweasel. **SERIOUSLY?** *NOW?* **JUST BEFORE I WENT LIVE ON-AIR FOR THE FIRST TIME?**

I tapped the screen and there they were: those three little words – the ones I'd been aching to hear.

I love you.

What did I tell you? The man's a scrote-bag!

TOM

I hadn't managed to get to bed – too busy working on *They F**k You Up* – so catching Harriet's first show was more of a late night than an early start.

I was used to hearing Dad on-air. As a kid, that's mostly how I remember him: a disembodied voice on the radio. He wasn't home much and never came to school plays or sports days. I never understood why. His shows lasted two or three hours, the time-slot varying according to whichever radio station he was working for, so how did he spend the rest of his time?

One night – I must have been twelve or thirteen – I hit on an answer that explained everything. He and Mum were always arguing (it never got physical but both were yellers and door-slammers) and the reason seemed obvious. If Dad wasn't at home and he wasn't on the radio, where was he? Answer: *with other women*. Once the idea took root, it quickly became the truth.

I didn't confront him – not till years later – but the

194

realization made sense of so many things: the constant rows ... Mum's epic sulks ... the treading-on-eggshells atmosphere at home. Above all, his absence from my life.

As the 6 a.m. news ended, I pushed the keyboard away, flopped onto my sofa with a mug of coffee and stroked Nelson's ears while listening to the familiar jingle kicking off Dad's new venture.

'*The Richard Young SHOW!*'

'Good morning, London,' intoned my father. 'Welcome to a brand new breakfast show with me, Richard Young ...'

'... and me, Harriet Brown. We've got all your favourite music, plus everything you need to start the day: news, travel, horoscopes and weather ...'

'... and we'll be doing our best to help out with advice on your personal and emotional problems so thanks for your emails ...'

'... but let's start as we mean to go on — with the best music in town: and it's a classic from Ol' Blue Eyes ...'

A Sinatra song began to play. 'The Lady is a Tramp', one of Dad's desert island discs. No doubt about it — it was a smooth start. Assured, relaxed, polished. Dad and Harriet sounded as if they'd been working together forever. And her luscious voice was made for radio.

I wish I could say I was happy for her and in many ways I was: this was a well-deserved break. But the truth was, I was jealous. I visualized the two of them sitting in the studio, headphones slung around their necks, sipping coffee and planning the next segment of the show while Sinatra crooned in the background. I could feel envy spreading through my system like caustic soda. No wonder Nelson jumped off my lap and disappeared through the cat flap.

I'd wished Harriet good luck by text and sent her a card c/o Silk FM. Dad would almost certainly have bought her flowers – a big bunch from a posh florist's. Perhaps they'd go for a celebratory breakfast after the show. Another image sprang to mind: him toasting Harriet with Buck's Fizz at The Wolseley (where else?).

Meanwhile, here was I – in stained trackies, surrounded by pizza boxes, dirty plates and empty Stella cans. I hadn't shaved for a week and judging by the reek from my clothes a shower was overdue.

On the bright side, my song-writing marathon was paying off. I'd discarded dozens of ideas, polished the four completed songs, drafted lyrics for five more *and* sketched out basic melodies for the final two. The libretto was taking shape, too, with the story arc starting to make sense and the characters developing clearly defined voices and speech patterns.

Jacking in the day-job had been reckless (giving no notice meant leaving *Double Glazing Monthly* without a reference) but sometimes you have to leap before you look. Or so I kept telling myself. From time to time – often as I was waking from a feverish sleep – I forced myself to get real and ask myself awkward questions: was I truly being bold or simply in the grip of a starry-eyed fantasy that would end in tears? And unemployment. And poverty.

Like someone unable to resist probing a painful loose

tooth, I forced myself to listen to the first half hour of Harriet's Silk FM debut. I was on the verge of switching off when I became transfixed by an ad-lib exchange on the subject of yoga. She was trying to explain to my father the difference between two poses.

'*Sarvangasana is when you're lying on your back with your arms supporting your back and your legs in the air.* Vriksasana *is when you stand on one leg with your arms raised above your head and your palms together.*'

'*And you do this for fun?*' asked Dad.

'*Yes, twice a week.*'

'*How much do they pay you?*'

'*Very funny,*' said Harriet. '*It's not expensive. You should try it.*'

'*Maybe next lifetime.*'

'*What's wrong with today? Or are you scared I'll put you to shame?*'

'*Is that a challenge?*' said Dad. I could imagine his raised eyebrow.

'*If you'd like it to be.*'

'*Challenge accepted.*'

'*This afternoon?*' said Harriet.

'*Perfect. We'll record what happens and report back tomorrow.*'

I had the impression this was a genuine off-the-cuff suggestion – one of those spontaneous 'magic moments' Dad's always talking about, the kind of flexibility he says makes working in radio more fun than TV.

I made the decision there and then. I knew where Harriet practised yoga – the studio opposite the park in Stoke

Newington. I googled its schedule and found the most likely class. If I got some sleep now I could be back in action by the time it started – 3 p.m.

No sooner had my head hit the pillow than the doorbell rang. I checked my watch. Just past six-thirty; too early for the postman. I pulled the duvet over my head. The bell rang again. I climbed out of bed and padded to the intercom.

'Yes?'

The voice was male.

'Is this Tom?'

'Who wants to know?'

'George.'

'George who?'

A sigh.

'Your grandfather.'

Suddenly, I was wide awake. I buzzed him inside, remembering Dad's text.

He's back. Don't give him any money.

I listened to him slowly climbing the stairs. As he turned onto the first-floor landing and came into view, I tried to remember the last time I'd seen him. Twenty years ago? More?

There were no photos of George Albert Brocklebank at the flat in Belsize Park. His name was never mentioned. It was as if he'd been airbrushed from the family history – the man who never was.

But here he was – 'Gorgeous George' – living up to his

nickname and climbing the final steps with a grace and agility that belied his age. Carrying a well-worn Aquascutum raincoat, he wore a bottle green corduroy suit, highly polished black brogues and a yellow silk pocket square, a look his generation would probably call 'natty'. His salt and pepper hair was in need of a trim. In a concession to age, his spectacles (*actual* rose-tinted glasses) dangled from a chain around his neck. His hands were liver-spotted, his nails immaculately groomed.

'I know it's horribly early,' he said, 'but at my age a proper night's sleep is a distant memory. Besides, your lights were on two minutes ago.'

He shook my hand – a knuckle-crunching grip.

'How did you know where I live?'

He tapped the side of his nose.

'That's for me to know and you to wonder.'

He walked past me, crossing the threshold of my flat, which suddenly felt too small to accommodate the two of us. He peered out of the window, scanning the street below.

'Looking for someone?' I said.

'You can never be too careful.' He turned and smiled. 'Don't worry, I shan't stay long.'

I closed the door. He cast a glance around what passed for my home. If he was shocked by the state of the place, he did a good job of disguising his feelings and pretending not to notice my dishevelled state. Ignoring the piles of washing-up and pizza cartons, he gestured towards the kitchen.

'Do you have any proper coffee?'

I set the kettle to boil. When I turned to face him, he was sitting on the sofa, polishing his glasses with a handkerchief.

'So,' he said. 'You've grown and I've shrunk. What else has happened since I last saw you?'

It turned out that my father's father had recently returned from what he called 'my grand tour, perhaps my last hurrah': driving Route 66 in America in a red Cadillac then travelling around Australia, the Far East and South America, stopping off to look at a gold mine in Peru. Unsurprisingly, there was a woman involved, a widow called Imelda. Her husband had been something to do with the oil industry and left her very well off (or as he put it, 'obscenely rich'). I dimly recalled a long-ago argument between Mum and Dad, when she'd called George a 'superannuated gigolo'.

'Imelda is a wonderful woman. Perhaps the love of my life.' He pocketed the yellow handkerchief. 'Well . . . one of them.'

'Lucky man,' I said, setting his mug on the coffee table.

'I'll invite you to our wedding,' he said. 'Chelsea Town Hall then lunch at the Savoy.' He peered at my grubby fleece. 'Think you can manage a suit?'

I ignored the dig.

'Have you told Dad you're getting married?'

The flinch was unmistakable. He shook his head and spoke softly.

'I'm hoping that you might tell him for me. We're on non-speaks.'

As if I didn't know. I tried to sound nonchalant.

'Because?'

He cleared his throat, clearly playing for time, but it was he who'd raised the subject of their estrangement so what was the point of skirting the issue?

'I can't recall,' he said.

An obvious lie but I let it go. He reached into the pocket of his raincoat and took out a notepad and pencil.

'Do you mind if I sketch while we talk?'

'Sketch what?'

He didn't answer but opened the notepad and began to trace the pencil softly over a blank page.

'How's your dear *maman*?' he said.

'In Goa. Having a midlife crisis.'

He looked up and arched an eyebrow.

'Another affair?'

I frowned.

'"Another"?'

He had the grace to look sheepish then gave a mischievous grin.

'Oops,' he said.

Insofar as I'd thought about my grandfather at all, this was the George Brocklebank I'd imagined. Here less than five minutes, he'd already let a family secret out of the bag. But I wasn't ready to have lifelong assumptions overturned by a man I barely knew.

'I think you're getting muddled up,' I said. 'If anyone has affairs it's Dad.'

He gave a small shrug, as if the matter were of no consequence.

'Suit yourself.' He gestured towards the Yamaha keyboard. 'Are you a pop star? That would explain the tattoo, I suppose.'

'No, I'm writing a musical, and I'm worried.'

'About?'

'That I'm no good at writing musicals.'

The skin around his eyes creased as he smiled.

'Do you have a vacuum cleaner, Tom?'

'Why, do you feel like doing some housework?'

He shook his head.

'Have you heard of James Dyson? The man who revolutionized the vacuum cleaner and became a billionaire?'

'What about him?'

'Do you know how many prototypes he built before he made a successful one?'

'Five? Ten?'

'Five thousand, one hundred and twenty six,' said George, still sketching on his pad. 'Repeat after me: "I'm not very good at writing musicals – *yet*."'

I smiled and did as instructed.

'Are you writing from the heart?' said George.

'Sort of.'

'There's your answer,' he said. 'Find a subject that comes from the heart and Lady Luck will shower you with blessings.'

I poured myself a cup of coffee and sat opposite him. Memories were stirring: George reading me a bedtime story (*Pinocchio*?). Eating ice cream on a pebble beach (Brighton?). Riding dodgems on a blustery pier. But that was all there was in the section of the memory bank labelled 'Grandpa'. The man had disappeared without trace when I was five, maybe six.

'What happened to you?' I said.

'Long story.' He put the notebook on the table, pocketed the pencil and took a sip of coffee. 'It's all in my autobiography.'

He reached into the pocket of his raincoat. This time he took out a tattered red exercise book.

'It's called *You Had to Be There*.'

'Have you got a publisher?'

'I'm working on it. But they tell me the book's too racy or that no one would believe it.' He pocketed the exercise book, put down his cup and cracked his knuckles. 'I tell them every word is true – every hard-earned scar, every stolen kiss, every narrow escape.'

I studied his face.

'Is my grandmother alive?'

The light seemed to leave his eyes.

'No, the poor thing died much too young. Run over by a hearse. Things would have been different if she were still around.'

'Is that true? About the hearse?'

'Who would make up such a thing?' He blew out his cheeks. 'But life is short, Tom. Eat the cake, buy the shoes, take the trip. Have you got a girlfriend?'

'I'm not sure.'

He raised a quizzical eyebrow.

'Boyfriend?'

'No,' I said. 'It's just ... complicated.'

'*Plus ça change, plus c'est la même chose*,' said George. 'Boy meets girl, boy gets girl, boy loses girl. Story of my life.' Finishing his coffee, he took off his jacket then unlaced his shoes. 'Mind if I grab forty winks?'

'Be my guest,' I said, getting to my feet as he stretched out on the sofa and propped a cushion under his head.

'Can I ask a question?' I said. 'Why does Dad resent me?'

He blinked.

'I'm sure he doesn't *resent* you, exactly. But life can be complicated.'

'What does that even mean?'

'*Tout comprendre, c'est tout pardonner*,' he said. 'To understand all is to forgive all.'

'That's the point,' I said. 'I don't understand.'

He shrugged and closed his eyes.

'*C'est la vie.*'

And that was that. I let the silence stretch.

'What should I call you?' I said.

He opened one eye.

'Anything but Grandpa.'

'George it is.'

There was warmth in his smile now, and a twinkle in his eye.

'Charming boy. You must take after your mother.'

He closed both eyes. Within seconds he was asleep.

I sat for a moment, considering the idea of tidying up but

what would be the point? He'd seen me at my worst and didn't care. I'd warmed to the man straightaway. He was nothing like the ogre my father had led me to expect.

I checked my watch: just after seven-thirty. Harriet's yoga class didn't start until three. I should have followed George's example and grabbed some shut-eye but his arrival had left me energized, my brain racing; there was so much to ask when he awoke.

I shaved and took a shower. When I emerged from the bathroom, George was snoring softly. I picked up his notepad and looked inside. His sketch was good, so accomplished it made me gasp. In a few strokes, he'd captured me perfectly – not just the contours of my face but my posture and expression: wary, on my guard. I replaced the notebook on the table then turned my attention to his jacket. A plum-coloured wallet jutted from an inside pocket. No – not a wallet, *a passport* . . .

I drew it out and flicked through the pages. A slip of paper fell to the floor. Four words in black ink. *Rochester House – Camden. Paddy.*

The passport photo showed my grandfather looking fit and tanned. There weren't many stamps and nothing to suggest recent trips to Peru, America, Australia or the Far East. Puzzled, I put it back, along with the slip of paper. My fingers made contact with something else in the pocket – a second passport. This told a different story. Every page was full. There were stamps from all over the world including the destinations on his 'grand tour'.

But the holder's name was not George Albert Brocklebank. It was Lord Anthony Buckingham.

RICHARD

Harriet did a great job on that first show. (The *Evening Standard* would later call her debut 'brilliant, a promising start to a glittering new career'.) No gaffes, no slips of the tongue, no awkward moments. Jennifer was beaming as we came off-air at nine o'clock, high-fiving the two of us on her way into a budgets meeting. Pam was pleased too, in her own low-key way, telling us we'd made 'a good start'.

Sitting opposite Harriet in one of Soho's few remaining greasy spoons (her choice not mine) I was glad I'd waited until we were alone before giving her her 'congratulations' gift. Her eyes widened as I pushed the distinctive turquoise box across the table and placed a muffin on top.

'Breakfast at Tiffany's,' I said.

Smiling, she untied the white ribbon and removed the lid from the box. Then she parted the tissue paper and gasped as she saw the silver bracelet nestling inside.

'Wow . . .'

She picked it up and examined the inscription I'd had

engraved. Nothing romantic (or, God forbid, suggestive), just today's date. Her first broadcast.

'I hope today is one you'll remember as a red letter day,' I said.

Okay, I sounded pompous but I had a sense that we were making memories. Finding the right words wasn't easy.

'It's beautiful,' she said. Her face darkened. 'But I can't accept it. It's too much. Besides, I haven't got anything for you.'

I waved her protest away.

'It's your big day, not mine.'

She chewed on her lip, a tic I was finding increasingly charming, along with her way of looping strands of hair behind her pink, perfect ear.

'Can I at least pay for breakfast?' she said.

'It's a deal.'

She slipped the bracelet onto her wrist.

'Thank you,' she said. 'For everything.'

I reached into my pocket and drew out an envelope addressed to Harriet.

'I meant to give you this earlier,' I lied. 'It's from Tom. I recognize his handwriting.' That part, at least, was true.

She opened the envelope. Inside was a Hallmark card. I took a sip of coffee and looked away as she read it. I knew precisely what my son had written because I'd steamed open the envelope the day before. (I know I should have felt ashamed but I didn't – merely a frisson of triumph.) I did my best to strike a casual tone.

'What does he say?'

'"Break a leg. I'll be listening."' She sighed. 'Sweet.'

It seemed clear she was underwhelmed, which I found reassuring. I'd been right to give her the bracelet before handing over Tom's card. The contrast between myself and the lad spoke for itself.

Our food arrived but we didn't eat much. To tell you the truth, ever since Harriet Brown breezed into my life I seemed to have little appetite. Meanwhile, she was still on a post-show high, dissecting our debut in detail. Like any actress, she was eager to know what I thought of her performance. Had she been professional? Did she sound warm enough? Should she talk more slowly? Did our banter strike the right balance? Was her laugh infectious or annoying? I reassured her on all counts.

'You did a brilliant job.'

She paid the bill then we walked towards Shaftesbury Avenue, taking the long way back to Silk FM through Soho Square. The rush hour was nearly over, the streets no longer seething with media types hurrying to work in the offices, studios and editing suites that had colonized the area. A couple of Japanese tourists pored over a map; a pale woman sat on a bench, offering her face to the autumnal sun; a busker strummed his guitar, playing an acoustic version of 'Stairway to Heaven'.

'God, I bloody love London,' said Harriet, kicking through a pile of leaves.

She seemed in no hurry, even though the Transport for

London PR woman had organized a ten-thirty photo-call at Tottenham Court Road tube station. Harriet was the star attraction. Her second debut of the day: the new Voice of London.

'Will you come?' she said.

I shook my head.

'It's your big day not mine.'

'I wouldn't be doing any of this without you.'

And there it was. The moment I'd been waiting for. I said nothing.

'Are things okay?' she said. 'Between us?'

'Why wouldn't they be?'

She stopped and sat on a bench. Something on her mind. 'Because I had ... feelings for you.' I wasn't crazy about her use of the past tense but bided my time, waiting for her to finish her thought. 'And I kissed Tom.'

'You didn't know he was *my* Tom,' I said.

'But you don't mind?'

'Of course not.'

Was she leading up to something? A declaration? Another kiss? I felt like a teenager on a first date. All that was missing was the awkwardness and acne.

'I know you ... like me,' she said.

'Of course I like you. I'd hardly have suggested you as my co-presenter if I didn't.'

She turned to look at me. 'I mean, you *like* me,' she said. 'And I *like* you.'

I played dumb. 'So ... what's the problem?'

'I *like* Tom too.' She drew breath and launched into what felt like a torrent of pent-up emotions. 'I could try and shut down how I feel about both of you and concentrate on all the amazing things that are happening – and I *so* don't want you to think I'm a hustler, playing you off against each other, because that's not how I am *at all* – but the truth is I'm confused and scared of messing up. Because that's what I do whenever things go right – I mess up. And now, on top of everything else, Damian's texting me a zillion times a day, saying he wants me back, so all things considered, I'm a bit of a fuck-up.'

I drew breath to reply but her mobile rang. She answered the call.

'Hello?' She listened. 'Sorry ... I'm two minutes away ... I'll be with you in a sec.' She pocketed her phone and got to her feet. 'See? I'm late for the photo-call. Day one of my new life and already I'm a diva.' She broke into a run, calling over her shoulder. 'Don't forget yoga! Three o'clock. Wear something loose!'

Then she was gone, running towards the gate and leaving me with only one thought.

Damian? Who the hell is Damian?

HARRIET

There must have been a dozen photographers on the platform, plus camera crews and reporters from local TV news. They crowded around me, barking questions: what was it like to be the new Voice of London? How did I feel about being on the radio? What time did I set my alarm for? Did I have a boyfriend? What did I think of Richard and **OHMIGOD I COULD JUMP ON THE RAILS RIGHT NOW AND FRY MYSELF ALIVE!**

It should have been exciting but I felt embarrassed and kept wondering what I'd let myself in for. Was this really what I'd wanted? Being well known for reciting a list of tube stops? For prattling about traffic on the radio? As doubts and The Thoughts competed for space inside my head and the paps snapped away, the trains came and went and my voice echoed over the tannoy.

The next train to Morden will arrive in two minutes.

The first time I heard myself I felt like crying. I sounded terrible.

Please stand back from the platform edge.

The second time was a bit less awful.

Please allow passengers off the train before boarding.

After fifteen minutes, I'd almost forgotten who the dis-embodied voice belonged to; she was simply That Woman.

Then it hit me. That text from Cockweasel was in danger of taking the shine off *everything*. I'd tried hard not to focus on it during the show but those three little words kept flash-ing into my mind's eye.

I love you.

FFS!

I hadn't replied. This was *my* morning – a moment in the limelight after years of rejection and failure. Today was proof that I wasn't invisible and had been a long time coming. I tried not to let the message overshadow everything. At the same time, it's hard to describe how much those three words meant. Two years of being in love with someone I'd believed to be wonderful. Of thinking I'd found The One. And what was the reality? Two years of being someone's dirty little secret.

I tried to give sensible or funny answers to the reporters' questions but one woman looked so bored I thought she was going to fall asleep and topple onto the track. Her lack of interest in my big day added to my growing sense of unease but I gave myself a stern talking-to: I was lucky not to be spending yet another morning cranking out cappuccinos and heating paninis filled with slimy cheese and ham. Just a month ago, I'd gladly have chewed off my own feet to have even one reporter show interest in my life – my ambitions, hopes, dreams – and now here I was, with half a dozen microphones in my face and a smiley TfL PR woman asking if I was okay and did I need anything? Bottle of water? Loo break? Diamonds on the soles of my shoes?

Okay, I made that last bit up but even this micro-taste of 'slebrity' was enough to help me understand why famous people can become gigantic cockwombles. It's not as if I think I've suddenly become some kind of VIP – I'm still just me, obvs – yet the smiles came more quickly and for the first time in my life people were focused on *me* and wanted *my* opinion – on London, on public transport, on how it felt to be 'an overnight success'.

The rest of the morning was a bit of an anti-climax, TBH. I went back to the greasy spoon for a break then wandered around Soho, trying to feel part of the 'media village' I'd fantasized about for so long. Walking along Shaftesbury Avenue, I took stock of the posters outside the theatres – all those talented actors, singers, musicians and dancers doing what I'd dreamed of doing since I was a kid.

One of Nan's sayings came to mind. *It's better to travel hopefully than arrive.* Not that I'd arrived anywhere. But being Richard's second banana had at least put me in the fruit bowl. What happened next was up to me.

The yoga studio was airy and full of light. Richard was the only bloke amidst a dozen of Stoke Newington's yummy mummies and me. As instructed, he wore a tracksuit and trainers. Both looked suspiciously new. He clipped a small wireless microphone to his top, and one to mine. Then he took a mat and sat cross-legged, copying the woman on his left. I nabbed the space behind him and unrolled my mat on the floor. The lack of sleep was catching up with me but I was determined to keep going till the evening and to keep The Thoughts at bay. An hour of yoga was just what I needed. Our instructor was Ayisha. Her slim figure and perfect posture spoke of years of practice. It was hard not to hate her and **I'VE NEVER SNOGGED A WOMAN BUT IN YOUR CASE I COULD MAKE AN EXCEPTION.**

'I see we have a new face,' she said.

All eyes turned to Richard. He gave a wave and cleared his throat.

'Hello, my name's Richard and I'm an alcoholic. Sorry . . . wrong meeting.'

I was the only one to laugh. The others seemed to take him seriously. Ayisha raised an eyebrow.

'Any aches and pains or injuries?'

'Am I that much of an old crock?' said Richard.

'Not at all,' said Ayisha, smiling. 'It's a standard question.'

As the class began, the smell of burning incense filled the room, along with the sound of Arvo Pärt's *Spiegel im Spiegel*. The simplicity of the piano and that sweet, soaring violin never fails to move me.

I could see Richard was having trouble following Ayisha's instructions, especially when it came to *sarvangasana*, a pose that involves lying on your back with your legs upright and your hands supporting your lower back. Hats off to him for trying, though, especially on his first class.

'May I make a request?' he said.

'Sure,' said Ayisha, even though no one talks in yoga, *ever*.

'If I die in this ridiculous posture will you pretend my last words were devastatingly witty?'

A couple of women giggled. I could see Ayisha smile but before she could reply the door opened. I was facing the other direction so couldn't immediately see who had walked in but I heard the new arrival whispering.

'Sorry I'm late.'

The man's voice sounded familiar. I lowered my legs and came out of the pose then turned to face the door. It was Tom.

TOM

It was all I could do not to burst out laughing. The sight of Dad flat on his back, desperately trying to keep his legs in the air almost made me forgive him everything. For being a crap father. For refusing to back down over Harriet. For hurting Mum with his affairs (although if Gorgeous George was right I might have to re-think that particular source of resentment).

Harriet's eyes widened in disbelief as I grabbed a mat and unrolled it at the front of the group, sitting on Dad's left. At first, he didn't notice me, too busy concentrating on main-taining his balance. But then he turned his head, saw me and immediately collapsed into a heap. His hair was a mess, his face ruddy – part exertion, part anger.

'What are you playing at?' he hissed.

Seeing the instructor's disapproving glare, I frowned at my father and raised a finger to my lips.

'Shhh.'

'Don't shush me,' he said.

Out of the corner of my eye, I caught Harriet's raised

eyebrow. The instructor cleared her throat and glared. Dad had little choice but to pipe down and continue with the class. Order restored, we shifted into *bhujangasana*, aka the cobra position. Craning my neck towards the ceiling and feeling my muscles stretch, I tried to imagine how hard this would be for a man twice my age. True, Dad was in decent shape – a regular tennis-player and walker – but yoga has a way of making you feel the burn in places you didn't even know you had places.

Not that I was in *any way* trying to convey a subliminal message to Harriet – e.g., that a twenty-five-year-old might be, like, fitter than a fifty-year-old IN ALL KINDS OF WAYS. Perish the thought. As if I would stoop so low.

As we moved to a kneeling pose, I could hear Dad's breathing becoming laboured as he did his best to keep up with a group of super-fit young women and me. Child's pose followed – the one that always makes me think of nap time in kindergarten. I could almost feel my father's relief. But then the instructor glided to the front of the room and adopted *vrikasana*, standing on one leg and raising the other, with her arms above her head and her palms together. She made it look easy but I knew it wasn't, even for someone accustomed to yoga. Studiously avoiding looking in Dad's direction, I tried to copy her, feeling my way into the pose. It's the balance that's tricky. As we get older, it becomes harder to stay steady – especially on one foot. I guess that's why so many elderly people 'have a fall'. Not that Dad is ancient (fifty is the new thirty and all that) but try as he might, he could not stand on one leg for more than a couple of seconds.

'You okay?' I whispered.

'Great. Thanks for asking.'

Maybe I was wrong but Harriet didn't seem to be taking any notice of us, totally focused on her own pose. I watched as Dad slowly raised his right foot, standing on his left leg for a couple of seconds before toppling over onto the mat.

'Don't worry,' I said, trying not to smirk. 'Probably just an age thing.'

'Shhh,' said Harriet.

'Sorry.'

Dad got to his feet and glared in my direction. 'I'm so glad you came.'

I swallowed a smile, watching as he attempted the pose once again. He stood upright, raised his left leg and lifted his arms above his head. Then he slowly placed his palms together. I held my breath. Three seconds. Five.

Seven . . .

Ten . . .

'Okay,' said Ayisha. 'And come down onto your mats and into downward-facing dog.'

The class did as instructed. With one exception. Guess who. Yes, my father was now into his *fifteenth* second standing on one leg, arms raised above his head, palms together.

Twenty seconds and counting . . .

I raised my head from my mat and stole a glance in his direction. He was staring straight ahead, eyes fixed on the bowl of burning incense.

Harriet didn't seem to have noticed his marathon effort to

impress her with his display of virility and strength. As the rest of the group followed Ayisha's instructions, my father held his pose for a full thirty seconds before slowly bringing his arms down by his side, lowering his left leg and bringing his feet together.

He looked at me and smiled.

'*Namaste.*'

RICHARD

Holding that bloody pose for a full thirty seconds nearly killed me but the effort was worth it, just to see the look on Tom's face.

From the moment Harriet issued her on-air challenge, drastic action was required. Yoga has never been my thing – even less so since Bonnie started going to classes every night, 'perfecting her practice', or so she said.

Fortunately, Pam was an aficionado so I asked for help. I needed to learn a single pose – something a beginner could manage, the trickier the better. She suggested something called *vrikasana*, a ludicrous posture that involves standing on one leg with your raised foot resting on your inner thigh, hands above your head and palms together. Not surprisingly, I kept toppling over, much to the amusement of everyone who passed the office, but after forty-five minutes of sweating and swearing I'd more or less got the hang of it – enough to maintain it for the half-minute needed to do the job.

I hadn't reckoned on Tom showing up. At first, I couldn't work out what he was playing at, then the penny dropped. He wanted to show me up in front of Harriet. Well, sod that for a game of soldiers.

During the class, I knew the lapel mic was capturing my every grunt and groan but that didn't matter – the gruntier and groanier the better. The plan was to play a couple of clips on Tuesday's show – a laugh at my expense, all good fun, new girl Harriet winding up good old Richard, ha ha, what a sport. This was in keeping with the way our double act was shaping up, which was fine by me and exactly what Jennifer and Pam had always had in mind for the tone of the show.

After what seemed like an eternity of stretching and aching, the yoga class drew to a merciful close. I saw Tom settling up with Ayisha. Then he came over to join me and Harriet.

'Hope you don't mind me dropping in,' he said. 'I heard you on-air and thought, "Dad doing a yoga class? Not to be missed!"'

Harriet grinned, taking him at face value. 'He did brilliantly.'

I swallowed a small smile of satisfaction and tried to sound nonchalant.

'Thirsty work. Who's for a cup of tea? The Milky Bars are on me.'

They both stared blankly, the reference to my favourite old TV ad wasted. Sometimes I hate young people.

*

The café in the park was almost empty, just a couple of school kids and an elderly man reading a paper. The three of us sat at a corner table, drinking tea and making small talk. Harriet kept checking her phone and replying to texts. I wondered if these were from the mysterious 'Damian' but decided not to ask.

'How's the musical coming along?'

'You always ask that,' grumbled Tom. 'Every time I see you. Like it's the only thing you can find to talk about.'

Not only was he testy, he looked pale and washed-out, as though he hadn't slept in a week. I wondered if he'd been taking drugs.

'I ask because I'm interested.'

He gave an exaggerated sigh. 'It's going well. Harriet's helping me put together the showcase.'

'Am I allowed to come?'

'Would you like to?'

'Am I invited?'

'Would you like an invitation?'

'Why wouldn't I?'

'I don't know, Dad, why wouldn't you?'

I smiled. He was playing me at my own game – answering a question with a question.

'Does that mean I'm invited?'

'*Yes*, Dad. You're invited.'

Taking a break from texting, Harriet looked from my face to Tom's then back again. 'Are you two always like this?'

We replied simultaneously.

'Like what?'

She rolled her eyes.

'Never mind.'

The three of us lapsed into an awkward silence broken by Tom.

'I had a visitor this morning. My grandfather.'

My stomach gave a lurch.

By the pricking of my thumbs, something wicked this way comes . . .

'Seems like a decent bloke,' said Tom. 'He kipped on my sofa then disappeared while I was out for a run. Oh, and he told me my grandmother died after being run over by a hearse.'

My knuckles whitened as I gripped the handle of my cup.

'You'd be wise not to believe a word that man says.'

Harriet looked up from her phone.

'Is it true? About the hearse?'

I shook my head. As more than one smart-arse has pointed out, I babble for a living. When being paid, I can prattle for hours but there are occasions when words fail me. This was one of those occasions.

'He's getting married,' said Tom.

I wasn't surprised. When it comes to that man, nothing is too hard to believe.

Harriet listened, bemused, as Tom and I discussed my father, a disgrace to mankind. Turned out he'd shown up out of the blue, which made sense, given that I'd recently changed the locks in Belsize Park. At first, I couldn't understand how he'd found Tom's address but then I remembered:

I leave my address book on the kitchen table. He must have gone through it during one of his visits.

'So you haven't seen him in a while?' said Harriet.

'Not since I was little,' said Tom.

She turned to me.

'How come?'

'Long story,' I said. I had no intention of telling it – at least, not the unexpurgated version.

'I'm in no hurry,' said Harriet.

'Perhaps another time.'

Tom gave a tight smile.

'Dad doesn't talk about my grandfather. Ever.'

'Because?'

I took a sip of tea, playing for time. Once again, Tom was the first to crack.

'George has two passports,' he said. 'One in the name of Lord Anthony Buckingham.'

I nearly spat out my tea. Harriet's eyes widened. She put her phone down.

'He's a lord?'

'No,' I said. 'He's a con-man with delusions of grandeur.'

'What sort of con-man?' said Harriet.

'The kind of parasite that attaches itself to wealthy widows then bleeds them dry before moving on. And that's not even the worst thing about him.'

'Wow,' said Harriet.

Tom turned to look me in the eye. He cleared his throat. Something on his mind.

'He told me it's Mum who has affairs, not you.'

I blinked in surprise.

'He said that?'

'Not in so many words but that's what he meant. Is it true?'

Harriet pocketed her phone and started to get up from her seat. 'You should probably have this conversation without me around ...'

I stayed her, placing a hand on her arm.

'No need to go,' I said. 'But yes, it's true.'

Tom blew out his cheeks.

'Is that why she's in Goa? She's having an affair?'

'Apparently.'

'Who with?'

'I believe her name is Alex.'

He blinked. 'Mum's a lesbian?'

'Sometimes.'

'Since when?'

'It might be best to ask her.' I smiled at Harriet. 'As you can see, we're one big happy family.'

Opening her mouth to reply, she was distracted by someone entering the café. I turned and saw a man in the doorway. In his mid-thirties, he was tall with thick blue-black hair, a candidate for the best-looking man I'd ever seen. Don't ask me how, but I knew I was looking at the man who'd been texting Harriet.

Or, as Tom and I would come to know him, *that bastard, Damian.*

HARRIET

Looking back, I should have known. He'd been texting all day, kicking off his campaign seconds before I went on-air for the first time.

I love you

Followed later by:

I miss you

Where are you?

Finally, I cracked and told him I was with Richard and Tom in the Clissold Park café.

You know the phrase 'my heart leapt from my chest'? Well, that's how it felt when Damian walked in. Instantly forgetting my sleepless night, I was filled with an energy I hadn't felt in months. He was still tall, dark and handsome, obvs, and his eyes were as blue as ever, but he seemed somehow different. Thinner. Older.

Sadder.

He gave me a peck on the cheek, like nothing had happened – like he hadn't lied through his teeth about being single – then he sat down and extended a handshake to Richard.

'I'm Damian. I heard your show. Wasn't Harriet great?'

Richard gave a smile that didn't reach his eyes.

'Brilliant, as expected,' he said before turning to Tom. 'This is my son.'

Tom mumbled something I couldn't hear because of the blood thudding in my ears and the galloping of my heart. Handshakes all round. I couldn't speak because **I JUST WANT TO RIP YOUR CLOTHES OFF, RIGHT HERE, RIGHT NOW.**

Damian took out an e–cigarette and started vaping.

I don't remember much about the next few minutes. I expect we all made small talk and I imagine it felt forced, as if two of us were waiting for the other two to piss off, which, of course, was exactly how Damian and I were feeling. My smile was wide enough to make my face ache, my whole body felt alive and tingly.

And all I wanted was to be alone with him. Somewhere dark. Somewhere private. **SOMEWHERE WITH A BLOODY BED.**

TOM

As rivals go, Damian Vance was every man's worst nightmare. Not only was he the best-looking bloke I'd seen outside of a Hollywood movie, he was also a maxillofacial surgeon.

'I should probably know what that means,' I said, managing half a smile. 'But I don't.'

He grinned, revealing the whitest teeth I've ever seen.

'It means I have a practice in Harley Street but travel a lot, mainly Africa and South America.'

'As a dentist?'

'Dentistry is part of it,' said Damian. 'I perform surgery on kids with severely disfigured faces.'

Harriet chimed in.

'He operates on children whose faces have been wrecked by injury, or diseases like cancer. Fixing defects in the head, neck, face and jaw. Gives them a shot at a normal life.'

'Wow,' I said, my cheeks hurting from the effort of smiling. 'Very cool.'

Dad refused to sound impressed.

'Who pays?'

'No one,' said Damian. 'It's *pro bono* work. "Giving back" and all that.'

In other words, the man was, like, half Ryan Gosling, half Mother Teresa. Which was wonderful. Just bloody wonderful. I was *so* happy for him.

'Tell them about your dad,' said Harriet, clearly thrilled at the opportunity to show off her 'fascinating' friend.

'I'm not sure they'd be interested,' said Damian.

'Try us,' said Dad, giving a smile as thin as my own. I don't think Harriet or Damian caught the ice in his tone of voice but it wasn't lost on me.

It turned out that 'Saint' Damian was not only a *wunderkind* with a social conscience that put me to shame, he also had a colourful family history *and* had managed to rise above a chaotic upbringing that might easily have seen him spend his life behind bars. Now dead, his mother had been a drug addict and his father was the late Jack Vance, rumoured to have been one of the masterminds behind the Mayfair safe deposit robbery. A gang of 'old geezers' had drilled into the underground vault and stole millions of pounds' worth of jewellery. No one knew exactly how much had been taken because the safe deposit accounts were shrouded in secrecy, but estimates ranged from five million to fifty million quid – maybe more. All but one of the perpetrators had been caught and banged up for years. 'Alfie' was the nickname the tabloids had bestowed upon the ringleader – the one that got away.

'But "Alfie" was actually Damian's dad, Jack,' said Harriet

proudly, as if claiming kinship with a cancer-curing scientist or an intrepid explorer of the North-West Passage. Damian tapped his e-cigarette.

'That's only according to rumour,' he said. 'Dad never confessed to me or anyone else.' He flashed that dazzling smile again, turning in Harriet's direction. She lowered her gaze, batting her eyelids, the way that Princess Diana used to look at a camera.

'You must be proud of *your* father,' said Damian. It took a moment before I realized he was talking to me. 'What's it like, having a famous DJ in the family?'

I was about to reply when Dad intervened.

'I don't think Tom's impressed by my job,' he said. 'If anything, he's always found it embarrassing.'

Had I? How would he know?

'It must be fun,' said Damian. 'Sitting in a studio, playing records all day.'

I felt my father tensing. Was Damian deliberately trying to put him down? To make his humble-bragging self seem even more important?

'What about Tom?' Damian turned to me. 'What's your line of work?'

I hate that question, even more so since I jacked in the day-job.

'Journalist by day,' I said. 'Songwriter by night.'

Damian arched an eyebrow.

'What kind of journalism?'

'Tom's writing for *Double Glazing Monthly*,' said Dad.

'Not any more,' I said, my cheeks burning. 'I'm focusing on song-writing.'

'Anything I'd know?'

I shook my head.

'I'm writing a musical. Harriet's helping. We're doing a try-out performance for a producer soon.'

'Cool,' said Damian. 'Can I come?'

Harriet turned to me, her eyes shining.

'Can he?'

'Why not?' I said.

Well, what was I supposed to say?

Damian turned back to my father.

'Will you be there?'

'I don't think I'm invited,' said Dad.

'Of course you are,' I said, hoping I didn't sound as pissed off as I felt. 'The more the merrier.'

I would later discover that if you spent enough time on Google you could make a strong case that Jack Vance and 'Alfie' the Mayfair mastermind were indeed one and the same. So on top of everything else – the career, the looks, the cash – 'Saint' Damian had a bank robber father who'd gone to his grave without anyone finding his stash of diamonds. Worth millions, apparently.

And the final straw? Damian owned a new silver Porsche, a poem on wheels in which he drove Harriet away without a backward glance.

Meanwhile, in other news, my mother was a lesbian and highly promiscuous, which made a mockery of everything I'd believed about her and Dad for the last twenty years and *apart from that, Mrs Lincoln, how did you enjoy the theatre?*

RICHARD

From the moment Damian Vance walked into the café I could see he was going to be trouble. It wasn't his looks or his job or even his vulgar car (and it certainly wasn't his naff e-cigarette), it was the way Harriet gazed at him. The wattage of her smile transformed her face; her body language changed in an instant, as if she'd been infused with a fast-acting love serum.

As Damian introduced himself with a bone-crunching handshake, I saw her cross her legs, flick her hair over her shoulder and moisten her lips with her tongue. Which meant only one thing. The days of *softly softly* were over. It was time to take my campaign to win her heart to a new level. No more Mr Nice Guy . . .

I listened as Damian told us about his voluntary work in poor countries. I wish I could claim the man was a nauseating braggart but he seemed like a decent sort who'd overcome a tough start and made something of his life, which, of course, made everything a thousand times worse. Tom seemed cheesed off, lapsing into monosyllables, but Harriet hung on the new arrival's every word and embarrassed him into insisting that he was only doing work many others did, too, and no, of course he wasn't a hero, just an ordinary bloke who happened to have made a few quid and wanted to share his good fortune with people who weren't so lucky.

As for his dad, well, I suppose having a criminal in the family gave us something in common – except for the fact that Damian seemed relaxed talking about Jack Vance's 'career', whereas I couldn't bear to mention my father's name.

And when it came to George 'dropping in' to Tom's flat, it was clear that trouble was brewing, but with no way of contacting the despicable old bastard, there was nothing I could do except hope he dropped dead soon and warn the lad to keep his distance. And worry.

HARRIET

In the weeks that followed, it felt as if life was on fast-forward. I was on a permanent high, keeping going thanks to a combination of coffee, exhilaration and adrenaline. The Silk FM show was a blast – I couldn't believe they were actually paying me – and working with Richard was a laugh, especially when I hit my stride towards the middle of the second week. Jennifer and Pam seemed pleased with my performance. The feedback from listeners was generally positive, except for the inevitable trolls. Richard told me to ignore the haters and stay off social media, which I was happy to do. I've always thought Twitter was for people with more time than sense. He showed me some of the emails he gets every day, gleefully telling him that he's the worst DJ *ever*.

As for the way he behaved towards me, he was nothing but a gent; there was no hint of any Awkwardness. Meanwhile, The Thoughts were muted, flaring up only occasionally and not once while I was on-air. So the only downside was the early starts; the four-thirty alarm took a lot of getting used to, especially as I never seemed to get to bed early enough.

(Okay, if you must know, I was spending masses of time *in* bed, just not enough time asleep, if you catch my drift . . .)

Having left his wife, Damian was renting a luxury apartment in the West End, within walking distance of his Harley Street surgery. His Porsche was parked outside the flat and his corner shop was Selfridges. Luckily, the journey from Oxford Circus to Nan's was a doddle on the Victoria Line, so I still popped in to see her every day while Damian was at his surgery. The journey gave me the chance to listen to myself on the tannoy. Hearing my voice never failed to give me the creeps. It felt like listening to myself talking from beyond the grave.

The next train to Walthamstow will arrive in two minutes. Please stand clear of the platform edge.

Best of all, Nan was on the mend, driving again, as well as following her other favourite, er, pursuits. (I could tell she was feeling better when I heard a buzzing sound from her room. If she was well enough to use her vibrator collection, she was well enough to get out of bed.) Mobile again, she told me to clear off and enjoy myself because I was only young once. 'They are not long, the days of wine and roses . . .'

Needless to say, I didn't tell her I'd started seeing Cockweasel again. No point upsetting her. The fact that I'd gone back on my word was hard enough for *me* to take; there was no sense in disappointing the rest of my family too. But from the moment Damian sauntered into the café, with his dancing eyes and whiter-than-white smile, I was a goner.

On top of everything else, there was Tom's musical. Not gonna lie, I was still wrestling with my decision not to play the lead, Roxanne. It's not that I was changing my mind (every time I thought about being onstage, The Thoughts started up again and I broke out in a sweat) but I hated myself for being so neurotic. The CBT woman's advice kept popping into my mind, like a zillion times a day, but I still couldn't bring myself to take it. 'Exposure therapy', where someone like me confronts fears head-on, may sound a doddle but the thought of actually *doing* it seemed as far off as ever – and with good reason, right? I mean, if your phobia is, say, spiders or rats, then how would you feel about lying still and letting them run all over your naked body? *Exactly!* And that's how I felt about appearing in front of a live audience, even a small one, so it made sense to help Tom to *fulfil* his ambition, not mess it up by ruining his one shot at impressing an important producer.

With the date of the showcase looming, I spent as much time as I could helping fine-tune the lyrics for *They F**k You Up*. When I couldn't make it over to Dalston, I'd FaceTime Tom from wherever I was and we'd spend an hour or so revising the songs. He offered me a percentage, but I said thanks but no thanks. This was his show – I was just chipping in the occasional suggestion and was more than happy to suggest someone else to play the role of Roxanne, my mate from drama school. Her name was Zara. She was a teacher, married with kids and desperate not to think of herself as someone who 'used to be an actress'. I know the feeling.

To be honest, the return of Damian overshadowed pretty much everything, including any feelings I'd had – or thought I'd had – for Richard or Tom.

Had I been on the rebound? Was I that fickle? Or was it like Nan says: nature abhors a vacuum? Either way, the good news was that neither Tom nor Richard seemed bothered by the fact that I was no longer 'available'. It was as if that whole weird flirty-brunch-with-Richard-and-kissing-Tom-in-the-rain stuff had never happened.

Phew!

TOM

I couldn't believe it. She was acting as if nothing had happened. Okay, so we were hardly Romeo and Juliet but there was definitely more to us than a couple of cocktails and a cheeky snog. Wasn't there? Or had I been benched?

Right from our first date, at Hampstead Observatory, I'd felt a spark. True, it needed nurturing, but it was *there*. There was promise in the air, a sense of foundations being laid for something real, something with potential to last – and that's without mentioning that I fancied the pants off her, or that the feeling seemed to be mutual. Unless I was behaving like a love-struck teenager. If so, what did that make Dad?

At least Harriet was keen to carry on working on the musical, which gave me an excuse to stay in touch on a regular basis. She'd suggested one of her friends from drama school, someone who would make a perfect Roxanne, so I met the woman. Her name was Zara. She was a primary school teacher with a nice smile and a lovely voice. When we started meeting for rehearsals she proved to be a great singer with terrific stage presence. For obvious reasons, I'd rather Harriet had taken the role, but if this was how she wanted things, I'd play along, glad she was keen to help make the show the best it could be. After one of our FaceTime sessions, during which she came up with a bunch of cracking ideas, I offered her a percentage of any profits but she wouldn't hear of it.

I invited her out several times – a movie, a new musical, lunch, a trip to Tate Modern – but she was always 'too tired' or 'too busy'. Sometimes, I could almost feel her slipping away – always 'up to her eyes' with the job at Silk FM or her Nan, or so she said. Of course, I knew exactly who she was *really* spending her time with, but had no idea how to turn things around.

And then George decided life wasn't complicated enough and everything started to spiral out of control.

RICHARD

So now there were three of us. If Damian Vance had been a bog-standard high street dentist – scale and polish, crowns and implants – he might not have presented much in the way of competition. But it was clear from our encounter in the café that he did a lot of voluntary work (all credit to him) and wasn't afraid to weaponize his noble heart.

All in all, Damian cut a heroic figure, which made him a more formidable adversary than my unemployed 'son' with his pie-in-the-sky dreams of becoming the next big thing on Broadway.

Nevertheless, Tom was still firmly in the picture, spending far too much time with Harriet as they continued to work on his so-called musical. With Damian in danger of crowding both of us out, it was clear that I needed to redouble my efforts and battle on two fronts simultaneously. At least my arsehole of a father hadn't reared his ugly head again. Be thankful for small mercies, and all that.

Harriet was settling in at Silk FM. For three delicious

hours every Monday, Tuesday, Wednesday, Thursday *and*
Friday I had her undivided attention and she had mine. The
Harriet-less weekends were empty, passing in a blur of wine
and old *Seinfeld*s but I knew it wouldn't be long before I
could once again savour her company, bask in the radiance
of her smile and breathe her perfume. For the first week or
so, we'd breakfast together. Our café. Our table. Almond
croissant for her, poached eggs for me.

Still, it was undeniably odd. On the one hand, our on-air
relationship was public property, listened to by hundreds of
thousands of Londoners. At the same time, when the microphones were off it was just the two of us in our little booth,
with Billie Holiday or Nina Simone or Tony Bennett sere-
nading us in the background. All well and good as far as it
went, which wasn't far enough.

And that's when I started behaving badly.

The first time I followed Harriet Brown was one Friday
morning, about a month after she'd started at Silk FM. I felt
like someone who'd accidentally strayed into a spy movie or
was playing at being a private detective. She'd started skip-
ping our breakfasts, hurrying off as soon as the show ended.
I tried to draw her out on the subject of her relationship with
Damian but she shrugged and told me, 'it's complicated' then
changed the subject.

Why did I follow her that particular Friday? Some might
put it down to jealousy. Nope. There was a world of difference between what I was doing and someone behaving like

an unhinged stalker. My motivation was simple: part curiosity, part concern.

She'd acted strangely throughout that morning's show, distracted verging on morose. While the microphones were off during an ad break I asked if she was okay. Her reply was instant. A flash of anger – something I'd never seen before.

'Mind your own business.'

She apologized straightaway but it was clear something was wrong. I decided to find out what it was.

The show finished at 9 a.m. and she was out of the building by five past. Donning my overcoat, I followed at a discreet distance, joining the hordes of commuters heading for work. She walked up Shaftesbury Avenue, towards Tottenham Court Road. It was a bright, clear day in November and I could feel the beating of my heart. What if she turned and saw me? No matter. I would invent an errand: breakfast with a friend, an appointment with my accountant.

She paused at a bus stop and checked her phone, the way people do when they have two seconds to kill. I slowed to a halt, feigning interest in a shop window. The bus arrived. She boarded via the front entrance, tapping her Oyster card on the reader then taking a seat. I considered hailing a cab but there were none to be seen. Besides, the thought of telling the driver to 'follow that bus' was ludicrous. I joined the queue at the rear entrance, using my Oyster card to board the bus and keeping my face turned towards the rear. Harriet's voice came on the tannoy.

Bus number ten to Hammersmith Broadway. Next stop . . . Great Titchfield Street.

I risked a glance in her direction but she was focused on her mobile and didn't seem to be listening. I assumed she was used to hearing her own voice. Perhaps she no longer even registered it. The bus stopped for passengers then moved on.

Next stop . . . Oxford Circus.

A longer pause this time, to allow people on and off, then onwards with a lurch.

Next stop . . . Selfridges.

Harriet rose from her seat and rang the bell. As the bus drew to a halt, I waited until she'd stepped off then followed suit. She walked quickly, turning into North Audley Street, where the crowds had thinned. Halfway down the street, she stopped outside a black doorway and pressed a buzzer. The door opened. She went inside a redbrick apartment building, five storeys tall, and closed the door. I counted to ten then approached the doorway. Ten buzzers, ten flats. The array of foreign nameplates suggested the occupants were from all over the world, with the exception of the first-floor flat.

I gazed up at the window and saw a *For Sale* sign on the wall. It advertised a 'two-bedroom luxury apartment'. Walking to the café on the corner, I took a table outside and turned to look back along the street. Damian's Porsche was parked opposite the building with the black door.

A waiter appeared. I ordered a double espresso and an ashtray. As I lit a cigarette, I could feel my stomach tightening, every instinct telling me my whole world was either about to change for the better or come crashing down around my ears.

HARRIET

In films, just when the hero and heroine are having a good time and relaxing, talking about how great life is, that's when you know everything is about to turn into seven sacks of shit. As in movies, so in life.

Damian didn't seem pleased to see me when I turned up in North Audley Street that morning, but I didn't care. My heart was beating at twice its normal rate and I desperately needed to get the words out, into the world, where they belonged. He closed the door of his flat and beat me to it.

'I need to talk to you,' he said.

'Um ...' I said, breathless from the stairs. 'Well, okay, but ...'

'There's no easy way to say this, Harriet, so I'm just going to say it.' He took a breath. 'I can't do this any more. It's not fair on my children. I'm going back to my wife.'

I blinked rapidly, hesitating before letting him have it.

'I hate to spoil your big moment but this isn't the best timing because I'M FUCKING PREGNANT!'

He blinked.

'How is that even possible? We always used a condom.'

'Except that time you didn't.'

'Which time?'

'Our reunion? The day you met me in the park café after my first show? The day we came back here and couldn't keep our hands off each other? The day we broke the lamp?'

His face crumpled, a picture of misery.

'Oh. *That* day.'

I nodded and tried to remain calm but **IF I PUSHED YOU DOWN THE STAIRCASE YOU'D CRACK YOUR HEAD OPEN AND DIE!**

I folded my arms across my chest. Pushing The Thoughts away, I started pacing back and forth on the parquet floor. (That's the thing about being an actor: even in moments of real-life drama, part of you is always observing the scene – the way you speak, how you carry yourself – and thinking, 'I must remember this. I can definitely *use* this.')

'I thought you'd sort out a morning-after pill,' he said.

'You didn't think AT ALL, Damian. Because that's who you are.'

Still, he had a point: he wasn't the only one who had been careless.

'I cannot *believe* I let this happen,' I said, still pacing. 'Or that I fell for you again, or ever believed a word you said.'

His shoulders slumped.

'So ... what will you do?'

I stared at him. In that instant, everything became clear.

It was never going to be 'What will *we* do?'; it would *always* be down to me. The man I loved with a tender, aching heart would walk away and leave me to clear up the situation. And the weirdest thing? I didn't feel angry or vengeful, just sad. Gut-wrenchingly, heart-crushingly sad.

'I'm keeping it,' I said defiantly. 'Will you help?'

He blinked again.

'Financially?'

'Yes.'

His jaw tightened. I knew what was coming.

'This isn't a good time, Harriet. She's found a new house. Two houses, actually – one here, one in Tuscany. The mortgages will kill me for a thousand years but it's a condition of my coming back.' His eyes welled with tears. 'And I *must* go back. I can't mess up my kids' lives. They don't deserve it.'

I felt numb.

'What about your father's money?'

He gave a pained smile.

'It's ... complicated.'

'So explain it.'

A sigh.

'There isn't any actual money – not as such.'

'Meaning?'

My blood was starting to boil, especially when he spoke very slowly, as if explaining to a child.

'Dad was hardly the type to bother with wills and bank accounts and probate.'

'So that's it?' I said. 'I'm on my own? Me and a baby?'

He spread his hands in a gesture of helplessness. I felt a surge of white-hot rage. I needed to leave before things turned nasty. He reached out a perfectly manicured hand.

'Can we talk about this?'

I looked into his eyes. I was livid with him, yes, but a thousand times angrier with myself. For going back. For believing a word he'd said. For hoping he would turn out to be the man I needed him to be. I stood on tiptoe and put my lips to his ear.

'Fuck off, Damian. And keep fucking off. And when you think you can't fuck off any more, keep fucking off till you come to a great big fuck-off sign that says, "No Fucking Off Allowed", then fuck off some more, until the end of time.'

I opened the door and slipped out of his life forever.

And if you believe that, you'll believe anything . . .

TOM

Harriet's text came out of the blue, just after 11 a.m.

Lunch?

I was eating Coco Pops, sprawled on the sofa. I pecked out a one-word reply.

Today?

Yep. *Got something to tell you.*

I showered, shaved and biked into Soho. When I walked into the café I saw my father sitting alone at a table. He frowned.

'What are you doing here?'

'Meeting Harriet,' I said.

'Oh. Me too.' His frown deepened. 'She invited you to lunch?'

I nodded. He gave a tight smile and nodded.

'How cosy.'

I sat opposite him and scrutinized his appearance.

'Cool haircut,' I said. 'Takes years off.'

'If you say so.'

I narrowed my eyes.

'Have you had work, Dad?'

'Define "work".'

'Your face looks different.'

He shifted in his chair.

'Probably the hair. Something about the way it frames my—'

'Is it Botox?'

'Certainly not.'

'Yes, it is. The lines on your forehead are different – thinner, smoother.'

He leaned forward in his chair.

'If you must know, I had a facial.'

'Looks like Botox to me.'

'It's a skin peel. It's no big deal. People have them all the time.'

'If they're trying to look younger.'

'If they take pride in their appearance.'

He cast a disdainful look at a thread trailing from the sleeve of my fleece and a grease spot on my jeans.

'It's a matter of self-respect,' he said.

'And trying to look younger.'

'Don't be boring, Tom.'

I swallowed a smile.

'Any particular reason for the makeover?'

'Such as?'

'Come off it, Dad – this is me you're talking to.'

I never got to hear his rationale because Harriet bustled

in and took the seat next to him. She looked as if she'd been crying.

'Thanks for coming.'

'Are you okay?' I asked.

'Not really.' She blew her nose on a tissue, flagged down the waiter and ordered tea.

'Nothing to eat?' he said.

She shook her head. I followed her lead. My father did the same, ignoring the waiter's disapproving glare.

'I've got some news,' said Harriet, her face deadly serious.

My stomach gave a lurch. Was she ill?

'I'm pregnant.'

From Dad's reaction – a glare at me – it was clear we were both having the same thought. *You bastard!* Harriet caught the look that passed between us.

'Will you get over yourselves?' she said. 'The father is Damian. But he doesn't want to know. In fact, he's going back to his wife – surprise, surprise – but I'm keeping the baby. I wanted to tell you both as soon as possible because, well, you know . . .'

She tailed off, leaving her thought unfinished but the meaning clear. The three of us hadn't known each other long but already there was history and baggage – above all, a bond about to be tested to the limit.

When I was eleven I fell for the girl next door, Elaine Buttrose. She only had eyes for Christopher Morris. Try as I might, I couldn't get her to pay me any attention – until the glorious day when Christopher was sent away to boarding school. Elaine moped around for a week or so then seemed to notice me for the first time. We began walking to and from school together and my heart skipped every time she smiled in my direction. It was the first time I was conscious of feeling truly happy. One summer afternoon – bright sunshine, blue skies – we were walking up Haverstock Hill, eating ice creams. A bus crawled past. Framed in the window was the last face I wanted to see: Christopher Morris's. He hammered on the window and I can still remember the sound of his voice above the noise of the traffic.

'Elaine! I've run away from school!'

I've never forgotten the expression on her face – one of utter joy – nor the way my stomach plummeted as I realized her heart belonged to my rival, and that life would never be the same again.

Now, sitting in the café, looking at Harriet's lovely face and listening to her talk about being pregnant with another man's child, I felt every bit as broken.

'Congratulations,' I said quietly.

It was the best I could do. Christ knows what my father was feeling ...

RICHARD

Pregnant?
PREGNANT?!

TOM

... but judging by the expression on his face we were as stunned as each other. I knew the next few moments might well determine how my relationship with Harriet panned out and was determined to rise to the occasion.

Her eyes glazed with tears.

'"Congratulations?"' she said. 'Really?'

I nodded, trying to sound more confident than I felt.

'Absolutely. You'll be a brilliant mum.'

'No doubt about it,' said Dad, doing his best not to put a foot wrong. He looked around for the waiter. 'Do you think they have champagne in this dismal place?'

A tear travelled down Harriet's cheek.

'It never occurred to me to celebrate. I only found out last night. I'm still in shock.'

I reached out and took her hand. Dad took her other hand.

'It's going to be fine,' he said.

'You think?' said Harriet.

'I don't think, I *know*.' He cleared his throat. 'Has he told his wife?'

'He's not going to tell her,' said Harriet. 'Neither am I.'

'But surely he'll be involved with the baby?' I said.

She looked stricken. Tears were not far away.

'Nope.'

Dad blinked several times, pausing before speaking.

'And you still don't want to tell his wife?'

Harriet gave another shake of her head. Her face filled with determination.

'He's got two kids. The boy's four, the girl's five. I don't want their unhappiness on my conscience and . . .'

She broke off and we all fell silent as the waiter arrived with tea. When he'd gone, Harriet spooned sugar into her cup.

'Everything became clear last night, after I did the pregnancy test. I knew what he was like when I went back to him. I knew he was still married. I knew there was a chance he'd go back to her.' She took a breath, steadying herself. 'And yes, we were careless, but I could have taken the morning-after pill, so maybe on some subconscious level I was *trying* to get pregnant. Either way, it's my fault as much as his. I've made my bed, now I've got to lie in it and put up with the shitty crumbs and tangled sheets.'

'But surely he should pay for the upkeep of—' began my father.

Harriet cut him short. She sounded calm and reasonable, as though she'd been thinking deeply and had reached an irrevocable decision. She put a hand on her stomach.

'I don't want him to have any part in this baby's life. Or mine. If either of you try to contact him, or his wife, I'll never speak to you again. I mean it.'

I said nothing. Dad remained silent, watching as she sipped her tea.

'I've got a decent job now, thanks to Richard,' she said. 'And who knows what might happen with the musical, right, Tom?'

I tried to sound optimistic.

'Broadway here we come.'

'Ealing or Tooting?' said Dad.

Lame, but it did the trick. Harriet smiled and seemed to relax.

'I'm going to stand on my own two feet and raise this baby, like millions of women every day. It won't be easy but I'll be fine. I've got Mum and Dad. And Nan.'

'And us.' The words were out of my mouth before I knew it.

Harriet's voice was a hoarse whisper, her eyes suddenly glazing with tears.

'Really?'

I could see my father cursing himself for not beating me to it.

'Tom's right,' he said. 'You've got your parents and your grandmother.' He cleared his throat. 'Most of all, you've got us.'

For a second, I thought Harriet was going to start crying but she gave a huge smile, reached across the table and pulled us into a three-way hug. Maybe it was wrong, but as the clinch continued I couldn't help thinking Dad had a point about Damian meeting his obligations. Dodgy diamonds or no dodgy diamonds, there was no shortage of money.

The clinch went on too long. He was the first to break it.

'Sod this place and the hell with tea. We need champagne.'

I opened my mouth to speak but he got there first.

'Don't start whining about foetal alcohol syndrome. I'm talking Veuve Clicquot at The Ritz – my treat.'

'Maybe one sip,' said Harriet, smiling.

It was hard not to smile back, especially as a wave of, like, clarity seemed to wash over me, bathing me in the warmth of a certainty I'd seldom known. If you love someone, you embrace their baggage, right? For all his faults, my father had accepted my mother's illness when he married her. For richer, for poorer, for better, for worse … etc., etc. Okay, they'd had a more complicated ride than he'd let on and their marriage was disintegrating, but at least they'd had something that had lasted, something *real*.

Glancing at him now, watching him don his stupid hat and clocking the crow's feet around his eyes, I felt a wave of something like tenderness.

TBH, there was also a flicker of renewed hope about my chances with Harriet. Bottom line? Damian was now out of the picture. One down, one to go …

RICHARD

PREGNANT?!

Tom got his response in first, appearing to take the news in his stride and volunteering *our* support, which was a colossal cheek but earned brownie points with Harriet. Clever sod.

A taxi took us to The Ritz, where I ended up downing most of the eye-wateringly expensive champagne myself. Apart from a few token sips, Harriet abstained, for obvious reasons, while Tom made a fuss about drinking no more than half a glass because he had to get to Soho for his pushbike then ride the bloody thing home. All in all, the impromptu celebration fell flat.

As for the big picture, the situation could have been worse. The baby's father could have been Tom, in which case I'd have had no choice but to retire gracefully and watch the woman I adored live happily ever after with the son I couldn't bring myself to like.

I'd done my best, believe me, but no matter how I tried

to tell myself that it was unfair to visit the sins of the father on the lad, there was something inside that made me need to keep him at arm's length. The shrink I saw tried to convince me that my feelings were only natural – the law of the jungle, an atavistic throwback neither good nor bad, simply a primal reaction to finding myself raising another man's child. That the other man in question was my own father made my feelings even less blameworthy – or so the shrink said – but I couldn't stop the guilt from overwhelming me. On bad days, the rage at George would rise to the surface before being replaced by guilt over how I'd treated Tom, and so the cycle would repeat and continue, repeat and continue, on and on, *ad infinitum, ad nauseam* ...

Walking along Piccadilly, Harriet declined my offer of a cab home, studiously avoiding any mention of The Wolseley, which was on the corner. I gave her a chaste hug then walked back to Belsize Park, mulling everything over as the thin, grey November light gave way to a gathering gloom and the champagne buzz morphed into a headache.

I spent the rest of the afternoon dozing fitfully on the sofa, waking from a nightmare about giant rats. The flat was in darkness.

I showered then donned my dressing gown. In the kitchen, I popped something in the oven (M&S's sticky sesame chicken with spicy potato wedges) and settled in front of the laptop, smoking one cigarette after another.

On a whim, I googled Damian Vance's name. There wasn't much. He didn't appear to have given any interviews about his good deeds, something I found both impressive and annoying. The man was noble *and* self-effacing – an irresistible combination. Certainly Harriet thought so.

A couple more clicks took me to a website called 'Joe Blogs', written by someone with a penchant for true crime. He had written about the speculation that Damian's late father, Jack, was the infamous 'missing man' in the Mayfair robbery, a heist that had titillated the whole country and resulted in a bunch of films and books. The crime had all the right ingredients: a bunch of 'old lags' tunnelling into a supposedly impregnable underground vault for 'one last job'. The beauty of the crime was twofold: nobody was hurt and no one knew precisely what had been stolen. The 'secure' safety deposit centre had been chock-a-block with items depositors wanted hidden from the tax authorities, ex-wives or the police. If the late Jack Vance was indeed the missing man, he had evaded capture, remaining on the run until his life ran its natural course. And if the blogger was right about rumours still circulating among the criminal fraternity, he'd managed to scarper with an impressively large haul of diamonds.

Shutting down the laptop, I raised a glass in a silent salute to the late Mr Vance then made a salad to accompany the sesame chicken, my thoughts turning to Harriet. For a change.

I've never been one for the unexamined life but despite my stint on the therapist's couch (in Crouch End, where else?) I seldom make much effort to ask myself how I'm *feeling*. In my experience, emotions bubble to the surface in their own time but take a while to catch up with events. In the case of Harriet's surprise lunchtime announcement, I found myself feeling oddly cheerful, verging on excited. She seemed to have decided that Damian was history, in which case perhaps the old Chinese saying was true: *every crisis is an opportunity.*

This was her crisis, of course, not mine – unless I chose to become involved. Just *how* involved would depend on two things: my willingness to help, and her willingness to let me. The latter would depend on how our relationship progressed. Were we destined to be 'just good friends' or, as I hoped, a great deal more? With Damian no longer in the frame, did that make Tom more of a threat or less?

As for helping to raise Harriet's child, wasn't it a price worth paying in order to be with the woman I loved – assuming I could win her over? I was forty-nine – hardly decrepit. And without wishing to sound smug, I was comfortably off, something that hadn't been the case when Bonnie and I had been starting out and Tom showed up, out of the blue.

I'm not suggesting that Harriet had a mercenary bone in her body but surely her new circumstances would make her look favourably on a bloke with a few quid in his pocket, not to mention a large, mortgage-free flat in a family-friendly neighbourhood. More good schools than you could shake a stick at. Walking distance from Hampstead Heath. Was I kidding myself or was I a decent prospect? The E-Type would have to go, of course, but perhaps that was a good thing.

I opened a bottle of wine and toyed with a few mouthfuls of food, trying to focus my thinking.

I wanted Harriet but did I really want to take on a baby?
How did I see the rest of my life panning out?

The questions seemed wreathed in mist, answers hard to discern through my foggy thinking. I went to bed, still ruminating.

It wasn't until the alarm went off at four-thirty on Friday morning that the matter seemed to have settled itself, as if a committee had convened overnight and delivered its decision. Mildly hungover, staring at my bleary-eyed reflection in the shaving mirror, I considered the verdict.

With Bonnie filing for divorce I was well placed for a guilt-free fresh start. Harriet's new circumstances surely offered me a second chance on the merry-go-round, perhaps an opportunity to get the whole parenting thing right – a shot at redemption after my failure first time round. To my surprise, I found that the prospect of a baby made no difference to how I felt about Harriet. Put simply, I adored her. As Shakespeare has it, 'love is not love which alters it when alteration finds'.

But while I was happy to support her and her baby, it seemed profoundly unjust that Damian should be allowed to saunter back to his wife and kids without meeting his obligations to Harriet – especially if there were any truth in those rumours about his father's secret stash. At the very least, he should provide a lump sum that could be put in trust for the child.

Harriet's warning was fresh in my memory.

I don't want him to have any part in the baby's life. Or mine. If either of you try to contact him, or his wife, I'll never speak to you again. I mean it.

I didn't doubt her sincerity. It was possible to imagine her honouring her contract with Silk FM, maintaining a pretence of normality while we were on-air but cutting me dead outside the studio, a prospect I would find hard to bear.

All of which meant subterfuge would be needed in getting Damian to cough up. Harriet might not thank me now for taking matters into my own hands but she'd be grateful *in the long run*. A trust fund for her child, guaranteeing his/her university education, somewhere to live and a future free from the financial insecurity that had plagued her own life. How could she not see me as her knight on a white charger?

How could I be anything other than Mister Right?

On impulse, I chucked away the antidepressants, my mind suddenly fizzing with excitement. Just weeks ago the future had looked bleak. Now I had a plan. All I needed was to figure out the answers to three questions. Had Damian inherited his father's cache of stolen diamonds? If so, where were they? And how could I get my hands on them without Harriet finding out?

HARRIET

I broke the news to Nan on Sunday morning. She was on
the sofa when I came downstairs, eating toast and watching
Omen III: The Final Conflict.

'I'm pregnant.'

She turned off the telly and peered over her glasses.

'Cockweasel?'

'Yep. He's going back to his wife.'

'Told your mum?'

'No. I don't want her to know, nor Dad, not till they
get back.'

A nod.

'Are you keeping it?'

'Yep.'

'Okay.' She patted the sofa. 'Need a cry?'

Too late. I was already crying.

Later, she served up the lunch she used to make when I was
little: cheese on toast with the crusts cut off.

'You can't do this alone,' she said. 'Kids are a money pit. Worse than old houses.'

'I'm not alone, Nan. I've got Mum and Dad and you.'

'We won't be around forever.'

'I'll be fine.'

'That's exactly what I said when your granddad buggered off. "I'll stand on my own two feet." And I did, but by Christ, it was hard.'

I took her hand.

'I'll be okay, honestly.'

She withdrew the hand. A steely tone entered her voice.

'I was seventeen,' she said. 'My dad chucked me out. I never saw him again – or my mum. Do you have any idea what it was like in those days? Single mothers weren't allowed to exist, not like today.' She closed her eyes and gave a small shudder. 'The things I did to survive ...'

She tailed off. When she opened her eyes, they were watering. I'd never seen her cry or heard her sound so serious.

'No one would blame you if you had an abortion,' she said. 'Then you could go to Hollywood, like you've always wanted.'

I couldn't believe what she was saying.

'What I've *always wanted* is kids,' I said. 'Annie, Dot and Freddie, remember?'

'What about your career?'

I sighed.

'I've been at it years, Nan, and look at me – I'm hardly Meryl Streep.'

She took a tissue from her sleeve and blew her nose.

'Harriet,' she said, 'I love your mum, and I've never regretted having her, not for one second, but if I'd made a different decision I'd have had a different life.'

I opened my mouth to speak but she was in full flow.

'I worry about you. You're too timid. You should go to Hollywood, give it a couple of years, see what happens.'

'And who'd look after the baby?'

She said nothing for a moment then admitted defeat.

'So you're keeping it?'

'Yes, Nan. I'm thirty-five and I'm earning a few quid for once, and if I went to LA I'd be just another wannabe actress, working as a waitress while trying to get a foot on the ladder, and what if I failed?'

'There's only one failure,' she said. 'Not trying.'

'I *have* tried,' I said. 'For years and years and *years*.'

I couldn't bring myself to tell her about The Thoughts, or how they made the idea of trying to crack Tinseltown impossible to imagine.

'Okay,' she said, tucking her tissue into the sleeve of her cardigan. 'I won't say any more – except babies *completely* take over your life so you're going to need all the help you can get, especially when it comes to money.'

'You did a great job with Mum. I'll do my best to be like you.'

'Fine words butter no parsnips, Harriet.'

'I'll buy my own parsnips.'

'It's not about fucking parsnips!'

It was the first time I'd heard her swear. She took a moment to regain her composure.

'From what you told me, Cockweasel's got plenty of cash. He needs to step up. Does his wife know?'

'No.'

'Then tell her.'

'I can't.'

'Why not?'

'Because it's partly my fault, too. And I don't want to wreck his marriage or blight his kids' lives.'

She blew on her tea and took a sip. I could tell she was making an effort not to lose her temper.

'Either you find a way to make him cough up or *I'll* tell his wife.'

I froze, eyes widening in disbelief.

'I mean it,' she said. 'If you don't tell his missus, I will.'

'You wouldn't dare.'

She met my gaze.

'Try me.'

I was still reeling from her threat when Tom and Richard texted within half an hour of each other, asking if I was okay and did I feel like lunch (Richard) or a trip to Columbia Road flower market (Tom).

I'd neglected both men over the last few weeks – too pre-occupied with Cockweasel – but had spent masses of time with Richard, if only at Silk FM, so I decided to hang out with Tom. If his dad was miffed, his text didn't show it.

OK, have a good Sunday. Hasta manana. x

Tom and I had seen each other semi-regularly, either in person or via FaceTime, restricting our conversations to the musical. He and Zara had been rehearsing and the show was really starting to take shape – although I still wasn't sure about the stuff set in prison. Tom knew masses about messed-up families, so he could write about them in a way that would connect with an audience. To me, the jailhouse stuff seemed an unnecessary complication, but it was his project, not mine, so I told him what I thought then left him and Zara to it. She told me she was having a blast and promised to take me to Nando's as a thank-you for getting her the gig.

I could tell Tom still *liked* me but I knew he'd backed off because of You Know Who. (Maybe Richard still *liked* me too, but he was harder to read.) Anyhow, things were different now. The baby changed everything. I was setting out on a solo adventure with no co-pilot. *Man plans, God laughs*, as Nan likes to say.

The flower market was a riot of colour with crowds of hipsters, families and old timers mingling in the November sunshine. I thought Tom might be planning to buy me a bunch of flowers but we just mooched around, taking a selfie or two before wandering into a tapas place and ordering food and drinks – beer for him, coffee for me. He didn't order any meat but I saw him casting an envious glance towards a plate of chorizo so I'm not convinced he's really a vegetarian, but it's nice of him to pretend. I can't say I felt relaxed but at least The Thoughts seemed to be having a day off.

'Can I ask you a question about Damian?' Tom said.

'If you must.'

'How does a dentist afford a Porsche?'

I sighed. What was *wrong* with everyone?

'He's not any old dentist, he's Harley Street.'

'So his wealthy patients subsidize his pro bono maxillo-facial work?'

I nodded.

'Do you know how much a full set of implants costs? Fifty grand.'

'Wow.' He turned to face me. 'Do you think Jack Vance was the one that got away? Was he really "Alfie"?'

I could tell where this was going. Damian had always been ashamed of his father but I knew Jack remained a source of fascination – as did the whereabouts of his stash.

'You're going to ask me if I know what he did with the diamonds.'

'Do you?'

'Do you think Damian would tell me, even if he knew?'

Tom sipped his beer. 'Hypothetically speaking, what if Damian *did* know? And what if Jack *has* left him the diamonds? Would it be so terrible if your baby got the benefit?'

I thought about it while chewing a piece of chargrilled aubergine.

'It's not going to happen,' I said.

'But if it did?'

'You mean, Damian gives me a wodge of his dad's haul, no questions asked?'

'Would you say no?'

'Depends.'

'On what?'

I sipped my coffee, playing for time.

'I need to do the baby thing my way, Tom.'

'It's just a hypothetical. Humour me.'

I rolled my eyes but Nan's threat was still fresh in my mind. *If you won't tell his wife, I will.*

'Okay,' I said. '*If* Jack Vance *was* who people say he was, and *if* he *did* get away with a bazillion pounds' worth of diamonds that were never going to find their way back to their rightful owners—'

'Because no one knows who the owners are—'

'. . . Exactly. And *if* he *did* leave them to Damian, and *if* Damian lobbed some of the proceeds my way, to help with the baby, then I wouldn't lose any sleep over it. Does that answer your question?'

'It does.'

'Good. But promise you won't ask Damian for money.'

'I promise.'

'Or go near his wife.'

'Ditto.'

Eager to change the subject, I asked about the latest news of his mum (he'd had an email from Goa) and his grandfather (no sign). We ended up laughing at the absurdity of families and agreeing there's no such thing as normal, let alone perfect.

As we left the market, he insisted on buying me a bunch

of lilies. I asked him to pose with me for a couple more self-ies. Silk FM have told me I've got to sign up for Twitter and start tweeting about my life at least twice a day. I think it's a waste of time, and I'm dreading the trolls, but anything to show willing.

Parting company at the tube station, I gave Tom a peck on the cheek. For a moment, I thought he was going to do The Lunge and move in for a proper kiss but it was just my imagination.

To be honest, although being with him all afternoon had given me goosebumps (hormones kicking in?) I felt relieved. Life was complicated enough – and about to get trickier still.

TOM

The idea of asking George about Jack Vance came while I was riding the night tube, listening to Harriet's announcements.

The next stop is Finsbury Park. Doors will open on the left hand side. Change here for the Piccadilly Line and National Rail services.

Performance-wise, she'd nailed it with that one. If Trip Advisor did reviews for tannoy announcements Harriet would get, like, five stars – no, six! Okay, I may have been not entirely sober when I had that thought.

I'd like to pretend I had a good reason to be on the Victoria Line at three in the morning but that would be a lie. The truth was I'd been working on the musical, alternating coffees and beers all evening. I was wired, drunk, and overcome with the urge to hear her voice. An aimless underground journey with pissheads and sleepy shift workers seemed to make perfect sense. The things we do for love.

As far as I knew, George wasn't a fully paid-up member of the criminal classes but with his reputation for fleecing wealthy widows he was the only person I knew with the right contacts. In fact, the more I thought about him, the cooler he seemed – an absolute ledge. So I rode the tube for, like, a couple more hours – listening to Harriet's voice and changing trains every so often, just to mix things up and stay awake. Around five-thirty, I headed for home, made a fresh pot of coffee and waited until a decent hour to text my father. *How can I contact George?*

He replied straightaway. *I have no idea.*

Seconds later there was another text. *Why?*

I pecked out a reply. *Maybe I should get to know him.*

The reply was instant. *Don't even think about it. Stay away.*

Still drunk, I was tempted to send Dad another message – an apology for having assumed the worst about 'his' infidelities; sympathy over the impending divorce – but decided against it. It was probably the alcohol making me sentimental. Instead, I replied to Mum's latest email from the Blue Moon Yoga Retreat on Patnem Beach, letting her know I was now in the picture about her and Dad, and about 'Alex' too. I decided not to say more, for now at least. That's the thing about a parent with bipolar disorder – you end up skirting important stuff in case it sends them off the deep end. I said I hoped she was okay and enjoying Goa. Then I lay on the bed, fully dressed, and crashed out for, like, ten hours straight.

My subconscious must have gone into overdrive because my waking thought was of George's passport and the note I'd found in his jacket pocket; those four words in black ink. *Rochester House – Camden. Paddy.*

A Google search told me that Rochester House was a hostel for homeless men. I wolfed down a bowl of cereal, showered and shaved, then biked to north London, arriving at the imposing Victorian building as dusk was falling. I chained my bike to the railings then buzzed the intercom. I heard a man's voice.

'Hello?'

'I'm looking for Paddy.'

'Paddy who?'

'I don't know. He might be a friend of my grandfather's.'

'What's your grandfather's name?'

'George Brocklebank.' I hesitated. 'Or maybe Lord Anthony Buckingham.'

I thought I heard a chuckle but perhaps I was mistaken. The buzzer sounded, the door clicked and I entered the building.

There was no sign of life. The place stank of fried food and disinfectant and the hallway was gloomy, lit by an overhead strip-light that flickered on and off, buzzing like an angry wasp. I walked through a fire door, into a corridor, and followed the sound of voices to an office. The door was ajar. Two men in their seventies were sitting by a two-bar electric fire, nursing mugs of tea.

'You're looking for Gorgeous George?'

The speaker looked ill – almost bald with wispy hair and sallow skin.

'Or Paddy,' I said.

'I'm Paddy.' He looked me up and down. 'I'm

273

guessing you're Tom? George said he was planning to try and find you.'

The second man drained his mug, placed it on the desk then shuffled out without a word. Paddy got to his feet, keys jangling from his belt. He was wearing a pair of exotic leather slippers, the sort you'd find in a souk in Marrakech. We talked as I followed him along a corridor lined with closed doors and up a flight of stone steps.

'Is George here?' I said.

He stopped at a door and gave me a wink.

'Let's find out.'

He knocked. No response. He knocked again. Silence, apart from a distant bout of coughing from down the hall. He selected a key and opened the door.

'Welcome to Shangri-La.'

He stepped aside and ushered me into the room. It was small with a single bed, a white plastic table and a chair. A flimsy rack served as a wardrobe. There were hardly any clothes. I recognized the bottle green corduroy suit George had worn during his visit to my flat. The yellow pocket square lay on the table, neatly ironed and folded.

'He lives here?'

'Sometimes,' said Paddy, shuffling inside and sitting on the bed. 'When he's not playing *cherchez la femme*.' Another wink. 'We go back a long way otherwise I'd tell him he's outstayed his welcome.' He opened a bedside drawer. 'Did you know your granddad used to be a pop star?'

He rummaged in the drawer and took out a vinyl

record – a 45 rpm single with a photo of George on the cover, looking moody. He was instantly recognisable in a sharp suit topped off with, like, a trilby set at a rakish angle. The song was called 'The Days Are Long (But The Years Are Short)'. To my surprise, I felt a lump rise in my throat as I stared at the picture. How old had he been? Twenty-five? Certainly no more than thirty; a man in his prime. I remembered the advice he had given me.

Life is short, Tom. Eat the cake, buy the shoes, take the trip.

Running a finger over the photo, I felt a sense of connection I'd never experienced before. Had 'Gorgeous' George's near-miss with stardom influenced my father's attitude towards music? Was this why Dad liked those old songs and had taken the job at Silk FM? I'd assumed his old-fogeyish attitude was a by-product of middle age but perhaps there was more to it. And maybe my own taste for musicals was part of a continuum – another branch of our gnarled and twisted family tree.

'He only made one record,' said Paddy. 'It didn't hit the charts but still – it was a moment in the sun.'

'He said he was getting married.'

Paddy rolled his eyes. 'Chelsea Town Hall?'

I nodded. 'Followed by lunch at the Savoy.'

'That was the plan.'

'Was?'

'Maybe still is.' He waved a hand around the room. 'Place like this, you don't ask too many questions.' He scratched his neck then turned to face me. 'I don't suppose he talked to you about a gold mine in Peru?'

'He mentioned it,' I said. 'Why?'

He ran his eyes over my clothes, taking stock of my dishevelled appearance.

'Never mind.'

I looked around the room, searching in vain for the red exercise book that had contained George's 'autobiography' then I heard a voice at the door. 'I see we have company, Patrick.' I turned to see my grandfather, smartly dressed in a pinstripe suit and black brogues. 'Splendid,' he said. 'Just in time for the cocktail hour.'

He didn't seem surprised to see me and there was no sign of embarrassment on his part.

'Shall we adjourn to the local hostelry?' he said. 'This place has its virtues but the bar is a disappointment unless you care for cocoa.'

Leaving Paddy to lock up, I followed George along the corridor and out into the fresh air. He peered along the street, looking in both directions.

'I take it you weren't followed,' he said.

'Who by?'

'Never mind.'

He took off at a pace that belied his age. There was a pub on the corner. We went inside. I offered to buy him a drink but he insisted on buying the first round – single malt for him, a pint for me. We sat at a corner table, exchanging pleasantries, neither of us mentioning his straitened circumstances. After a moment or two, he turned to face me.

'Have you a girlfriend, Tom?'

'Not at the moment.'

'Someone in your sights?'

'You could say that, yes.'

'Excellent.' He sipped his whisky. 'It does a chap good to have a young filly on his horizon. Keeps him fresh, sharp.'

I smiled. 'How are the wedding plans?'

'I'll keep you posted.' He drained his glass. 'Did your *papa* send you?'

'Why would he do that?'

'To tell me to bugger off.'

'He doesn't know I'm here.'

He raised an eyebrow.

'In which case, to what do I owe the pleasure?'

I leaned forward and lowered my voice.

'Do you know anything about a man called Jack Vance?'

George studied my face, as if bringing me into focus for the first time. A sly smile crept over his features.

'What would you like to know?'

RICHARD

Monday's show went well, despite a hangover that defied coffee and Nurofen. During the final hour, with Perry Como crooning 'Magic Moments' as Harriet and I chatted off-air, I like to think I did a decent job of hiding my feelings about the photo of her at a flower market with a smug-looking Tom – the one that showed up on her new Twitter feed on Sunday afternoon. (Cyber stalking? Me?)

'Looks like you had fun at the weekend,' I said, doing my best to strike a casual tone.

She said something about how sweet Tom was and how she loved lilies.

'I associate them with funerals,' I said then worried I might have sounded as if I was trying to put Tom down (which, with hindsight, I suppose I was).

She skipped breakfast – again – and hurried off after the show; a doctor's appointment, or so she said. I pretended not to mind, took myself to a café and booted up my laptop. Sipping a latte, I emailed my solicitor, telling her to expect to hear from Bonnie about the divorce. I can't pretend it wasn't a melancholy moment. Twenty-five years of marriage reduced to an exchange of emails and dry legalese.

To cheer myself up, I googled articles about the Mayfair jewel robbery and found several obituaries of the late Jack Vance. The man seemed to have spent most of his life behind bars, progressing (if that's the word) from domestic burglaries to Post Office robberies followed by a series of increasingly audacious bank and safe deposit heists. Not surprisingly, there was no clue as to what he might have done with his share of that final haul.

I'd just ordered a second cup of coffee when my mobile rang. Usually, I ignore unknown numbers but this time I answered on impulse. God, how I wished I hadn't. There was no preamble but the man's voice was unmistakable.

'The lad came to see me.'

I froze.

How long since we'd spoken. Twenty years? More?

Resisting the urge to hang up, I gathered my wits, letting the seconds tick by before finding my voice.

'How did ...' I tailed off. My voice was little more than a croak. I cleared my throat and tried again. 'How did he find you?'

'He's clever,' said George. '*Comme papa, comme fils.*'

Silently, I counted to ten. The trouble with a charm offensive by my father is it's all offensive and no charm. I did my best to rise above the most crass insult I'd ever heard but my hands were trembling and I could feel the blood thudding in my ears. How often had I fantasized about this conversation? What I would say, how scathing my words would be, barbs filled with recrimination and wounding wit. But when the moment finally arrived – this thunderbolt from the blue – it was as though the years had worn away the worst of my fury, like the ocean slowly but surely eroding a shoreline. I was still livid, yes, but most of all, I felt overwhelmed and exhausted by the effort of carrying so much rage, and for so long.

'What do you want?' I said.

I heard him clear his throat. 'Tom's taking a risk. I thought you should know.'

It seemed an unlikely pretext for breaking a silence that had lasted two decades. All of a sudden, the penny dropped: the man was dying, eager to re-establish communication before it was too late, to explore the possibility of redemption, even absolution, as if *that* could ever happen. In spite of everything – the rage, the weight of wasted years – I felt a pang of sympathy, recalling a phrase I'd come across in one of Bonnie's self-help books. *Forgiveness means giving up all hope of a better past.* But if forgiveness was out of the question (and by God it was) then my father had succeeded in piquing my curiosity by telling me that Tom was at risk.

Employing a technique I use when trying not to lose my cool (e.g., with police officers who pull me over for speeding, or hapless call centre workers in Bangalore), I decided to pretend that I was on-air, performing for my unseen audience. For the duration of the call, I wouldn't be Richard

Brocklebank – heartbroken son nursing a life-shattering grievance – I'd be Richard Young, radio pro.

'What sort of risk?' I said.

'He's in love, poor sod. The girl's up the duff. Not by him, apparently, by some toerag who's trying to wash his hands of the whole affair. Poor Tom is badly smitten. He wants to help her.'

'Help how?'

'Money,' said George. 'He wanted to pick my brains.'

'About?'

He hesitated. 'Is this line secure?'

I fought the temptation to hurl the phone across the café.

'I don't think GCHQ care about a call between a DJ and an ageing gigolo. What did Tom want to know?'

'He asked about an old lag, Jack Vance. Tom said you were up to speed about this – the girl too. I take it you know who I'm talking about?'

'Yes.'

'Rumour has it Vance was involved in something big a few years ago. Tom seemed to think I might know people who knew him.'

'Why would he think such a thing?'

'I assume you've told him I'm some kind of crook.'

If only 'crook' were the worst of it . . .

'I made some calls,' continued George. 'Jack's wife has been dead for years. There's one son, Damian. Word is his old man shuffled off having made sure his son was *extremely* well provided for. His way of apologizing for being a lousy father.'

'A father apologizing?' I said, allowing the mask to slip. 'Whatever next?'

A pause. When George spoke again he had the grace to sound chastened.

'Yes ... Well, we are where we are.'

'Which is where exactly?'

'Tom's keen to get his hands on what you might call Vance's bequest, assuming there is one. He wants to give any proceeds to the *jeune fille*, to help her out with the baby.'

He was right: Tom *was* smart. Then again, I'd had the exact same thought.

'It's his way of trying to win her affections,' continued George. 'I asked what was wrong with a box of Milk Tray.'

'Hilarious.'

'He seemed to think so,' said George. 'He wants to search the flat where Damian is staying. Either for the haul itself or something in writing – a will or a clue to "buried treasure".'

'And he wants you to teach him how to be a burglar?'

'Not exactly.'

'What, then? Are you going to break in?'

'Not my style, despite what you may believe. But from what Tom told me there might be another way to gain access to the flat. Ideally, the ruse needs three people. I thought you might like to help. Keep it in the family, so to speak.'

'Some family,' I said, my performance starting to falter.

He sidestepped the dig. Was his refusal to rise to the bait a sign of desperation?

'Will you help him or not?' he said. 'It's for the girl and

her baby, remember, not for me.' He paused before delivering the clincher. 'But mainly it's for the boy. Our boy.'

I closed my eyes tightly, silently cursing. He'd always known how to appeal to my better nature. Part of his shtick.

'Help how?'

He sounded cagey. 'Are you in or not?'

I considered my options. This was no longer just about Tom and Harriet. The stakes were now much higher. If George *was* dying, it was essential to make sure he took to his grave the secret that had wrought nuclear winter in the midst of our broken family, a secret so toxic it still had the power to wreak havoc. If the bastard was gripped by a sudden determination to play happy families – with Tom at least – then I needed to keep them both under close observation, to fend off potential catastrophe.

And there was another consideration. If I spurned George's request, not only would I risk things spiralling out of control, I would deny myself this opportunity to curry favour with the woman I adored, leaving the field clear to Tom. All things considered, it was what he would call 'a no-brainer'.

'I may live to regret this,' I said, 'but the answer is yes. So stop playing around and tell me – what am I letting myself in for?'

HARRIET

If you don't tell his missus, I will.

There was no doubt that Nan meant every word. I knew I didn't have long before she carried out her threat so after the show on Monday I skipped breakfast with Richard, saying that I had an appointment with the obstetrician. I knew he wouldn't ask questions.

I hurried to Oxford Circus and hopped on the first tube to Brixton, cringing every time an announcement came on the tannoy. Perhaps it was to do with being pregnant but hearing my voice echo along the platform made me feel extra vulnerable and exposed.

I wouldn't like to give the impression that I'd repeatedly stalked Candida Vance as my relationship with Cockweasel had crashed and burned, or that I'd been driven crazy by jealousy, but let's just say I knew where they lived – a five-bedroom, Farrow-and-Ball-decorated house within walking distance of Brixton tube, giving Damian an easy half-hour commute, including the six-minute stroll to his Harley Street surgery. I knew where their kids went to school. I knew what time Wifey dropped them off in her maroon Range Rover Evoque. I also happened to know she went to the gym on Mondays, Wednesdays and Fridays, emerging just after 10 a.m. then treating herself to a caffè Americano in the Starbucks down the road. (Oh, and she was partial to a cinnamon swirl, too, but only on Fridays.)

I bought a cappuccino and took a seat by the window. Sure enough, she walked in at six minutes past ten, ordered her coffee and flicked through a copy of *OK!* magazine while taking delicate sips through a straw, careful not to smudge her lipstick. She was blonde, of course. Her tan looked real. I vaguely remembered Damian saying something about how she always visited Marbella during autumn half term. She looked like one of those saddoes who enjoy paying extra for priority boarding so they can walk past the rest of us, nose in the air.

'Hey,' I said, taking the seat next to her. 'I'm Harriet.'

Candida looked up from the magazine.

'Do I know you?'

'No. But I know your husband.'

She gave me a glare, as if I were something unpleasant stuck on the sole of her shoe.

'Christ,' she sighed. 'Not another one.'

'Excuse me?'

She narrowed her eyes.

'Actually, this is good news. He's already said yes to the new house and the villa in Tuscany. Now I'll get the new car, too.'

'I don't get it.'

'That's because you don't get Damian,' she said, leaning closer. I could smell the coffee on her breath, and her expensive perfume. 'Not like I do. Which is why he always comes back.'

'From where?'

'Whichever slag he's been shagging. You're not the first, darling, and you won't be the last. Which is why our arrangement works so well.'

I blinked, determined not to lose my cool.

'What arrangement?'

A thin smile. She was tapping her acrylic nails on her brand new iPhone, focusing on its screen as she searched for an app.

'He'll never leave his family. Know why? He's half man, half rosary. Each time I catch him out he's so overwhelmed by Catholic guilt that he can't sleep. That's when I get an upgrade.' Without pausing for breath, she held up her mobile and took a photo of me. 'I had a Mini then a Golf then a Beemer. Last year he bought me the Evoque.'

'Wait,' I said, leaning forward and holding up a hand to staunch the flow of words. 'He was seeing someone *else*? Last year?'

She pocketed her phone and faked a yawn.

'There's always more than one on the go, darling. Lucy, I think her name was. Or was it Lottie?' She shrugged. 'Not that it matters; they all look the same.' She leaned closer still. 'A bit like you.'

I could feel the bile rising in my throat.

'He told me he'd left you,' I said.

She shook her head and gave a world-weary smile.

'I threw him out when I found out about Lucy ... or Lottie or Laura. Told him he needed a few months on his own, to get stuff out of his system before he could come home. I love it when he's not around. Gives me breathing space.' She sighed. 'To tell you the truth, I'm dreading having him back but the kids miss him so what can you do? I've said he can come home in a few weeks, in time to put up the Christmas tree and play happy families.' Candida got to her feet, folding the glossy magazine into a roll and tucking it into her Louis Vuitton bag. 'What did you say your name was?' I opened my mouth to speak but she beat me to it. 'Don't bother. You'll always be "Lexus" to me.'

She headed for the door. I called her name.

'Candida.'

She turned.

'Yes?'

'What did you do to them?'

She frowned.

'To who?'

'Your parents.'

The frown deepened.

'I don't get it.'

'They must have hated you,' I said. 'Why else would they name you after a yeast infection?'

She opened her mouth to speak then changed her mind.

The best she could muster was pursed lips and a middle finger. Then she was gone.

The whole thing – the showdown I'd been rehearsing for months – no, *years* – had lasted less than two minutes. She hadn't even finished her coffee.

I sat for a while, feeling poleaxed, then felt a surge of white-hot anger coursing through every fibre of my being. By the time I walked out of Starbucks I was seething, fit to burst **AND I COULD PUSH THAT WOMAN AT THE BUS STOP UNDER A BUS, AND HER UGLY BABY TOO!**

The journey back to Soho passed in a blur. It was nearly eleven-thirty by the time I got to the Silk FM office. Pam said Richard was back from breakfast and was recording trailers in studio B. I waited till the red light was off then pushed open the soundproofed door and went inside. He looked surprised by my reappearance.

'How was the doctor?'

'I didn't go,' I said. 'I went to see Damian's wife instead.'

'And?'

I took a deep breath.

'I've changed my mind. About making him pay towards the baby.'

He smiled. 'You're sure?'

I nodded, fighting back tears.

'I've never been more sure of anything in my life.'

TOM

I have only one childhood memory of 'Gorgeous' George. A rainy Sunday afternoon spent sitting on his lap, eating Maltesers while watching *The Sting*. Bored by the movie (I was five), I remember George punching the air in triumph as the grifters played by Paul Newman and Robert Redford pulled off their elaborate con and netted a fortune.

That was the last I saw of him until the day he arrived at my flat and fell asleep on the sofa. After his disappearance from family life, I remember quizzing Mum and Dad as to his whereabouts but they were always tight-lipped and quick to change the subject, so I stopped asking, sensing a no-go zone. Exactly why the man had become, like, *persona non grata* I had no idea. I'd assumed it was because of the way he lived – bed-hopping from one rich widow to the next, lotus-eating his way around the world. But now he was back. And determined to make his presence felt.

The scam to gain entry to Damian Vance's flat wasn't on a par with *The Sting* but its simplicity was pretty cool. Harriet had mentioned the rented North Audley Street apartment during one of our FaceTime chats and I 'just happened' to cycle past on a couple of occasions, at different hours of the day and night, glancing up to see if the lights were on.

Okay, I was seething with jealousy, unable to resist the temptation to check on her whereabouts and tormenting myself with visions of the woman I loved undressing before Vance's hungry eyes. And perhaps I went too far but anyone who's been under attack from the green-eyed monster will understand. Won't they?

Earlier in the day, George had done what he called 'a reconnaissance op' outside Damian's apartment then insisted on the face-to-face meeting with my father so we could figure out how to get inside.

My grandfather seemed nervous in the Uber that took us from Camden to Belsize Park. A muscle twitched repeatedly under his eye, something I would come to recognize as a sign of stress.

'We won't mention Rochester House to Richard,' he said. 'As far as he's concerned I'm living the life of Riley. Wine, women and song.'

'Whatever you say.'

Dusk was falling as we arrived at the white stucco building that housed Dad's apartment. I pressed the buzzer on the intercom. The door clicked and opened. George ushered me inside then followed me up the staircase in silence. He exuded an air of solemnity, as if something momentous was about to happen. When I look back at that father–son encounter – their first after a twenty-year estrangement – I can only imagine how he must have felt. Into the lion's den . . .

Dad was waiting at the door, his expression betraying no hint of how he was feeling. I'd been expecting some acknowledgement of what was a highly significant reunion but there was nothing, not a handshake or a smile and certainly nothing resembling a hug, which wasn't unusual as far as Dad was concerned. He'd never been one for showing physical affection, at least not to me.

'*Bonjour*,' said George blithely. 'Good to see you.'

'Let's get on with this,' said my father.

The surprise came when I walked into the living room. Sitting on the sofa, holding a mug of tea, was Harriet. I'm ashamed to admit my first impulse was to jerk my head towards the door to Dad's bedroom, to see if the bed was rumpled. How exactly had they spent the afternoon? No sooner had the thought crossed my mind than I told myself off for being so suspicious. In the first place, I had no reason to believe she was sleeping with my father. In the second place, she was pregnant with Damian's baby. The important question was: what did my suspicions say about me? I didn't like the answer.

I'd taken to listening to their show, searching for any telltale change in the nature of their banter – something to suggest they were growing more intimate – but there was nothing I could pinpoint, just Dad's banal babble leavened by the warmth and wit of his 'second banana'.

The bedroom door was closed. I smiled at Harriet.

'I didn't expect to see you here.'

'Richard invited me,' she said, smiling. 'I told him I've changed my mind. About Damian and the baby. Turns out he's a bigger bastard than I thought.'

She put down her mug and got to her feet as Dad gestured towards George.

'Harriet, I'm afraid I'm going to have to introduce you to my father.'

George took her hand. I thought he was going to raise her fingers to his lips but he settled for a twinkle-eyed smile.

'*Enchanté*. Now I understand why Tom is so eager to help.'

Dad puffed out his cheeks, cleared his throat and gestured towards the coffee table. Two bottles of wine – one red, one white – sat next to a sad-looking platter of vegetarian canapés from Marks and Spencer. I cottoned on to his game immediately.

'No cocktail sausages, Dad? I thought they were your favourite.'

He ignored me, filling his glass and leaving me and George to serve ourselves. We made stilted small talk – traffic, the weather – with Dad showing zero interest in how his father had passed the two decades since they'd last met. He seemed ill at ease, as if trying to keep a lid on his temper.

'So, George,' he said, 'why are you here?'

My grandfather sat next to Harriet and smiled.

'I put the word out about Jack Vance. Two sources say he's left his son set up for life.'

'Anything more specific?' said Harriet.

'Diamonds. A lot of them.'

Her eyes widened.

'So now what?'

'The simple approach is best,' said George. 'The apartment Damian is renting is up for sale. I've made an appointment to view it tomorrow lunchtime. Tom and I will go together. I'll distract the estate agent, leaving Tom free to search the place and find whatever there is to be found.'

Dad frowned.

'Where do I come in?'

'You'll stay in the street, keeping lookout. We don't want Damian showing up out of the blue.'

'Won't he be working?' said Harriet.

'Better safe than sorry,' said George.

I saw Dad's jaw tighten.

'Thank you for that blindingly original observation.'

My grandfather let the put-down pass. I had the feeling he was determined to stay on, like, best behaviour, no matter how severe the provocation.

'Surely it would make sense for me to go inside, too,' said Harriet. 'I know where Damian keeps stuff.'

'*Bonne idée,*' said George. 'In which case, why doesn't Tom act as lookout?'

I shrugged.

'Cool.'

George turned to my father. The muscle beneath his eye twitched again.

'It seems we don't need you after all.'

But Dad had other ideas.

'I said I'd help and I will.'

'There's really no need,' said George.

A testy tone entered my father's voice.

'Tom and I can both keep lookout.'

George gave a resigned shrug.

'If you insist.' He got to his feet. 'Mind if I use your bathroom?'

Dad gestured towards the hall.

'Second on the left,' he said. 'As if you didn't know.'

He waited until George had left the room then turned to me and whispered, 'Have you given him money?'

'He hasn't asked for any.'

'He will.'

We turned to watch George walk along the hall and disappear into the bathroom. I've never claimed to be on the same wavelength as my father but in that moment I had the strangest feeling we were both thinking the same thing.

What the hell is George up to?

RICHARD

It was all I could do not to punch the man in the face.

Good to see you ... As if we were old friends meeting at a party.

Un-fucking-speakable.

Un-fucking-forgivable.

As for Tom, I could tell he was taken aback to find Harriet on my sofa. At the risk of sounding uncharitable: tough. His feelings on that score were the least of my worries (although on another matter they were the greatest).

If my father opened his big mouth – if he dropped the slightest hint about the secret I'd nursed since Tom's sixth birthday – I would not be responsible for my actions. Allowing him into my home was no prelude to reconciliation, let alone forgiveness, it was a case of 'keep your friends close but your enemies closer'. I needed this enemy in plain sight, where I could keep tabs on him and make sure he wreaked as little havoc as possible. As I watched him slip into my bathroom, a series of lurid headlines flashed into my mind's eye.

DJ MURDERS FATHER

20–YEAR–OLD FAMILY SECRET LEADS TO MURDER

GIGOLO KILLED OVER SKELETON IN FAMILY CLOSET

It's an odd thing, coming face to face with someone who, not to put too fine a point on it, ruined your life. Okay, I was far from destitute and Bonnie and I had managed to muddle through, against all odds – but the combination of love, apathy and guilt that had kept us together was no recipe for happy ever after. As for Tom, had he been mine – properly mine – it was hard to imagine how different our lives might have been. It crossed my mind that had the boy's very existence not soured every waking moment, I might have backed down when it came to pursuing my one shot at late-life happiness in the shape of Harriet Brown. But as the poet says, 'Shit happens'.

Needless to say, neither Harriet nor I mentioned George's master-plan the following morning, while we were on-air, our conversation inhibited by the presence of Pam and the rest of the team. We did the show as if it were just a normal day.

At this point, I need to make a confession. Knowing of Harriet's interest in astrology it's possible that I may have accidentally-on-purpose tampered with the forecast for her sign, intercepting the email from our 'official' astrologer (puh-leeze!) and adapting his mumbo-jumbo to suit my agenda. Avoiding Harriet's gaze, I switched on the mic and addressed the listeners.

'Aquarius: a day of potentially dramatic developments. You'll prosper as long as you put your trust in an older, wiser advisor. Now is not the time to rely on people younger than yourself – especially anyone born under the sign of Libra.'

Which happened to be Tom's sign.

I know.

So sue me.

After the show, Harriet and I went our separate ways until the rendezvous in the North Audley Street café. Tom was already there when I arrived, eating a sandwich and drinking coffee. There was no sign of George. I felt a flicker of relief. The last thing I needed was for him and Tom to become bosom pals.

I looked away as Harriet greeted Tom with a hug and a peck on the cheek. I was on high alert for any sign that their relationship had stepped up a gear during rehearsals for his musical – a look, a tell in their body language – but there was nothing. Which proved sod all. With Harriet carrying Damian's baby it was hard to predict if she was more or less likely to succumb to Tom's charms – or mine, for that matter. That she was growing increasingly angry with Vance was a good sign but would her ire make her more or less keen to go it alone?

As for Tom, how would he feel about taking on another man's child? Was he the jealous type? Or did he, like me, view her pregnancy as a chance to show what he was made of? There was only one way to find out – ask – and that, of course, was out of the question.

Tom drained his cup. I checked my watch. 1.25 p.m. The appointment with the estate agent was for 1.30. Vance's apartment was less than two minutes' walk but there was no sign of George.

'Is he reliable?' said Harriet, chewing the inside of her lip.

'Quite the opposite,' I said.

'He'll be here,' said Tom.

His sangfroid grated on my nerves. To make matters worse, he was right. As if on cue, George sauntered through the door wearing dark glasses and a bottle green corduroy suit with a yellow pocket square.

'You look like a gangster,' I said.

He gave a thin smile.

'Is there no end to your charm?'

Without waiting for a reply George turned to Harriet.

'Did you bring a handbag?'

She raised a large leather bag for his inspection.

'Perfect,' he said. Then he did the oddest thing. He took hold of her arm and drew her closer.

'You're nervous,' he said. 'Am I right?'

Harriet nodded. I noticed for the first time that she was trembling.

'The thing is . . .' she said then fell silent. George smiled.

'Yes?'

Harriet took a breath then continued.

'The thing is, it's a performance. I know it's only an audience of one, and if it was the radio show I'd have no problem, but it's an *actual person*.'

George smiled.

'Try not to think of him as a person,' he said. 'Think of him as an estate agent.'

Harriet shook her head.

'Snobbery doesn't help,' she said.

George's expression grew serious.

'In my experience,' he said, 'the whole of life is a perform-ance, what Americans call a high-wire act. A tightrope walk, if you like. Do you know what prevents tightrope walkers from falling, Harriet?'

She shook her head.

'The secret is simple,' said George. 'Just keep going and *never look down*. Got it?'

Harriet blinked and smiled.

'Got it.'

'Say it,' said George. 'Keep going and *never look down*.'

She looked him in the eye.

'Keep going and *never look down*.'

'Excellent,' said my father, his smile broadening. 'So, are we ready?'

Harriet nodded.

'Ready.'

Tom left a tip then headed for the door and left the café. As Harriet followed in his wake, George raised an eyebrow in my direction.

'We can manage without you, if you'd rather stay here?'

I took a step closer and breathed in his ear.

'Tell him and I'll kill you.'

He looked stricken. I hadn't planned on saying anything but it was clear that my words packed a punch. Hardly surprising. They'd been a long time coming.

'You have my promise,' he said.

'Which is worthless.'

A sigh. 'I'm trying to do a good deed in a wicked world, Richard. Let's get this done.'

'Then what? Your wedding? Chelsea Town Hall? Lunch at the Savoy?'

'Are you coming or not?'

I walked past him, out into the street where Tom and Harriet were waiting. George sent Tom to the corner of Oxford Street, to keep watch in one direction. I was dispatched to the other end of the road, nearer Grosvenor Square, to stand lookout in the unlikely event of Damian deciding to pop home at lunchtime.

George was right, of course – better safe than sorry – but there was something about the enterprise that felt both shabby and absurd. All the same, I could feel my pulse quickening as I watched my father and Harriet approach the black front door and shake hands with a sharp-suited estate agent before crossing the threshold of what might prove to be an Aladdin's cave.

HARRIET

Keep going and never look down . . .

I'd lost count of the number of times I'd been inside the flat, and being there with George but without Damian felt weird. The estate agent droned on as the three of us wandered from room to room. *The master bedroom is south facing and has plenty of light . . . The ensuite bathroom has underfloor heating . . . blah blah blah.*

Like most rental apartments, the place was sparsely furnished. Damian had always been fussy about tidiness so there wasn't much clutter. After a couple of minutes I started to lag behind, as arranged with George, leaving him to fire a barrage of convoluted questions designed to distract attention from what his 'granddaughter' was up to.

Alone in the kitchen, I tried to ignore the pounding of my heart and feigned interest in the 'soft close' mechanism of the drawers, all the while keeping my eyes peeled in a way I never had during previous visits. I knew the rumours about Damian's father, of course, but the idea that Vance Senior might have bequeathed his son a dodgy legacy had never crossed my mind. What was I searching for anyway? Cash? Jewellery? A will? No one knew what the Mayfair vault had contained but the best guess seemed to be diamonds. Lots of 'em.

I left the kitchen and joined the others in the sitting room, feigning interest in George's queries about the feasibility of extending the lease and trying to ignore the voice inside my head that was telling me **HOW EASY IT WOULD BE TO OPEN THE DOOR ONTO THE BALCONY AND JUMP OFF**! Pushing The Thoughts away, I braced myself for the next phase of the performance, George's words playing in my ears.

Never look down . . .

'Mind if I look around by myself?' I said.

George turned to the estate agent.

'Okay by you?'

The man smiled.

'Of course.'

So I left them to it and walked into Cockweasel's bedroom. Not so long ago, I'd spent many deliriously happy hours here. As a human being, Damian had turned out to be less than zero; as a lover, he scored top marks. Perhaps it was the hormones, but quelling The Thoughts and running my hand over a pillow, I felt a surge of sadness so intense it almost made me fall to the floor and weep. The fact that it was followed *immediately* by an equally powerful craving for a Scotch egg slathered in mayonnaise confirmed what Nan said about pregnancy: baby wants what Baby wants.

Damian had always been a neatnik but I'd never seen the place so tidy. I checked the drawers, careful not to disturb his belongings as I rifled through his neatly folded socks, boxers and T-shirts. The wardrobe was next. I patted down his shirts and the pockets of his suits then checked inside his shoes. Nothing.

I could hear George in the adjoining room, asking about the differences between leasehold and freehold. Despite the circumstances, there was something about being in the company of this old man that made me feel safe and secure. I thought back to the horoscope Richard had read on-air. *You'll prosper as long as you put your trust in an older, wiser advisor.* George was certainly older. Whether or not he was wiser remained to be seen.

I checked the pillows and looked underneath the bed, then slid my hands between the mattress and the divan. Kneeling down, I detected the smell of Damian. His body. His hair. He was everywhere. The duvet. The sheets. The pillowcases.

I felt another bitter-sweet pang of sadness then a surge of anger. I had adored this man – trusted him – and he had let me down. But did the betrayal justify snooping through his belongings – with intent to steal?

I summoned the memory of well-heeled Wifey. Our Starbucks showdown.

There's usually more than one on the go. Lucy, I think her name was. Or was it Lottie? Not that it matters; they all look the same. A bit like you.

The thought stiffened my resolve. I called to the other room.

'Okay if I use the loo?'

The estate agent called back.

'No problemo.'

I walked into the bathroom and bolted the door. Everything was immaculate, like an ultra posh hotel suite. Cockweasel may have been a shit-bag but when it came to personal hygiene he was a prince among men, just the right side of prissy. I can't pretend that I didn't scrutinize the medicine cabinet for traces of other women but there was nothing to arouse suspicion and no sign of a second head for the electric toothbrush. Somehow, I managed to resist the urge to examine the shower's plughole for traces of long hair.

I flushed the loo then studied my reflection in the mirror. My cheeks had a rosy glow. Another telltale sign of the hormones raging through my body? Thinking longingly of that Scotch egg (and maybe a pork pie with piccalilli), I washed my hands while letting my eyes rove over the contents of the chrome rack. A bottle of shampoo. Conditioner. A can of shaving foam.

Peering more closely, I frowned. Despite his fastidiousness, Damian had never been the type to use moisturiser. In fact, he mocked men who did. So why was there a tub of Nivea? On impulse, I took it from the rack and slipped it into my bag. Then I unlocked the door and joined the others in the sitting room. My mouth was dry. My pulse was racing.

TOM

It was Harriet who insisted on taking a taxi all the way from North Audley Street to Walthamstow. An Uber not a black cab, but even so, I remember thinking, *She's changing, going up in the world*. Dad offered to pay, flashing his cash as usual, but she wouldn't hear of it.

'I'm earning decent money for a change so I'm paying my own way.'

Independent, smart, kind, funny, talented and gorgeous. I mean, come on – what's not to like?

George was quiet, staring out at the traffic. He piped up once, as we were driving along Walthamstow High Street and passing an estate agent's window.

'That used to be a bakery,' he said. 'Best sausage rolls in the world. Pastry like you wouldn't believe.'

I raised an eyebrow.

'You don't strike me as someone who spends much time in Walthamstow.'

He smiled. 'There's a lot you don't know, my lad.'

305

'Look at that pigeon,' said Dad.

I followed his gaze but there was nothing out of the ordinary. I had the feeling he was trying to, like, change the subject.

It wasn't until we were inside Nancy's kitchen and introductions had been made that Harriet told us about the pot of Nivea from Damian's bathroom.

'It's probably nothing. I acted on impulse.'

She drew the blue tub from her bag and placed it on the table.

'Does it rattle?' said George, his voice filled with hope.

Nancy frowned. 'It's cream. Why would it rattle?'

Harriet unscrewed the top of the tub then peeled back the foil seal and scrutinized the contents. Her face fell.

'It's cream.'

'Got a sieve?' said Dad.

As Nancy rummaged in the cupboard under the sink, I thought I saw George checking out her legs.

'Will a colander do?' said Nancy.

'Perfect,' said Harriet.

George dipped his fingers into the tub and slopped a dollop of white gunk into the colander.

'Put it under the tap,' said Dad.

Harriet did as instructed, turning on the tap and holding the colander under the running water. I held my breath, watching as the cream washed away, leaving ... nothing. George's face fell.

'Try again,' he said.

Harriet followed his example, scooping another handful

of cream into the colander then holding it under the gushing water. We watched it disappear. Leaving some kind of residue. Like small shards of glass . . .

'Ohmygod . . .' said Harriet.

'Bloody hell,' said Dad.

'Blimey,' said Nancy.

'Hallelujah,' said George.

Harriet scooped the remainder of the Nivea into the colander and repeated the rinsing exercise revealing more diamonds.

At a guess, I'd say there were fifty or sixty stones, the size of coffee beans. George took a pair of black-rimmed spectacles from his pocket and peered at them. The stunned silence was broken by Nancy.

'Will someone tell me what's going on?'

While Harriet brought her grandmother up to speed about Jack Vance and the legacy he'd left his son, George busied himself making a pot of tea. He didn't ask permission, just made himself at home, finding teabags, mugs and milk.

'Do you take sugar?' he said, turning to wink at Nancy. 'Or are you sweet enough?'

She blinked at him, as though seeing him for the first time.

'Do I know you?'

'I don't think so,' said George.

She peered closer.

'Didn't you used to be a singer?'

My father gave a snort of derision but George smiled from ear to ear.

'I was hardly Elvis,' he said, 'but I did once cut a record. It reached number eighty-six in the hit parade. It was called . . .'

'"The Days Are Long . . . "' interrupted Nan.

'" . . . But The Years Are Short",' finished George.

'I loved that song. You had a good voice.'

'I could tell you were a woman of taste.'

Dad rolled his eyes then turned his attention back to the diamonds.

'What are we supposed to do with these?'

Nancy prised her eyes from George's face and frowned at my father.

'Don't ask me. I'm a dinner lady not the Pink Panther.'

'I might know a chap,' said George.

Harriet raised an eyebrow.

'A fence?'

'Yes. I could have a word.'

'Absolutely not,' said Dad.

'I don't know about you,' said Harriet, 'but stolen diamonds aren't my thing.'

'Nor mine,' said George. 'But I know people who know people. I could have a word, find out what these beauties might be worth. It's not as if you can take them to Bond Street and get an estimate.'

My father shook his head.

'Out of the question.'

'Isn't that Harriet's decision?' said George. 'Surely the whole point of the exercise was to provide funds for her baby.'

All eyes turned to Harriet. She stared intently at the diamonds, as though unable to believe what she was seeing.
Upending the colander, she tipped the gems back into the
blue plastic tub.

'I think I'm in shock,' she said.

George handed her a mug of tea and gave an avuncular
smile. 'Perfectly natural.'

She returned his smile and in a flash I could see how the
man's charm must have worked its magic on women all over
the world. Like my father, he was a man who genuinely
liked women – he listened to what they had to say and came
alive in their presence. I studied Harriet's face. Even with
everything that was going on, it was clear she felt calmer,
grateful for his reassurance. I could feel my spirits sinking.
Could I ever make her feel that way?

Nancy opened the fridge and took out a pot of peach
yoghurt. She poured the contents into the tub of Nivea, covering the diamonds.

'So it doesn't rattle. Can't be too careful.'

'Wise woman,' said George, handing her a mug of tea.

She peered at him.

'What did you say your name was?'

'George.' He held out his hand. '*Enchanté.*'

'Likewise.'

'And you're Nancy. Like the song: "Nancy With the
Laughing Face".'

George began to hum the melody. My father clenched his
jaw, struggling to keep his temper.

'Can we get back to the matter at hand?' He stared at the motley crew in the small kitchen. 'Two radio presenters, one copywriter, one ageing roué and a dinner lady. What are we supposed to do with a stash of stolen diamonds?'

RICHARD

I hate to admit it but the old bastard was right: it *was* Harriet's decision. The North Audley Street sting had been planned with her and the baby in mind. It was hardly unreasonable for her to decide she needed time to work out how to handle the riches that had landed in her lap.

I could scarcely believe that the plan had worked so smoothly. At the same time, I was annoyed it had been George who'd devised the ruse: a false name and phoney contact details had conned the estate agent, and Harriet had done the rest. A simple ploy but I should have thought of it. Still, at least the brainwave hadn't been Tom's, earning him points with you-know-who.

As Harriet gazed at the diamonds, I studied her lovely face. In just a few weeks she'd gone from working as a minimum-wage barista to being the Voice of London *and* co-host of the most popular show on Silk FM. She'd captured the hearts of two men and rekindled an ill-fated romance with a third, resulting in heartbreak as well as the pregnancy that would

311

change her life. All this she'd taken in her stride, making the most of each opportunity or rolling with the punches without being fazed or overwhelmed, or so it seemed. And now, with a fortune in 'hot' diamonds she was still acting cool, as if everything was normal. Bloody brilliant.

After some discussion, we agreed to think things over and talk again the next day. As my father and Tom were saying goodbye to Nancy, I took Harriet to one side.

'Do not let George take the diamonds to a fence,' I whispered. 'Warn your grandmother too.'

She frowned. 'Are you sure?'

I nodded. 'What did your horoscope say?' Her frown deepened as she tried to remember. I jogged her memory. '"You'll prosper as long as you put your trust in an older, wiser advisor."'

'Meaning you?'

'Could be.'

She thought for a moment, chewing on her lip. 'But what if the advisor is George?'

Hoist by my own petard . . .

'You cannot imagine what that man is capable of,' I said.

I could see she thought I was being melodramatic but I didn't care. I couldn't trust the bastard, especially where money and women were concerned. Turning to go, I was tempted to kiss her on the cheek but I caught sight of Tom glaring in our direction. Or perhaps it was just my imagination.

GEORGE

Let's be clear: love turns the brain to mush. Even the sharpest mind can be blunted by a weakness for a pretty face. A shy smile, the curve of an ample bosom, the shape of a delicate ankle. Ask Antony and Cleopatra. Or Bill Clinton and 'that woman'.

All my life, *cherchez la femme* had been a code to live by, a means to a mostly enjoyable end, but time was fast running out and there was an increasingly urgent need for the where-withal to see me out in the style to which I had become accustomed. I'd never taken the long view, preferring to live in what a long-dead Buddhist lady-friend had insisted on calling 'the now'. The fact that her 'now' had been an eighteenth-century palazzo in Venice was neither here nor there. I'd accumulated neither property nor cash and my line of work had never come with a pension.

Ever since Imelda had declined to invest in my invisible friend's non-existent Peruvian gold mine, my sleepless nights had been troubled by a sense that I'd been looking in all the wrong places. How many times had I dined at the Savoy or the Carlyle or the Hôtel de Paris courtesy of a platinum Amex belonging to a woman whose generosity was matched only by her means? How many nights had I whispered sweet nothings into expensively perfumed ears? How often had I turned left upon boarding a plane, settling into a soft leather seat thanks to the widow of the week? As the saying goes, there are two kinds of class: first-class and no-class. Yet how many times had I popped the cork from a bottle of Cristal only to find myself bored witless by the benefactress *du jour*, eager to move on to the next conquest, the next 'eternal' love?

In my eighty-first year, I'd come to a conclusion that I should have reached decades earlier: the life of the lotus-eater was fine as far as it went, which, it turned out, wasn't very far at all. You can take the boy out of Walthamstow . . . etc.

Now here I was, George Brocklebank aka 'Lord Anthony Buckingham', in a two-up, two-down, making a pot of Typhoo for a woman my own age – 'Nancy With the Laughing Face' – and feeling more at home than I had in years. It was a sobering realization. Had I not fallen prey to delusions of grandeur and a determination to live the high life, Harriet's grandmother (a fellow Walthamstownian) was just the sort of woman I might have made a life with. A little life, perhaps, but would it have been so bad? My father had been a butcher, working six days a week to put food on the table and a roof over our heads. He never took a holiday. His one pleasure was his allotment, his life's companion my mother. I'd aimed higher and travelled further but had I been happier? I doubt it. Yet still I remained hungry for one final victory, determined to go out with one glorious last hurrah. And those diamonds in Nancy's kitchen were dazzling . . .

HARRIET

I stashed the pot of Nivea under my mattress and hardly slept a wink. I'd never stolen so much as a Mars Bar let alone jewels. What was I supposed to do now? What would be the repercussions of stealing Cockweasel's twenty-two-carat 'legacy'? What about Richard and Tom? And Nan and George? Had I dragged them into a situation that could backfire any minute? Or was it the other way round? Had these three men steered me along a treacherous path I should have avoided?

In the meantime, what the actual eff were Richard and Tom playing at? Was either of them seriously *still* hoping to be more than 'just good friends' or had they resigned themselves to being friend-zoned by a preggers nut-job? The more I thought about my horoscope, the more it made sense. *'You'll prosper as long as you put your trust in an older, wiser advisor* (George, obvs). But there had been more – something about now not being *'the time to rely on people younger than yourself – especially those born under the sign of Libra'*, which must surely mean Tom, the only Libran on my radar.

As for the diamonds, what options did Damian have? To call the police and report that his father's ill-gotten gains had been stolen? As if! He'd be charged with handling stolen goods. I knew George had given the estate agent a phoney name (Lord Somebody-or-Other) backed up by a fake passport and contact details that didn't exist. The likelihood of Damian tracing the theft to Brocklebank Senior or his 'granddaughter' seemed non-existent. Would there be a midnight knock on the door? Unlikely. Could I be sure there would be no repercussions? Nope.

Tossing and turning at 2 a.m., I came to the conclusion that any guilt I felt was down to having helped out with George's scam. But did I feel bad about ripping off Cockweasel? No way. The confrontation with Candida still rankled every time I remembered her smug smile – the way she'd taken pleasure in making me feel so shabby.

There's usually more than one on the go . . .

I can't have slept more than two hours so it was no surprise that I felt crabby throughout the show with Richard, although I did my best while we were on-air. For obvious reasons, he didn't mention the previous day's escapade while we were in the studio – even when the mics were off – and neither did I, but as we emerged at nine o'clock he ushered me into an empty office and closed the door.

'Have you decided what to do?'

I shook my head. 'I hardly slept. I feel like shit.'

He smiled. 'You look gorgeous.'

I felt a flicker of irritation. Seriously? Flirting? *Now?* Acting like everything was normal?

'How did I get myself into this situation?' I said. 'The diamonds. The pregnancy. The *everything*.'

He spread his hands. 'As John Lennon said, "Life is what happens while we're making other plans." It's too late for second thoughts.'

'I'm not sure I was having any thoughts at all. I'm not a criminal mastermind, I'm just trying to do what's best for my baby and now I've got a tub of stolen diamonds under the mattress. I wish I'd thought this through. Or *someone* had.'

Richard looked away, sidestepping the implied accusation.

'Promise me you won't let George con you into letting him help,' he said. 'Trust me, the man is only interested in helping himself.'

My irritation cranked into top gear. Was that all he could say? If 'Gorgeous' George was so untrustworthy why had Richard allowed him to get involved in the first place? I could feel myself starting to simmer . . .

'I need to go,' I said, opening the office door and heading out into the corridor. Richard called after me as I walked towards the staircase.

'Fancy a bite of lunch? My treat?'

I pretended not to hear.

The tube journey to Nan's took half an hour. Exhausted, I dozed off a couple of times, zoning in and out of consciousness. The sound of my voice on the tannoy had already ceased to be a novelty. It now seemed to blend seamlessly with The Thoughts and whatever surreal nonsense was swirling around my head, producing a hallucinatory effect.

This is the Victoria Line to Walthamstow Central . . .

Just as well Mum and Dad are away . . .

THAT MAN IS SO UGLY AND HIS BABY IS EVEN WORSE

Next stop: King's Cross St Pancras . . .

They'd be so ASHAMED of you for stealing . . .

Doors will open on the right hand side . . .

I COULD JUMP ON THE LIVE RAIL AND FRY!

How will you tell them you're pregnant?

Nan was in the bath when I got back, singing 'Nancy With the Laughing Face' at the top of her voice. I made tea and toast and sat at the kitchen table. When she came down she seemed surprised to see me.

'Oh. You're back.'

'Yep.'

'How was the show?'

'Fine.'

She sat at the table and poured herself a mug of tea, still humming under her breath.

'You're in a good mood,' I said.

She smiled and buttered a piece of toast. Everything that happened yesterday seemed to have slipped her mind.

'What am I going to do, Nan?'

'About what?'

319

'The bloody diamonds, what else?'

Her smile vanished. She fixed me with a glare, picked up her mug and got to her feet.

'I'm not psychic, Harriet. I don't know what's going on inside your head. And judging by what's been going on lately, neither do you.'

She left the kitchen and went upstairs. I tried to finish my breakfast but I'd lost my appetite.

I decided to count the diamonds. Maybe I could google what they were worth. If I knew how much they'd fetch, the future might begin to take shape and maybe I'd feel better. I took the colander from the cupboard and went up to the spare room where I'd passed the semi-sleepless night. The bed was unmade, as I'd left it. I closed the door and knelt down, stretching my hand under the mattress, feeling for the tub of Nivea. For one horrible moment I thought it had gone. My stomach gave a lurch. I explored further, my hands stretching as far as I could reach. I felt a surge of relief as my fingers made contact with the plastic pot. I drew it out and unscrewed the lid. The peach yoghurt smelt sickly sweet.

In the bathroom, I closed the door and placed the colander in the basin. I upended the plastic tub. The yoghurt oozed out. I turned on the tap, watching the gunk wash away. My stomach plummeted.

The yoghurt had disappeared.

There was no sign of the diamonds. Heart hammering, I frantically scraped the inside of the tub with my fingers. Still nothing. I could feel the blood thudding in my ears. I stared at my reflection, trying to think straight, but my head was filled with white noise. And that was when I saw it, reflected in the mirror.

The toilet seat. It was up.

I flung open the door and stood outside Nan's bedroom.

'Nan?'

She sounded apprehensive.

'Yes?'

'Has someone been here?'

There was a pause.

'What do you mean?'

'Exactly what I said: has someone been here?'

'Like who?'

'A man.'

Another pause. I heard the bed creak then the door opened. She emerged from her room, eyebrows arched, fists on her hips. Ready to do battle.

'Why do you ask?'

'Because the loo seat is up.'

She looked away. A sheepish note entered her voice.

'He forgot his glasses.'

I frowned.

'Who did?'

'George. He came back for them. About half-seven, while you were on the radio.'

I felt as if I was about to throw up. Looking past Nan, I could see her dressing table. Amid the clutter of creams and lotions, above the open drawer that contained her collection of dildos, sat a vase filled with white lilies – an expensive bouquet from a posh florist. There was a pencil sketch on a page torn from a notebook. It captured Nan's face perfectly and made her look beautiful. She turned and followed my gaze.

'Been a long time since a man gave me flowers,' she said. 'Such a gent.'

I closed my eyes.

'Christ, Nan. What have you done?'

TOM

As soon as Harriet called I dropped everything and headed for Walthamstow. Sitting in the Uber I tried George's mobile.

Number unobtainable.

I closed my eyes trying to calm my racing mind. How had life become so complicated? A few weeks ago I'd had a job, a flat and a cat. Now I was unemployed, battling my own father and racing across London in response to Harriet's SOS because the granddad who'd disappeared when I was six had conned his way into a stash of diamonds bequeathed by a career criminal to his philandering son, a maxillofacial surgeon who had impregnated the woman my father and I both adored.

Was this Chaos Theory in action? I had only the vaguest idea what the term meant – some branch of mathematics beyond my understanding – but it seemed to fit. There are times when life feels like you're at a rodeo, riding a bucking bronco and all you can do is try not to get thrown off and trampled underfoot. This was one of those times. But it had never been about the diamonds. They were just a means to an end – winning Harriet's heart – and retrieving them seemed like the most important thing in the world. It may sound melodramatic but sitting in that car I felt as if I was embarking on a mission, a knight on a white charger determined to prove his worth to the woman he loved. Win the treasure, win her heart.

I called Rochester House and asked to speak to George or Paddy. A bloke told me they weren't there and had no idea when they were likely to return.

I was on the verge of phoning Dad but something held me back. I wish I could say it was something more noble than feeling chuffed to bits that Harriet had reached out to me, not him, in her hour of need, but that would be a lie. It's not that I wasn't taking seriously the fact that George appeared to have ripped off Harriet and Nancy, but in spite of the circumstances, I took her call as a positive sign. Perhaps I was finally moving into pole position.

Which is why my heart sank when I arrived at Nancy's house only to find my father clambering out of a black cab. Paying the driver, he caught sight of me and frowned.

'The man's a snake,' he said. 'Don't say I didn't warn you.'

I felt a rush of anger.

'You're not seriously blaming me?'

'Who brought him on board?' said Dad. 'Who insisted on playing happy families? You think he's a harmless old goat but he's nothing of the kind.'

I drew breath to answer but Harriet appeared at the door, glaring. She ushered us into the hall then folded her arms.

'Tell me you've found him.'

I shook my head.

'No answer from his mobile.'

'Probably a pay-as-you-go,' said Dad. 'I wouldn't be surprised if that's the last we hear of him. Once a shyster, always a shyster – as I've warned Tom many, many times.'

Nice. Blaming me for his father's behaviour. I knew why, of course – anything to make me look bad in her eyes.

She stared at him.

'That's all you have to say?'

He blinked, taken aback by the hostility in her voice. Then he cleared his throat and peered over her shoulder, into the kitchen.

'Can we have a word with your grandma? Perhaps she can shed some light on what happened.'

'We *know* what happened,' said Harriet, her voice rising in anger. 'Your thieving bastard of a father came when he knew she'd be alone. He sweet-talked her into bed then stole the bloody diamonds.'

I raised an eyebrow. 'He seduced her?'

Harriet held up an empty foil blister pack; the pills had been removed. 'His Viagra. It was in the bin.'

My father closed his eyes and let out a slow exhalation of breath. 'Did he tell her where he might be heading? Any clue at all?'

Nancy's voice came from upstairs. 'Stop asking daft questions.'

I looked up and saw her on the landing, twisting a handkerchief in her hands, a picture of anguish.

'If I knew where he was going I'd have told Harriet. Or the police.' She descended the stairs and fixed my father with a glare. 'He's your bloody father. You'd better find him.'

Dad gave a pained smile. 'If only it were that simple.'

Nancy shot him a dirty look. She turned to me. 'Have you got his address?'

I sidestepped the question. 'I'm going to do everything I can to find George and get those diamonds back.'

I saw a flicker of relief on Harriet's face. She seemed mollified.

'At least there's one person I can rely on.'

I could feel Dad seething. Time to press my advantage and present myself as a man of action.

'This isn't over,' I said, opening the door. 'I'll keep you posted.'

Dad looked bemused. 'Where are you going?'

I ignored him and stepped outside. Walking in the direction of the tube station, I wondered if it was a mistake to leave him behind. Would he try to ingratiate himself with Harriet, to smarm his way back into her affections? Judging by her frame of mind he'd have an uphill struggle. And while he was launching another charm offensive, I was the guy with a head start. The one *doing* something. Trying to make things right.

Sitting on the tube, I listened to Harriet's voice on the tannoy, counting down the stations from Walthamstow to King's Cross St Pancras. Was it my imagination or did I detect something different in her voice – a note of irritation?

As I changed to the Northern Line and waited for a train to Camden Town, I had the strangest feeling that I was under observation. I scanned the platform but there was no sign of anything untoward, just the usual gaggle of tourists and commuters. Once again, I heard Harriet's voice boom from the station's speakers.

The train now approaching is to Edgware. Please stand back from the platform edge.

Emerging into the fading light of a gloomy north London afternoon, I turned my collar against the drizzle and made my way to Rochester House. To my relief, Paddy had returned. He was in the office, drinking tea and doing the *Evening Standard* crossword.

'Have you seen George?'

He shook his head. 'His door was closed when I passed an hour ago. He's probably having a nap.'

Getting to his feet, he led me along the corridor, shuffling in his Moroccan leather slippers and rapping on my grandfather's door. No response. Paddy produced his keys and unlocked the door. His face fell.

'Blimey.'

He ushered me inside. The room was empty, the clothes rack bare. No suits, no shoes, no belongings. No trace of the 'harmless old goat' who had conned Nancy, Harriet, Dad and me before vanishing with a fortune in stolen diamonds.

RICHARD

Tailing Tom on the tube felt ridiculous – as though I'd strayed into a spy movie. He nearly spotted me on one occasion, suddenly turning in my direction, forcing me to slow my pace and melt into the crowd. After the first leg of his journey he changed platforms and waited for a Northern Line train. I maintained my distance, listening to Harriet's golden voice on the tannoy.

The train now approaching is to Edgware. Please stand back from the platform edge.

Those mellifluous tones stiffened my resolve, reminding me why I was playing silly buggers and following my son: only by tracking George down did I stand a chance of setting things right and winning Harriet over. Unlike me, Tom seemed to have some kind of plan. I was determined to find out what it was.

The train arrived. As he stepped aboard, I slipped into the adjacent carriage, my face hidden behind a copy of the *Evening Standard*. I kept watch through the glass panel. He got off at Camden Town. I followed suit, maintaining a discreet distance.

Outside the station, heading away from the bustling high street, he walked past a row of Victorian houses then turned onto a deserted side street. I followed, peering around the corner in time to see him entering a large redbrick building. It looked as if it might once have housed an institution, a school, perhaps, or a working men's college. The door closed behind him. I waited a moment before taking a few steps closer. There was a sign above the door. *Rochester House.*

Returning to the corner of the street, I lit a cigarette, leaning against the railings and keeping watch on the door. After a couple of minutes, it opened and a man emerged. In his late forties, he was dishevelled and shabbily dressed, hobbling along the street and into an off licence. Moments later he was back, opening a can of Special Brew and taking a long, thirsty swig before limping away and disappearing around a corner.

Half an hour and two cigarettes later, the cold was starting to chill my bones. Giving up on Tom, I was on the verge of heading for home when I saw him emerge from the redbrick building and walk in my direction, head down, hands tucked into his pockets. I made a hasty retreat, diving into a newsagent's and feigning interest in a rack of magazines. Seeing him walk past, I counted to ten before peering out of the doorway. He'd disappeared, presumably making his way to the tube. I returned to Rochester House and pressed the buzzer. A male voice answered.

'Yes?'

'I'm looking for George Brocklebank.'

'And you are?'

'His son.'

There was a pause followed by a sigh. 'You'd better come in.'

The man's name was Paddy. Sitting in his shabby office, he told me that 'Gorgeous' George had been one of the hostel's occasional residents but had vanished, taking all his belongings. I blinked as the man's words sank in.

'My father was homeless?'

'This *was* his home,' said Paddy. 'At least, when he wasn't "working".' He leaned forward in his chair. 'I'll tell you what I told Tom. I've no idea where George is but he's one hell of a character.'

For several seconds I was lost for words. When I managed to speak, there was a catch in my voice. 'May I see his room?'

Paddy led me along the corridor. He pushed open a door. The room was tiny, almost cell-like. A single bed, a clothes rail and a rickety chair held together by string.

How had the old man sunk so low? Where were the Savile Row suits, the Jermyn Street shoes, the silk pocket squares? What had become of the Havana cigars, Cartier lighters and Rolex watches?

Any sense of pity lasted only seconds, replaced by a surge of fury. For decades this man had lived the life he chose – selfish and callous, maybe even sociopathic, wreaking havoc and misery in his wake. My life would have been better if he'd cleared off as soon as I was born. So would Bonnie's.

As for Tom . . .

I could barely bring myself to consider how much happier the boy's childhood would have been had his very existence not served as a daily reminder of George's betrayal. I'd tried to forgive Bonnie – succeeding most of the time – but forgetting was another matter.

Poor Tom.

Blameless Tom.

For twenty-five years, I'd done my best, every waking moment of every day. True, I'd lost the plot on the day he turned six, the day the truth had come to light. For a year I'd been unable to so much as look at 'my' son without searching for signs of George. My father was in every hair on Tom's head, every mannerism, every facial tic.

George . . . George . . . Fucking George . . . !

'Are you okay?' said Paddy.

I turned to study his face. 'Are you sure you don't know where he is?'

'I am.'

I reached for my wallet and took out all the cash: just over two hundred pounds.

'Positive?'

His hesitation lasted a split-second.

Ten minutes later, I was in a cab, sifting through a Tesco bag retrieved from the hostel's bins. Paddy had managed to identify the rubbish removed from George's room. The bag contained bits of paper covered in doodles, two dog-eared paperbacks and a sheaf of receipts from London's swankiest restaurants.

Best of all, the cache contained a copy of *The Times* dated just over a year ago. Someone (presumably George) had circled a name in the obituary column. A billionaire, Bernie Shine, had died at ninety-four after a stellar career at the top of the oil industry. Shine was survived by two daughters and a third wife, Imelda. According to the waspish obituarist, Widow Shine was renowned for enjoying the high life and keeping a permanent riverside suite at one of London's finest hotels.

I thought for a moment then tapped on the glass partition and called to the driver.

'Change of plan. We're going to the Savoy hotel.'

HARRIET

The road to hell is paved with good intentions – another of Nan's sayings and one that fitted the bill when it came to Richard and Tom.

Okay, they meant well. Maybe I shouldn't have blamed them for the fact that 'Gorgeous' George had conned his way into God knows how many bazillions of pounds' worth of diamonds (not to mention Nan's bed) but I couldn't help the way I felt. Guilt by association.

On the other hand, if George hadn't come up with the estate agent scam, I'd never have got the jewels in the first place. That he was devious was never in doubt. But it wasn't as if we could shop him to the police without being prosecuted for theft and/or handling stolen goods. Bottom line: I was *sooooo* pissed off with everyone involved, including Nan and myself. I was also knackered, my breasts were sore and I'd spent half the afternoon throwing up. This pregnancy lark was no day at the beach.

To make matters worse, Cockweasel was on the doorstep

when I got back from my first antenatal appointment. At first I thought I was hallucinating but no, there he was, leaning against his Porsche, smoking one of his stupid e-cigarettes and scrolling through his phone. He looked up as I approached the house.

'Your grandma wouldn't let me in.'

I said nothing, reaching for my keys while trying not to let anger get the better of me.

'How are you?' he said.

'Pregnant. Thanks to a crap shag with a knob-jockey.'

He had the grace to let his chin sag onto his collarbone, a picture of shame. When he spoke again his voice was barely audible.

'Are you going to tell Candida? About the baby?'

I closed my eyes.

'Piss off, Damian.'

'I wouldn't blame you if you did but please don't involve my kids in—'

'I've no intention of telling your children. They've enough on their plate being related to a shit-weasel like you.'

He cleared his throat, fiddling with his key-ring. Something on his mind. His voice took on an edge.

'I know it was you,' he said.

I pretended not to hear and put my key in the lock. He stepped towards me and lowered his voice.

'The estate agent described the people who viewed the flat. You and an old man – "Lord Buckingham" – who doesn't exist. There's a Duke of Buckingham but he bears no resemblance to the bloke who helped you burgle my flat.'

I turned to meet his gaze.

'I've no idea what you're talking about.'

I could tell the human skid-mark didn't believe me. He was trying to remain calm. On one hand, he wanted his stuff back; on the other, he couldn't lay into me without risking setting me off. Who knew how I'd respond to pressure? Another visit to Wifey? A scene outside his house? At his kids' school?

'I know I've behaved badly,' he said, 'but Dad left those diamonds to me. The only decent thing he did.' His voice had fallen to a whisper. 'God knows how he thought I could turn them into cash – and it's not as if I can go to the police and tell them what you did – but the point is, *they belong to me.*'

'Like your new house?' I said. 'And the one in Tuscany?'

'Both mortgaged to the hilt.'

I turned to face him.

'Let me guess,' I said. 'You were planning to wait a few years then quietly flog the diamonds through a fence and use the money to pay off both mortgages.'

The expression on his face told me I'd scored a bullseye. He clenched his jaw.

'Look me in the face and swear you don't know where the diamonds are.'

A command I was happy to obey. I met his gaze.

'On Nan's life,' I said, 'I have no idea.'

Then I went inside and closed the door.

TOM

Leaving Rochester House, I walked to the pub where I'd had that first pint with George. I left twenty minutes later, none the wiser. No one had seen the old sod or knew where he'd gone.

Heading for the tube, I turned up my collar against the drizzle and reflected on what Paddy had confirmed: my grandfather was the kind of man who would have the contacts to fence stolen diamonds and turn them into cash. How much were they worth? Thousands? Millions? Enough for George to see out his days in Palm Springs or the South of France?

It was hard not to feel a sneaking admiration for his chutzpah. If he hadn't stolen the gems from Harriet I might have wished him good luck. But this wasn't simply an old rogue's last hurrah, this was a devastating blow to the woman I adored. Did the fact that George had seduced Harriet's grandma make things worse? Only one person could answer that question – Nancy herself – and she wasn't talking, at least not to me.

Fumbling for my Oyster card, I was about to pass through the ticket barrier at Camden Town when I realized I had no idea where to go. Harriet was barely speaking to me, and my father was more unapproachable than ever. I stared at my phone for five minutes before accepting the inevitable: like it or not, Dad and I were in this together. I tapped his name. He answered straightaway.

'Have you found him?' he said.

'I wish. Have you?'

'No.'

'Where are you?'

He hesitated.

'Let's just say I'm on the case.'

'Where?'

'That's for me to know and you to wonder.'

I could feel a knot of anger tightening in my stomach.

'Either you tell me or I'll wait outside your house and follow you until we find him.'

No response. I let the seconds tick by until he caved in and broke the silence.

'The American Bar at the Savoy.'

'Is he there?'

'No, but his girlfriend is.'

'Girlfriend? You make her sound sixteen.'

'Try ninety,' said my father. 'Better get a move on before she snuffs it without telling us how to find her toy boy.'

RICHARD

Now in her eighty-first year, Imelda Shine was a strikingly beautiful woman with perfect posture and a bob of immaculately coiffed golden hair. Perched on a stool at the bar, she sipped from a flute of champagne then tapped a manicured fingernail on the ice bucket. Judging by the slur in her voice, she'd been drinking long before I showed up at her hotel.

'Suppose I know where Georgie Boy is, why should I tell you?'

'I'm his son. I'm concerned about his welfare.'

She gave me a sideways glance. 'And I'm Little Red Riding Hood.'

I studied the woman's tanned face, checking for signs of 'work' or Botox but there was nothing, merely evidence of good genes and money. Plenty of money.

The billionaire's widow had sounded terse when she'd answered the phone in her suite, agreeing to meet me in the American Bar 'as soon as I can drag my bones to the lift. Order a bottle of Dom Perignon. Put it on my tab.'

I'd paid for the champagne myself, of course, trying not to wince at the price. The rich can smell a sponger straightaway and I'd no intention of allowing myself to be bracketed with my father.

'Do you know those people?'

I followed Imelda's gaze. Tom and Harriet were shuffling into the bar, escorted by a wary-looking woman I took to be a receptionist.

'I'm afraid so,' I said.

Seeing my companion, the flunkey held back, hovering by the door as Tom and Harriet crossed the room to join us at the bar. Satisfied that the jeans-clad newcomers posed no threat to the hotel or its clientele, the receptionist glided away and exited.

As I performed the introductions, I could see Imelda appraising the new arrivals but finding them not to her taste. The lack of grooming. The lack of money.

She pointed to a corner table and addressed a waiter. 'We'll sit there.'

The man performed a curt bow and gathered our ice bucket and glasses while taking an order from Tom and Harriet; a negroni for him, a Diet Coke for her.

'Perhaps if you'd shown interest in Georgie sooner,' said Imelda, settling carefully into a velvet banquette, 'things might have been different.'

She held my gaze. There was a challenge in her stare. I wondered how much she knew. Already on edge, her next utterance sent my anxiety levels soaring.

'So,' she said, gazing at Tom, 'this is the famous "grand-son".' She used her forefingers to mime quotation marks. Tom looked quizzically at her.

'Famous in what way?' he said.

'Georgie talks about you a lot.'

'Oh?' said Tom.

'How's the musical coming along?' said Imelda.

'He told you about my show?'

She nodded, her voice turning into a camp drawl worthy of a *grande dame* of the theatre. 'He told me *lots* of things, sweetheart.'

She glanced in my direction, a coquettish smile playing on her lips. I could feel my palms growing sweaty. An intervention was required.

'My father is not all he seems,' I said.

'I'm aware of that,' said Imelda, bestowing a withering glare. A trio of gold bracelets jangled on her bony wrist as she reached for her glass.

'Meaning what?' said Harriet.

Mrs Shine took a sip of champagne before replying. 'If you've come to tell me that "Lord Anthony Buckingham" doesn't exist, you're too late. George is as aristocratic as my *derrière*; I knew he was a fraudster the moment he picked me up in the casino at Monte Carlo.'

'He picked you up?' said Tom.

The woman nodded. 'I was on a losing streak. He promised to change my luck if I allowed him to take me to dinner at Le Louis XV. I knew he was a con-man from the start, but what I couldn't know was how much fun we'd have and how much I'd missed *fun*.' She crossed her shapely legs in a move that marked her as a graduate of the finest finishing schools.

'My husband had all the money in the world – grand houses, palazzos, planes, helicopters, super-yachts – but no sense of humour.' She leaned forward and placed a bejewelled, liver-spotted hand on Tom's knee. 'When it comes to women there are two things a man needs to know: how to make her laugh and how to make her come.'

Harriet's eyes widened in mock outrage.

'You know you said that out loud?' she said, earning a thin-lipped smile.

'I'm just glad George has finally come into some good luck,' said Imelda. 'We celebrated last night – oysters, caviar, champagne, the "whole enchilada" as he put it, delivered via room service . . . if you catch my drift. Then he told me that he was sorry but he needed to move on to pastures new. "Time for one last hurrah".' She sipped her champagne. 'I can hardly blame the old trout. Perhaps if I'd accepted his proposal of marriage ages ago it might have been a different story, or if I'd believed his nonsense about a gold mine in Peru, but no matter – it pleases me to see him standing on his own two feet. And if he's found another lady friend – someone to "see him out" – well, *c'est la vie*.' She shrugged. 'Plenty more fish, as they say.'

You had to admire the woman's spirit.

'Who's the new "lady friend"?' said Tom.

'I believe it's someone he "bonded" with,' said Imelda.

'Someone from a similar background.' She stifled a yawn. 'I suppose what he says is true: "You can take the boy out of Walthamstow et cetera" – even if the "boy" is as old as Methuselah.'

Harriet cleared her throat.

'When you say "lady friend" I think you might be talking about my grandmother. And George's "good luck" might refer to diamonds.'

'A girl's best friend?' said Imelda, waggling a diamond-ring-laden hand and raising a quizzical eyebrow.

'Not this girl, unfortunately,' said Harriet, her expression unreadable. 'George conned my Nan out of a lot of diamonds. They belong to me.'

'Is that so?' Imelda's lips twitched with amusement. 'Or would it be more accurate to say they don't officially belong to anyone – with the possible exception of anonymous holders of safe deposit boxes in Mayfair?'

Georgie Boy, it seemed, had told Imelda everything. And if her teasing remark about her paramour's 'grandson' was anything to go by, the woman couldn't be trusted to remain discreet about anything.

As though reading my mind, she turned to Tom and fixed him with an alcohol-addled smile, her talons poised to mime another set of quotation marks.

'So,' she said, 'what do you make of your "grandfather"?'

HARRIET

What was the creepy old cow playing at?

As if being on Planet Posh wasn't unnerving enough, the weirdo in the Chanel suit seemed to be involved in some kind of game with Richard and Tom – like she was talking in code. And why did she put everything in quotation marks?

They talked about George a bit longer – his track record with women didn't seem to faze Mrs Shine. But I had the sense that she was toying with Tom's dad, talking in a secret language only they understood. Richard seemed on edge and desperate to change the subject, tapping his fingers on the table and looking relieved when the woman got to her feet.

'A pleasure meeting you all,' she said. Her champagne was unfinished. It was clear we were being dismissed. She turned to me, giving me the once-over.

'What about you?' she said.

'What about me?'

She arched a perfectly groomed eyebrow.

'George tells me these two chaps have been making a play for your affections. I've heard of "keeping it in the family" but don't you think you're taking things a little far?'

I blinked.

'We're just good friends.'

She gave a knowing smile.

'In my experience, there's no such thing – not between men and women. May I ask how old you are?'

'Thirty-five.'

'And Richard is, what, fifty?'

'Forty-nine,' said Richard.

'And Tom?'

'Twenty-five,' said Tom.

The woman's lips twitched in amusement. She turned her gaze to me.

'And you're leading them both a merry dance.'

I felt a stirring of anger.

'Not that it's any of your business,' I said, 'but I'm pregnant. The father isn't in the picture but Tom and Richard are being very supportive.'

'Both of them?'

'Yes.'

She arched her eyebrow once more, looking at the two men, both of whom were now on their feet, eager to leave.

'How droll,' said Imelda, staring at the three of us. 'A very modern *ménage a trois*.'

'It's not like that,' I said. My cheeks were burning, my pulse quickening. She gave me a pitying look.

'If you say so. But this has nothing to do with dia-monds, does it?'

'I don't know what you mean,' I said.

She gestured towards the men at my side. Her voice was slurred.

'I know about Richard and Tom from Georgie Boy. As far as these two chaps are concerned, this isn't about jewels.' She leaned forward; I could smell the alcohol on her breath. 'It's about *you*. A father and son with scores to settle, and they've made you piggy-in-the-middle. It's "eyes on the prize" – that's you – and winner takes all.'

Tom's brow was furrowed. 'What "scores"?'

His father cleared his throat, glancing anxiously towards the barman. He kept his voice low.

'Let's not make a scene here.'

Imelda's eyes widened in mock horror. 'A scene? At the Savoy? Heaven forbid!'

Tom was still frowning. 'What "scores" do we have to settle?'

The woman jabbed a finger in his chest.

'You've never forgiven your father for being a cold fish. And he's never forgive you for not being—'

'*MRS SHINE!*' Dad's shout made the woman jump. She blinked twice in quick succession, swaying slowly on her feet. Then she picked up her clutch bag from the banquette.

'I may need a lie-down before dinner.'

She headed for the door, weaving her way across the bar in a pair of impossibly high heels. I called after her. 'Mrs Shine?'

She stopped and turned.

'Yes?'

'Are you sure you don't know where George is?'

She hesitated then shrugged her shoulders.

'Try Paris,' she said. 'And remember what they say: "*Tout comprendre, c'est tout pardonner*". "To understand all is to forgive all".'

Then she turned on her Louboutin heel and was gone.

TOM

The encounter with Imelda Shine was weird not least because of the way she kept, like, staring in my direction and miming finger-quotes every time she referred to my 'grandfather'.

Outside in the hotel's courtyard, Dad gave what sounded like a sigh of relief then climbed into a taxi, the door held open by a doorman.

'Anyone need a lift?' he said.

I ignored the question.

'What did she mean about settling scores?'

Dad gave a small shrug, feigning nonchalance. 'Probably the booze talking.'

Perhaps – but the woman had been right about one thing: I would always find it hard – no, *impossible* – to forgive my father for being so cold and behaving as though my existence was a slap in the face. But maybe Imelda had a point about that saying: 'to understand all is to forgive all'. If I could understand why Dad was the way he was perhaps I could meet him halfway.

The cab driver was growing impatient. 'Where to, mate?'

'Let me guess.' Harriet turned to my father. 'You're going to suggest we all go to Paris to find George.'

'Actually,' said Dad, 'I was thinking of getting something to eat.'

I looked at Harriet. She was shaking her head, as if unable to comprehend his peculiar behaviour. Then she closed her eyes and wrapped her arms around herself.

'Are you okay?' I said.

She chewed on her lower lip and took a moment before opening her eyes.

'Was that woman right?' she said. 'Is that how you see me? Both of you? Some kind of "prize"?'

The taxi driver was drumming his fingers on the steering wheel. My father ignored him and stepped out of the cab.

'This is not the time or the place,' he said to Harriet. 'I can't speak for Tom but I think you know how I feel.'

'Do I?' said Harriet. 'Or am I some kind of sports day "prize" in the father–son tug-of-war? Is that why I got the job at Silk FM? Is that why I'm helping with Tom's musical? Is that why you're both offering support for the baby? Are you both patronizing me just so you can get into my knickers?'

I saw Dad wince at the vulgarity. 'Again, I can't speak for Tom, but—'

She held up a hand, cutting him off mid-sentence.

'What a family,' she said, shaking her head from side to side. 'Grandfather, father and son – birds of a feather.'

Dad flinched, as though he'd been stung by a wasp. 'I am *nothing* like my father.'

'Makes two of us,' I said.

She stared at us for a moment then her face, like, crumpled and she began to cry, shoulders heaving, tears trickling down her cheeks. The doorman stared in horror then moved away, ushering another hotel guest into the waiting taxi. The driver had given up on my father.

'I don't know why I'm crying,' said Harriet.

'Probably something to do with hormo—' began Dad, but she cut him short.

'If you say "hormones" I'll kick your head down the street.'

'I only meant—'

'I know what you *meant*,' said Harriet, fumbling in her pocket for a tissue. 'I'm pregnant so *obviously* I'm over-emotional and yes, you're right – I probably *am* hormonal – but has it ever occurred to you what the last few months have been like for me?' She blew her nose as the tears continued to fall. The seconds ticked by as Dad and I waited for her sobs to subside. Then she blew her nose again and took a deep breath.

'Before I met you two,' she said, 'I worked in a café then watched films with Nan – end of story. Yes, it was boring and the money was crap, and yes, I *really* want to act and sing for a living, but at least life was simple. Now I barely sleep. I'm on the radio, I'm on the tube and I'm on the buses. Meanwhile, my ex – the man who promised "happy ever after" – lied through his teeth then broke my heart. He *whooshed* back into my life for a few weeks then *whooshed* out again, leaving me up the duff. I've had a showdown with his wife who told me I'm just another "bit on the side". I've also helped a con-man to burgle my ex's flat, so we could steal God knows how many stolen diamonds – and now "good old Georgie Boy" has seduced my grandmother and buggered off to Paris.'

I drew breath to speak but she wasn't finished.

'Meanwhile, throughout everything that's happened, you two have been sweet and supportive – or so I thought.' Her face darkened as she looked from my father's face to mine then cast a glance at the small crowd that had gathered in the queue for taxis. 'But maybe that old sourpuss was onto something. Because right now I'm being stared at by a load of posh people, crying like a baby and feeling like piggy-in-the-bloody-middle – and you know what?' She paused for breath before delivering her parting shot. 'It feels like shit.'

She walked off, heading for the Strand. I was about to call her name but Dad put a hand on my shoulder.

'Let her go,' he said.

For once, he was probably right.

RICHARD

After she'd gone, I turned to Tom and composed my features into a smile.

'Hungry?'

'Starving,' he said.

'Good. The Milky Bars are on me.'

He rolled his eyes. 'Whatever *that* means. Can we go somewhere non-posh, somewhere normal?'

'Define "normal".'

'Burger and a beer?'

'A burger? Would Harriet approve?'

'I won't tell if you won't.'

We exchanged half a smile then made awkward small talk as we walked into Covent Garden and found a table in Joe Allen's diner, a basement relic from the eighties. The encounter with Imelda Shine had left a lingering 'bad vibe', leaving us both on edge. There was no mention of 'eyes on the prize' or, thank God, Imelda's near-catastrophic indiscretion.

Tom ordered a cheeseburger, I chose swordfish and a

bottle of house white; my Amex had taken enough of a hit at the Savoy.

The restaurant was busy with late-afternoon drinkers making an early start on the weekend, a relief from the stultifying atmosphere at the American Bar. I remained on high alert, waiting for Tom to raise the subject of Imelda's remarks about his 'grandfather'. Was the whole fragile edifice of what passed for our family life about to come crashing down?

Oh, what a tangled web we weave when first we practise to deceive . . .

'Heard from Mum?' he said, slathering ketchup onto his plate.

'Not for a few days,' I said. 'I imagine we'll be communicating through lawyers from now on.'

'Does it have to be like that?'

'Divorce doesn't bring out the best in people.'

I pushed the swordfish around the plate. My appetite had dwindled to the point of no return. Briefly, I considered going back on the antidepressants, but the thought didn't last long.

'What happened on my sixth birthday?' said Tom.

The question caught me off-guard. I almost choked on my wine.

'I expect you had a party,' I said, trying to sound calm despite the sudden fluttering of my heart. 'Cake, balloons, the usual stuff.'

'Not much of a party,' said Tom. 'You stormed out.'

'Did I?'

He met my gaze. 'And you stopped speaking to Mum – for a year.'

I forked a piece of fish into my mouth as my mind worked overtime, groping for a plausible explanation.

'I had a lot on my plate,' I said, lamely. 'Working hard, bringing home the bacon.' A feeble response but it was the best I could do.

'So you were busy and decided to take it out on me and Mum?'

I took a moment to consider my answer. 'I'm sorry. I've never claimed to be Father of the Year.'

He chewed on a chip. 'When Harriet has her baby let's hope I do a better job.'

I stiffened. 'Assuming she chooses you,' I said.

He gave me a sideways look. 'Is that what this is about?' he said. 'You're hoping for a second chance?'

'At what?'

'Being a father. Bedtime stories, sports day, school plays. All the stuff you never did with me. Redemption.'

I stifled a sigh.

Walk a mile in my shoes then tell me about how to behave . . .

'There was always food on the table,' I said. 'Clothes on your back, a roof over your head.'

'You sound like something out of a Charles Dickens novel.'

'Mum was always there. You were never starved of affection.'

He shook his head from side to side, shooting me a disdainful look.

353

'Wow,' he said softly. 'Larkin was bang on. Your mum and dad *do* fuck you up.'

'You seem pretty well balanced to me.'

'So you're not going to back off?'

I took another sip of wine and considered the question carefully. I'd never been one for falling in love every five minutes and I was hardly ancient but how many chances at love were likely to come my way? Tom had his life ahead of him. Even if Harriet did upset him by choosing me, he'd bounce back. There would be other women, other chances to meet his Ms Right.

'She's a grown-up,' I said. 'Perfectly capable of making her own decisions.'

'And you see nothing wrong in competing with your own son?'

I sighed. 'The heart wants what the heart wants, Tom. It's unfortunate that we both seem to have fallen for the same woman but I can't help how I feel any more than you can. The bottom line is this: *I* have no choice in the matter. The choice is Harriet's. If she chooses you then so be it. I'll take it like a man and move on. I hope you feel the same.'

He was about to reply when our mobiles beeped simultaneously. He checked his message. I checked mine. A text from Harriet.

Nan's gone! SO HAS HER PASSPORT!

HARRIET

There was a note on the kitchen table in Nan's handwriting.

Off for a dirty weekend. Don't wait up.

A weekend in Paris with the man who'd ripped us off? What was she *thinking*? Okay, so she'd bought his record, 'The Days Are Long', but that was a lifetime ago. Wasn't she a bit old to be acting like a groupie?

I texted Richard and Tom then got busy with the hoover while waiting for them, my guilt about involving them in yet another drama competing with my concern for Nan. I hadn't asked them to come to *my* rescue, like cavalry riding over the hill to save a damsel in distress, but Nan hadn't travelled further than Southend since about 1832, so if she was gallivanting around Paris with a con artist, something had to be done. Who knew how low 'Georgie Boy' would stoop? Her life savings? Her house?

In the event, only Tom showed up. I answered the doorbell and stood in the hallway, arms folded.

'Where's your dad?' I said.

'Guess.'

'Paris?'

He nodded.

'He's on the last Eurostar. I told him he was overreacting but he said he didn't trust George not to . . .'

He tailed off.

'Not to what?'

'Lead Nancy a merry dance.'

'You mean, rip her off – again?'

'Yes. But I think he's being melodramatic. George doesn't prey on people without money.'

'Who says Nan doesn't have money? She's got savings and jewellery and a house worth half a million quid. I wouldn't put it past the bastard to sweet-talk her out of every penny. Besides, I think your dad is being a hero.'

Not what Tom wanted to hear. He scratched his chin.

'I'm ninety-nine per cent sure George is going to give Nancy the time of her life, not rip her off,' he said. 'According to Dad there's only a handful of luxury hotels in Paris. He's going to try them all. Does she have a mobile?'

'It's switched off,' I said. 'I don't know what to think. It's not as if she doesn't know he's a crook. So why has she gone off with the man who stole from us?'

Tom cleared his throat then put a foot on the doorstep, clearly angling for an invitation to cross the threshold. I wasn't in the mood for company.

'How about a veggie lasagne?' he said. 'I could get the stuff from Tesco.'

I shook my head.

'Not tonight.'

His face fell. Sensing him plucking up courage to press the point, I felt on the back foot, like that awkward moment when someone's about to move in for an unwanted kiss.

'I thought . . .' He tailed off then made a second stab. 'We could have a quiet night in. Sofa. Telly. Bottle of wine.'

No mistaking what he had in mind. *Netflix and chill* . . . I tried to let him down gently. He deserved that, at least.

'I appreciate you coming but it's been a hell of a week and I'm knackered.'

His smile faltered then he did his best to rally.

'No problem. Anyway, I should get some work done.'

'How's it going with Zara?'

'She's doing okay,' he said. 'And Paul Mendoza's PA says he wants to see the show as soon as possible. I'll book a room upstairs at my local pub. A week tomorrow, if you're free?'

'Sounds great.'

And that's when I felt my throat constricting and the tears glaze my eyes. *Sodding hormones!*

'Are we okay, Tom?' I said, fumbling for a tissue.

His smile was back.

'Absolutely,' he said.

'Good,' I said, blinking back tears. 'Let's hope we can say the same for Nan.'

TOM

Heading home on the Victoria Line, maybe it was the three whiskies I'd downed in the pub near the tube station but Harriet's voice sounded different – firmer somehow, bordering on hostile. Or perhaps it was my imagination. Either way, when I stumbled onto the overground at Highbury & Islington, there she was again. Even the briefest announcement – *'next stop, Dalston Junction'* – seemed to have taken on a brittle edge, as if she'd decided to give me, like, the cold shoulder. Just me, of course. No one else. Too much Johnnie Walker will do that to a man.

Next stop, Dalston Junction. And no 'lasagne', thank you, Tom Brocklebank. As for 'sofa, telly and a bottle of wine' – who do you think you're kidding?

We'd both known what I'd meant by 'a quiet night in'. Was I disappointed by her rebuff? Of course. Surprised? No. It wasn't the ideal moment to make a pass, but with my father en route to Paris I could see she was impressed by his man-of-action shtick and I couldn't help wondering how many more chances there would be to have her to myself. In hindsight, the doorstep lunge was a dumb move, doomed to fail. Dad's reaction to George whisking Nancy off to Paris was much smarter. That he stood little chance of finding them was irrelevant. He was *doing something*. What was my response? A lame pass. Meh.

All the same, there was still time to save the day. By now, my hopes of making progress with Harriet – of pulling off a coup that would throw serious shade on my father – were pinned on the musical. The songs were in good shape, even if I said so myself. And not only had she helped me to get the show ready, perhaps she'd done me a favour by, like, rebuffing my overture.

I now planned to work all weekend, finessing the lyrics, honing the melodies, perfecting the libretto. Every word counted, every note, every beat. The date of the showcase was in Paul Mendoza's diary, all I had to do was book the room above my local and make sure the show was ready. Zara and I needed more rehearsal time but no impresario would expect us to be 'off the book'. The point wasn't to show him a polished production ready for opening night, but to whet his appetite and persuade him to invest seed money in *They F**k You Up* – to put some skin in the game.

By the time I got home, the cat was asleep, annoyed to be woken as I sat at the Yamaha and started running through the opening bars of a new song, 'Co-dependent Blues'. Or maybe it was the smell of my Big Mac that roused her – the quarter-pounder-with-cheese that was my response to being snubbed by Harriet. If I couldn't have her, at least I could have *meat.*

(Men think this way, especially when drunk. I *know.*)

Nelson gave the Big Mac a disdainful sniff then let herself out through the cat flap. Alone with, like, half a bottle of whisky, a pack of Marlboro Lights and exercise books filled with scribbled scores and lyrics, I sat at the keyboard, plugged in my headphones and settled down to work.

Over the last few weeks, I'd grown accustomed to the show being an obsession – a distraction from thinking about Harriet 24/7. But at 3 a.m. – with the whisky and cigarettes gone – the truth hit me like a speeding truck. *They F**k You Up* was no distraction. It was *everything* – the personal and the professional inextricably bound, one dependent on the other.

I'm not sure when I moved onto the sofa – probably around 4 a.m. – but I know when I was jolted awake: 8 a.m. on the dot. My phone rang. Dad's name flashed onscreen.

'Sorry to wake you,' he said.

I tried to speak but my tongue felt as if someone had shoved a tobacco loofah in my mouth, and my skull was threatening to burst open.

'It's about George,' he said.

I sat up, blinking against the daylight, my head throbbing. 'Have you found him?'

'Yes. And Nancy.'

'And?'

'I've got bad news.'

RICHARD

I stepped off the train at the Gare du Nord just before midnight. Climbing into a taxi, my first stop was The Ritz. The receptionist declined to reveal if Monsieur George Brocklebank was a guest at the hotel. The same applied when I enquired about 'Lord Anthony Buckingham'.

'I'm sorry, m'sieur. We cannot divulge such information.'

Two hundred euros later it was a different story. Cash talks, especially at establishments frequented by the wealthy, where treatment of staff is often poor and the pay even worse.

Keeping the taxi on standby, I repeated the exercise at the Hôtel Plaza Athénée, Le Meurice, The George V, Hôtel de Crillon and Le Bristol. I didn't bother with the Mandarin Oriental. My father would have dismissed it as a 'palace of bling'. He was an old school *bon viveur* with a ton of money and no time to lose. Only the best would do.

There was nothing to admire about a man who had committed the ultimate betrayal, and yet I couldn't help feeling a sneaking regard for one aspect of his Parisian adventure: in spite of everything, it *mattered* that he'd decided to share it with a woman his own age rather than younger models who would have happily helped him to enjoy his ill-gotten gains.

It was harder to understand Nancy's motive for joining him on the jaunt. What kind of woman colludes in stealing from her own granddaughter? Or perhaps the truth was more complicated.

It was 2 a.m. before I decided to take a break. Paying the cab driver, I found an all-night café and sat outside with a glass of Ricard and a cigarette, huddled in my coat, glad of the fedora clamped to my head. I contemplated sending Harriet a text but decided against it. The best outcome would be to find Nancy and George together, fit and well, then retrieve Harriet's cash, or what was left of it. Mission accomplished, I could return to London triumphant. Would my boldness sway her? Would it seal the deal? Doubtful, but it could do no harm – and anyway, it was the right thing to do, not least because it was a way of keeping tabs on George ... and of doing everything possible to ensure the man kept his mouth shut about Tom.

Strolling by the Seine, I recalled the last time I'd visited Paris with Bonnie, twenty years ago. Tom was five. We'd left him with her parents and spent a springtime weekend eating in out-of-the-way restaurants and making love with an intensity we hadn't known since our early days.

'Making love' was the correct term for it, too, not 'having sex' or 'shagging'. And 'romance' was the *mot juste* for what we'd had all those years ago. I'd been in love before, of course, and so had she, but even as our honeymoon period had segued into something more mature we'd managed to remain smitten. Love letters, poems, Post-its on the pillow or stuck to the bathroom mirror. Lingering looks, flowers, a brush of fingertips under the table at a dinner party. Surprise gifts – nothing extravagant, but thoughtfully chosen books and CDs, or tickets to a sought-after concert or play – in the good times, maybe even a surprise plane ticket to Venice, Amsterdam or Rome. The fact that life had been so enjoyable had made Bonnie's betrayal harder to bear, but also meant there was so much to walk away from. That weekend in Paris had been our final carefree jaunt, our last weekend of innocence before the revelation that had blighted not only Tom's birthday but the rest of our lives. In the end, I'd stayed not for his sake but for my own.

My melancholy was interrupted by the chirruping of my phone. I stared at the caller's name, taking a moment before answering. I'd tried George's mobile several times since discovering his vanishing act, but now here he was, his name flashing onscreen.

'Damn you to hell,' I said. 'What are you playing at?'

A pause then a woman's voice.

'Richard?'

'Who's this?'

'Nancy. Is there any chance you might be able to help me?'

'Is my father with you?'

'In a manner of speaking.'

'How do you mean?'

She cleared her throat. 'He's with me, yes. We're in Paris.'

'Me too. I came to find you.'

'Oh,' she said. 'In that case, perhaps you could come straightaway?'

She gave me the address of a hotel in the fifth arrondissement. I flagged down a taxi. The streets were almost empty and the journey took less than five minutes. As we turned into a narrow cobbled street and pulled to a halt outside the nondescript building that housed the three-star *L'Hôtel Hortense*, I saw Nancy in the doorway.

'I'm so sorry,' she said as the taxi drove away. 'Your father's gone.'

'Gone where?'

She put a hand on my shoulder. 'He passed away. Two hours ago. I'm so sorry.'

I'd half-expected it, of course, but her words still had the power to take my breath away. I leaned against the hotel door and sank to a crouch.

I don't recall a great deal about the next few hours. I remember the apologetic smile on the face of the hotel manager; the cosy room on the top floor where George lay in bed, naked; Nancy sweeping his little blue pills into a bin. The rest is a blur.

I must have contacted Tom and Harriet, and I guess I called Pam to tell her I wouldn't be at work for at least a week (repatriating a body is no simple matter). As dawn broke over the rooftops I knew that even as I was discharging my duty, formulating plans for the funeral, I'd already decided there would be one notable absentee – me.

Among many bizarre moments (the woman from the British Consulate who giggled at inappropriate moments, the struggle of the funeral directors to carry George's body down the narrow staircase) the thing that sticks in my memory is being drawn aside by Nancy and ushered into the bathroom.

'He said this is where he used to come with your mum,' she said. 'I thought it was sweet, after all his fancy hotels.' She nodded towards the shower. 'That's where you were conceived.'

I must have flinched.

'Don't worry,' she said. 'I expect they've given it a squirt of Mr Muscle.' She managed half a smile then her eyes filled with tears. 'I'm sorry for your troubles,' she said. 'He told me about Bonnie, how he regretted that affair more than anything. And don't fret – I won't breathe a word to Tom.'

I watched as she opened the cupboard under the sink and drew out a canvas holdall. It bore George's initials. G.O.B. George Albert Brocklebank.

'Before I agreed to come I made him promise that he would return this to Harriet,' said Nancy. 'It's probably best if you give it to her.'

I unzipped the holdall. It was filled with fifty-pound notes.

'Nine-hundred-and-twenty-two thousand, eight-hundred-and-fifty quid,' said Nancy. 'Lord knows how he fenced those diamonds, and I've no idea how you're going to get it back to London but you'll think of something. Harriet says you're resourceful.'

I said nothing, watching as the woman extracted a notepad from the side pocket of the holdall.

'Better this than months in a hospital with tubes up his nose,' she said. 'And it could have been worse. He told me the pacemaker had given him an extra ten years.'

'My father had a pacemaker?'

'You didn't know?'

I shook my head.

'I expect he didn't want to worry you.'

As if. Did she seriously think he gave a damn about anyone but himself? She opened the notepad to reveal one of his pencil sketches: a picture of a baby – a boy.

'It's Tom,' I said, running a finger over the baby's face.

Nancy shook her head. 'It's you.'

Underneath my father's signature was an inscription.

For R with love. Better late than never.

I turned the pages. Another drawing: me as a baby. And another: older now – perhaps two or three. I flicked through the notepad. Each page contained a sketch of me, drawn by my father recording my childhood, from infancy to adolescence. Funny thing was, I had no recollection of him drawing me, ever.

As I stared at the sketches, I dimly remember Nancy leaving the bathroom then returning with my father's yellow pocket square. She held it out but I shook my head.

'I'm fine,' I said. 'Just something in my eye.'

Despite her presence, I felt more alone than at any time in my life. There was only one person I wanted to be with, one person I could think about.

Being around death has a way of concentrating the mind, of shifting the focus to what really matters. Had George not died, I would almost certainly not have done what I did when I got back to London, so I suppose I have him to thank for spurring me into action, but was I sorry the old bastard was gone? No. It would take every ounce of self-control to prevent me from dancing on his grave.

HARRIET

Nan came home on Sunday night. Tom and I were waiting. Sipping tea in the kitchen, she told us about the holdall full of fifty-pound notes. Apparently George had whisked it through customs without breaking a sweat. Richard was planning to smuggle it back into the UK, hiding it in his father's coffin. Even Tom had to admit the idea was ingenious.

For the next few days, while Richard was arranging the repatriation of George's body, I did the breakfast show with his stand-in, a smarmy bloke called Chris. Nice enough, I suppose, but we didn't have the same rapport and I was relieved when the week was over.

Richard called twice, once on Tuesday and once on Friday evening. He sounded drunk both times and said there was something he needed to talk to me about.

'What?' I said.

'Not now. Next time I see you.'

On Saturday night, I suggested to Tom that he might like to cook us all a (non-veggie) meal but he was busy, putting

the finishing touches to *They F**k You Up*, so I settled for
a Chinese takeaway. When I got back from collecting it,
Richard was sitting at the kitchen table, the holdall at his feet.

'Is that what I think it is?' I said.

Nan planted a kiss on my cheek. She was wearing a new
perfume. It smelt expensive.

'Before I agreed to go to Paris,' she said, 'I made George
promise you'd get all the cash. I didn't think you'd mind if
he spent a few bob on me first – on *us*, I suppose – but now
it's yours, all of it. You and the baby.'

I raised a quizzical eyebrow in Richard's direction. He
nodded. 'Every penny.'

Bending down, I unzipped the holdall and gasped, feeling
as if I'd strayed into a heist movie.

'Nearly a million quid,' said Nan.

My heart was trying to fight its way out of my chest.

'Shouldn't we give it back?' I said.

'Who to?' said Nan. 'Damian's dad? He's pushing up dai-
sies. Damian doesn't deserve a penny. Or maybe you'd like to
try to track down some tax-dodging toerags who lost a safe
deposit box full of dodgy diamonds?' She shook her head. 'I
don't know what you'll do with it, Harriet – it's not as if you
can swan into the estate agent's and buy a house for cash –
but you'll work something out. If you ask me, at thirty-five
it's a nice problem to have.'

She said she had a headache and was going upstairs, to
watch *The Texas Chainsaw Massacre*, but I had the impression
that Richard had asked her to make herself scarce, so he

could get me on my own. I served up the food and tucked into a plate of crispy beef while he toyed with a spring roll.

'Will you go back to being vegetarian?' he said. 'After you've had the baby?'

I shrugged.

'Maybe. Right now I'm doing whatever my body tells me.'

He wiped his mouth with a paper napkin.

'Quite a week.'

'Yes,' I said.

'The funeral's on Wednesday.'

'Same day as Tom's musical,' I said. 'Are you coming?'

He gave a tight smile. 'We'll see.'

I could tell he had something else on his mind and I was right. He cleared his throat and put down his fork.

'I've been doing a lot of thinking.'

'I'm not surprised,' I said. 'Nan says a death in the family makes you take stock.'

'So does divorce.'

'Is Bonnie coming to the funeral?'

He shook his head.

'Won't Tom be disappointed?' I said.

'It's complicated,' said Richard. 'And Goa is a long way.'

'They have planes.'

He shrugged. 'It's best she stays away.' He cleared his throat. 'But that's not what I wanted to talk to you about.'

'You're making me nervous.'

And that's when he reached across the table and took my hand.

'My father had a saying I agree with: "Life is short. Eat the cake, buy the shoes, take the trip." This isn't the ideal time but I think you know how I feel about you.'

OH

MY

GOD

'I think you like me, too,' he continued.

'Um. Of course.'

JESUS

H

CHRIST

'So . . . I was wondering . . .' He tailed off then tried again. 'I was wondering if – when the divorce is finalized, obviously – you might do me the honour of becoming my life.'

'Your what?'

'My wife.'

'You said "life".'

'A Freudian slip. Let's try again. I wonder if you would do me the honour of becoming my wife.' I drew breath to respond but he put a finger to my lips. 'It sounds crazy and I know there's something rather Jane Austen about proposing to someone you've only kissed in the back of a taxi, but you're right: a death in the family – even my motley crew – makes you think about what's important. And the answer is very simple: I love you.'

I was aching to speak but he wasn't finished.

'Don't answer now,' he said. 'We've been through a lot – especially you – but things are looking up. You've plenty of money so you won't think I'm proposing because of old-fashioned ideas about sweeping you up into a big house and showering you with gifts, like a delicate doll who can't take care of herself. Yes, I want to look after you – and the baby – but you're an independent woman and I know you're going to be a success, whatever you decide to do.' He held my gaze. 'I think we could make a good life together. So will you think about it? At least until after the funeral?'

I met his gaze and smiled.

'Yes,' I said. 'I will.'

TOM

I knew Dad and George were on bad terms but to boycott your own father's funeral? Seriously?

Dad texted just after nine, as soon as the Silk FM show ended. I'd tuned in to the final hour, to check he was still in one piece after Paris. If he was upset, he didn't let it show on-air. His text was short and not very sweet.

Hope today goes well. Will try and come to your show tonight.

So he wasn't planning to go to his own father's funeral and would only 'try' to attend the biggest night of his son's life.

Cheers, Dad.

Mum emailed to say she wouldn't be flying back for George's send-off. It was 'all for the best' and he was 'one of a kind – a force of nature'. Whatever *that* meant.

At first, I thought no one aside from me, Harriet and Nancy would turn up to send him on his way. The north London crematorium was almost deserted as we arrived on the dot of 11 a.m. A couple of stragglers were left from the

373

first funeral of the day but made themselves scarce when they realized we were next on the conveyor belt.

And then 'our' mourners began to arrive – almost all women. They came singly and in couples, on foot, in chauffeur-driven cars, minicabs and taxis – all well-heeled women of 'a certain age'.

To begin with, most stood awkwardly on their own, until a stylish redhead sporting five-inch stilettos and a black hat initiated a bit of small talk. A hubbub of conversation began to spread around the grounds of the crematorium, then the laughter started and the atmosphere began to change, going from funereal to cocktail party.

'How did they know where to come?' said Harriet.

Nancy blew her nose. 'Word spreads. A good man is hard to find.'

The women didn't introduce themselves to me, the only family member present, but I didn't take offence. This was a Brocklebank funeral but the mourners had known George far better than I had. If condolences were due it was to them, not me.

Imelda Shine was the last to arrive, stepping from her chauffeur-driven Bentley and crossing the courtyard at a brisk pace. She placed a bony hand on my arm.

'At least he died doing the work he loved,' she said.

Nancy's nostrils flared. 'Are you the Shine woman?'

Imelda's eyes flickered towards Nancy's handbag and shoes. Both had seen better days. 'You must be Nancy. I gather he was with you when we lost him.'

'If we'd *lost* him I'd have sent out a search party,' sniffed Nancy. 'The old bugger died.'

Imelda stared for a moment then began to laugh. She pointed at Nancy. 'You're sitting with me.'

Linking arms, they walked into the chapel. Their fellow mourners followed, as if they'd been waiting for the arrival of their queen bee. I was about to follow suit when Paddy sidled up and drew something from a carrier bag.

'He wanted you to have this.'

He handed me a red exercise book. I flicked through the dog-eared pages. Copperplate handwriting. Black ink. Proper fountain pen.

'His autobiography,' said Paddy.

I remembered George telling me the title. *You Had to Be There.*

'People say the book's too racy or that no one would believe it.'

'He was no God-botherer,' said Paddy, 'but he asked me to tell you that "the truth shall set you free".'

'Meaning?'

He was about to reply but Harriet tapped me on the shoulder. I turned and followed her gaze. A horse-drawn hearse was entering the courtyard, driven by two coachmen in top hats. The coffin was festooned with white lilies. Without warning, tears sprang to my eyes. The cover of George's record flashed into my mind – his shot at stardom, the photo of him as a young man sporting a trilby and a smile. I'd never heard the song, a ballad accompanied by a simple piano solo, but would always remember its title: 'The Days Are Long

(But The Years Are Short)'. I assume it was thanks to my father that it was playing as the coffin was carried inside, the crowd listening to George crooning lyrics filled with melancholy and regret.

> The days are long
> But the years are short
> Life's game must be learned
> But cannot be taught
> Forget and forgive
> That's how we must live
> The days are long
> But the years are short

It was a humanist service, conducted by a celebrant called Julia. She appeared to know a good deal more about the 'dear departed' than was the case at most funerals. Perhaps she too had been a member of George's 'fan club', as she referred to the mourners. There were no hymns, just a couple of songs – Nat King Cole's 'Let There Be Love' and, inevitably, Sinatra's 'My Way', with which we all sang along. I was half-expecting eulogies from one or two of the women but Julia was the only speaker, talking of George's 'indefatigable lust for life', a turn of phrase that provoked sniggers from the back row.

After forty-five minutes, we emerged from the chapel into the drizzle and cold. Having planned the funeral to the last detail, it seemed that Dad had drawn the line at arranging a wake. Most of the mourners left immediately, leaving a handful of dawdlers to congregate in the courtyard, exchanging email addresses and numbers. Those who stayed seemed more relaxed now that the main event was over; there was almost a party atmosphere. Several women came to shake my hand, one or two telling me how much I reminded them of my grandfather, something I found a) comforting and b) weird since I'd never thought there was much resemblance.

As Nancy and Paddy were driven away in Imelda's Bentley, Harriet enfolded me in a warm embrace. It was the first time we'd been so close since that kiss in the rain, the first time I'd smelt her hair in weeks. I closed my eyes and inhaled.

'I've called an Uber,' she said softly into my ear. 'Would you like to come home with me?'

I opened my eyes and raised an eyebrow.

'Sorry . . .' she said. 'I didn't mean it like that.'

'It's okay,' I said. 'It's just today's crazy . . . the funeral . . . and the show tonight.'

'Which is why I thought you could use some down time.'

'"Down time"?'

While I was trying to work out if she was speaking in code, she twirled a strand of hair between her fingers. Not for the first time, I reflected that being around death makes people behave differently. Things seem more vivid somehow — there's an urge to be honest, to make every second count.

'I love you, Harriet,' I said.

She looked startled then her face settled into a smile.

'I love you too.'

'Really?'

She leaned forward and gave me a kiss. On the cheek, but even so.

'How could anyone not love Tom?'

I decided not to press my luck. 'It's been quite a few weeks,' I said.

She nodded.

'So what time do you want me?'

Now? Always?

'I'm meeting Zara at the pub at six o'clock,' I said. 'Mendoza's due at eight so we'll have time to run through everything.'

'Six it is. Will you be okay till then?'

'I'll be fine.'

I saw her off in the cab then called one for myself and waited in the portico, sheltering from the rain. The court-yard was deserted and silent. I contemplated texting Dad to tell him everything had gone according to plan but decided against it. He'd done his duty but no more than the bare minimum, so, as the saying goes, fuck him and the horse he rode in on.

Leaning against the redbrick wall, I flicked through the exercise book. George's 'autobiography' was in the form of a diary. Straightaway, my eye was drawn to an entry written on the date of my sixth birthday. The chapter mentioned a gift he was planning to give me, a rocking horse. It was headlined in capital letters.

THE DAY THE SHIT HIT THE FAN.

RICHARD

Taking a seat in the empty Silk FM studio, I reached into the envelope Paddy had sent me, slipped the record from its sleeve and set it to play. As the piano solo began, I studied George's photo on the cover. His trilby. His smile. His shot at immortality.

The days are long
But the years are short
Life's game must be learned
But cannot be taught
Forget and forgive
That's how we must live
The days are long
But the years are short
We all make mistakes
And I'm no exception
Oh, how my heart aches
For my cruel deception

So now here I am
Down on my knees
My pleas for forgiveness
Lost on the breeze
There's no one to blame
I lost at life's game
The days are long
But the years are short

The song ended. Silence descended. I sat for a moment then lifted the stylus and set the record to play again.

HARRIET

Tom's declaration of love caught me off guard. So did Richard's marriage proposal, but life without these two blokes was now hard to imagine. So where did that leave me, apart from thirty-five, up the duff and minted? Over the years, I'd had enough junk male to last a lifetime, but had I found more than my fair share of Mr Rights?

As Richard had said, his proposal was 'a bit Jane Austen', and as for Tom, I'd only snogged him once or twice, but did that matter? Weren't friendship and trust the best basis for love? Wasn't my so-called 'relationship' with Cockweasel a warning from the future? *Carry on as you are and this is the best you can expect.* I couldn't help remembering a line from *Thelma and Louise*, one of Nan's favourite non-horror films: 'You get what you settle for.'

If I *settled* for Tom or Richard would that be so terrible?

I was at Nan's when Zara called. She sounded like she'd been crying, which was hardly surprising. Apparently a speeding van had sent her flying while she was on a zebra crossing so she was calling from hospital, nursing two broken legs, a smashed pelvis and God knows what else. There was no way she could do Tom's try-out and she'd been desperately trying to call him but he wasn't answering and **OHMIGOD OHMIGOD OHMIGOD!**

So I phoned Tom but the call went straight to voicemail. Five minutes later I tried again and left another message. Then I sent a text.

Zara in hospital! She can't do your show tonight. Call me! NOW!

But he didn't.

It was pouring with rain so I jumped into an Uber and went straight to Dalston, hoping to find him at his local, but no one had seen him. The room above the pub was empty apart from crates of fizzy drinks and boxes of Kettle Chips. By 6 p.m. I'd left four voicemails and sent three texts but Tom still hadn't responded, so I texted Richard. He told me not to worry – his son was prone to cutting things fine. Hmmm ... Today's vanishing act didn't chime with the Tom I knew – dependable, trustworthy Tom. It was partly his reliability that had drawn me to him in the first place. Most blokes are flakes, so to find one who showed up on time and kept his word was brilliant. WTF had happened to him?

My thoughts were interrupted by a burst of laughter from the bar downstairs, followed by footsteps on the creaking wooden staircase. Tom entered, holding his keyboard under his arm. I could see he was drunk. His face was flushed, his hair wet and his eyes were red-rimmed, as if he'd been crying.

'Sorry,' he slurred. 'Hell of a day.'

I swallowed my impatience, forcing myself to remember he'd just buried his grandfather.

'Did you get my messages? About Zara?'

He nodded and mumbled something about planning to send her flowers.

'So what are you going to do about the musical?' I said.

He turned to face me.

'That depends on you.'

'Me?'

'You know the show by heart. I need you to take her place.'

Okay, I know I should have seen it coming but what with the Silk FM show and George's funeral and Zara's accident and everything else, the idea of me stepping into her shoes hadn't crossed my mind – well, maybe for a nanosecond, but then **THE THOUGHTS THE THOUGHTS THE THOUGHTS** had surfaced and I'd forced myself to focus on other things. Now, here we were, on the biggest night of Tom's life and all I could think was, **PLEASE DON'T ASK ME TO DO THIS, PLEASE, PLEASE, PLEASE!**

'Is there an audience?' I said.

He nodded.

'The pub's put the word out among the regulars. Should be about fifty people.'

FIFTY? MIGHT AS WELL BE FIFTY MILLION!

He carried on talking but I'd stopped listening and **THE WINDOW IS OPEN AND I COULD PUSH YOU OUT BEFORE YOU COULD STOP ME, OR I COULD JUMP, BECAUSE ANYTHING WOULD BE BETTER THAN PERFORMING IN FRONT OF *FIFTY* PEOPLE AND THE THOUGHT MAKES ME WANT TO PISS MY PANTS.**

He was saying something. I tried to focus.

'You're the only one who can help, Harriet.'

'I'm sorry,' I said. 'I can't. I just can't.'

His face fell.

'I don't understand. I thought we were friends. More than friends.'

And suddenly, I was racing out of the room, down the wooden staircase and out onto the main road. The rain was falling harder now, stinging my cheeks as I ran along the pavement. Crossing the road, I splashed through a puddle then ran on, my feet pounding the concrete, my heart racing and **THE THOUGHTS THE THOUGHTS THE THOUGHTS** and next thing I knew, I slammed into a man emerging from a kebab shop, ricocheted off him and toppled off the rain-slicked kerb, into the path of an on-coming bus. The blast from the horn was deafening. The driver swerved, missing me by inches as I collapsed in the gutter. Kebab Guy was saying something, tugging me by the arm and hoisting me up, back onto the pavement, then he was gone. Slumped in a doorway, my heart hammering, tears and rain pouring down my face, I tried to catch my breath. Glancing up to the skies, I saw a cable – some kind of electrical wire – strung across the street, from one roof-top to another, like a tightrope. And I remembered what George said about walking a tightrope and keeping going and *never looking down*, and that brought back everything the CBT woman had told me about 'exposure therapy', where you confront your worst fears – *not* doing everything you can to *avoid* what frightens you most but *immersing* yourself in *the very thing that scares the shit out of you.* In that instant I knew this was one of those moments that I could either look back on for the rest of my life and hate myself for not doing all I could, not just for Tom but for myself, or I could find the courage to tackle the tightrope.

As my breathing returned to normal, I got to my feet and retraced my steps. In the room above the pub Tom was on his mobile.

'Can I call you back?' he said into his phone. 'She's just walked in.'

He hung up and took a step towards me, his face etched with worry as he took stock of my appearance.

'Jesus, are you okay?'

I managed a nod.

'We've got an hour,' I said, heading for the loo. 'Give me five minutes to sort myself out.'

'Then what?'

I smiled, trying to sound braver than I felt.

'Then let's get this show on the road.'

His face lit up and I thought he was going to tell me he

loved me again, but he just said, 'Thank fuck for that,' and reached for his phone.

In the loo, I splashed water on my face and stared at my reflection in the mirror.

'Fuck off', I said, not to myself but to The Thoughts. 'Fuck off, fuck off, FUCK OFF, *FUCK OFF!*'

I'd love to be able to say it worked like a charm, silencing the voices forever, but what happened was the opposite: a sudden escalation of The Thoughts that felt overwhelming, like a psychological tsunami. Every foul thing you can imagine – every vile thought, every negative emotion, every self-punishing, self-sabotaging idea – was clamouring inside my head, growing louder and nastier and more and more intense with every second. Instead of doing what I normally do, which is push everything away, I kept staring at my reflection and telling The Thoughts to *fuck the fuck off with fuck off sauce and fuck off sprinkles*. Then I took a deep breath, turned away from the mirror and walked out of the toilet.

In my absence, Tom had tidied the room, created a small stage area and arranged chairs for the expected audience. He was sitting at the Yamaha, picking out the intro to the opening song, 'Boy Meets Girl'. I've never seen anyone look quite so miserable.

'Has something happened?' I said. Without answering, he gave a thin smile that didn't reach his eyes. I could smell the alcohol on his breath.

'The show must go on,' he said then he turned back to the keyboard and began to warble the first line of the opening song. I joined in, managing to drown out The Thoughts in my head by focusing one hundred per cent on the lyrics and the melody.

We ran through 'Boy Meets Girl' with just a couple of hitches – nothing to worry about, just a consequence of my being rusty. If anything, Tom's playing was even better than usual, looser and more impassioned. Moving on to the second song, 'Co-dependent Blues', I hit the high notes in the middle-eight without any difficulty at all. By the time we ran through the title song, a ragtime pastiche called 'They F**k You Up', we were properly warmed up. I took a deep swig of mineral water and checked my watch. Five to eight.

YOU'RE A RUBBISH SINGER, ABOUT TO HUMILIATE YOURSELF IN FRONT OF A BIG PRODUCER AND A BIG CROWD, INCLUDING TOM AND HAHAHAHAHAHAHA

'What if he doesn't come?' I said.

He shrugged.

'That's the least of my worries.'

I frowned.

'Is this about George? Or your father?'

He cocked his head to one side.

'Define "father".'

Before I had the chance to ask WTF he was talking about, footsteps announced the arrival of one of the barmen, who ushered in the first few members of the audience and **OHMIGOD OHMIGOD OHMIGOD IS THIS REALLY HAPPENING?** Tom and I made ourselves scarce, moving behind the bar area. Over the next few minutes, the room filled with a friendly-looking crowd, clutching drinks and chattering among themselves.

Before I knew it, it was time for the arrival of Paul Mendoza – the most handsome dude I'd ever seen – and his two female assistants, both in their twenties. After making the introductions, Tom went downstairs to fetch drinks for the new arrivals while I made small talk, fielding the producer's enquiries about my acting credits and involvement in the show, all the while silently telling The Thoughts to **fuckofffuckofffuckofffuckoffFUCKOFF!** Paul's easy-going manner helped. He said he was workshopping three plays, had two musicals in development and another set to open at the Sheffield Crucible in the new year.

'To recoup its investment,' he said, 'a midscale musical needs to run for at least a year and sell half a million tickets. That's a lot of bums on seats.'

'So no pressure,' said one of the assistants, giving me a smile that didn't feel genuine. I wondered what her agenda was.

BITCH BITCH BITCH!

By the time Tom got back with the drinks he still looked washed-out but showed no sign of being drunk. One of the women – the nicer of the two – tapped her watch, a signal to Paul.

'Okay, let's see the magic,' he said, rubbing his hands together.

'Don't you want to wait for Richard?' I asked Tom.

'He's not coming. Long story.'

Whatever *that* meant.

The bitchy assistant cleared her throat.

'Paul has another appointment at ten so . . .'

She tailed off. It was now or never. The producer took a seat. His assistants followed suit, positioning themselves on either side of their boss. All three crossed their legs. The crowd fell quiet as a sense of anticipation filled the air.

'So,' said Paul, leaning forward in his chair. 'Tell us about your show.'

Tom sat at the keyboard and cleared his throat. He took a deep breath then stared into the middle distance for what seemed like an age. I had the strangest feeling he was on the verge of tears. When he finally spoke, he did so fluently and eloquently, reciting the 'elevator pitch' we'd spent days perfecting, but his voice was unsteady, almost tremulous.

'Thank you all for coming. You're about to get a taste of an integrated musical in three acts called *They F**k You Up*, which, as I'm sure you know, comes from the Philip Larkin poem, 'This Be The Verse'. The show is set partly in a prison, which serves as a metaphor for the way we're all prisoners of our backgrounds – and that's the core theme: family dysfunction and how we all need to break free from parental expectation and find fulfilment by living life on our own terms.'

Paul nodded, scribbling on a notepad as I took my opening position and **fuck off fuck off** *FUCK OFF*! and Tom picked out the first few notes of the opening song. He stopped playing and turned towards the door, frowning.

'Is someone there?'

I followed his gaze. There was silence for a moment then a floorboard creaked and Richard stepped into the room, looking as if he'd been caught out.

'Sorry,' he said. 'I didn't want to interrupt.'

I saw Tom clench his jaw, as though trying to keep a lid on his temper, then he gestured towards an empty chair.

'Take a seat,' he said.

I found it weird that he didn't introduce his dad to Paul Mendoza. Nerves? Or had Richard lurking outside put him off his stride?

Moments of clarity are rare and tend to arrive without warning. Later, I would wonder what it was about seeing father and son together in that shabby room above the pub that brought a rush of emotion to the surface. Something about the expression on Tom's face, the one that made him look five years old – lost and vulnerable? Or was it the sheepish way Richard shuffled in, avoiding his son's eye, as though burdened by a need to make up for lost time, hoping this better-late-than-never appearance could atone for bedtime stories unread, school plays missed, sports days unattended? In that moment, I felt a surge of affection for both men.

But at the same time, perhaps it was the tang of ambition in the air that told me I wasn't ready to give up on my dream of becoming a bona fide actress, and of finding someone I could love with every fibre of my being. For once, The Thoughts were silent as the realization hit home with the force of a punch: I could *never* commit to a happy-ever-after with Richard or Tom. Now I knew the truth – now I could *name* it – I must tell them how I felt. Not tonight but soon.

I watched as Tom reached into his rucksack and pulled out a red exercise book. He tossed it to Richard.

'In case you get bored,' he said.

Richard caught the book and frowned, clearly puzzled. As Tom turned to the keyboard and began to play I caught a glimpse of his father out of the corner of my eye. He was flicking urgently through the exercise book. I turned away, to avoid being distracted. Then I started to sing.

For the next twenty-five minutes, I did my best, despite my clammy palms, a galloping heart and The Thoughts swirling inside my head. **YOU'RE UGLY AND TALENTLESS AND WHAT THE HELL MAKES YOU THINK ANYONE WANTS TO HEAR YOU SING?** Somehow, I managed to keep going, song after song. I wouldn't be so big-headed as to say I was on top form but the experience reminded me that there are times when giving a performance feels like you're walking on air; this was one of those times. The audience helped. They'd been briefed that this was a try-out, so they knew what was at stake and were generous enough to applaud and whistle after every number, even when I hit a bum note in the middle of the title song. While Tom's keyboard playing was full of passion and flair, his singing voice was no more than adequate, but that wasn't a problem. Mendoza wouldn't be expecting polished performances, just a flavour of the musical and a sense of whether or not it had 'legs'. Was the story fresh? Did it have universal appeal? Were the melodies memorable? Did the lyrics have depth, wit and wisdom? Were the characters likeable, or at least relatable? Bottom line: was this a show that would persuade investors and punters alike to part with their hard-earned cash?

As we finished the final song, Paul led the applause (there were wolf whistles too) and Richard joined in with what looked like genuine enthusiasm. The Thoughts were still circulating inside my head **THEY'RE JUST BEING NICE, CLAPPING FOR THE SHOW AND TOM, NOTHING TO DO WITH YOU, YOU TALENTLESS ARSE-WAZZOCK** but they seemed more muted now and were rivalled by another voice competing for my attention **YOU DID IT YOU DID IT YOU DID IT!**

The audience filed out, chatting among themselves and heading back down to the bar, leaving just Mendoza and his assistants. If we'd been in one of Nan's films this would have been the moment when the big-shot producer would have asked us both to sign on the dotted line, setting us on the road to fame and fortune – so it came as a blow when Paul delivered his judgement.

'Thank you both,' he said, pocketing his notebook. 'It's a good show – a nice idea, well executed – but I'm not looking for good, I'm looking for great.'

Tom's face fell. Mendoza put a consoling hand on his shoulder.

'You've got talent. Don't waste it. Let me know if you

have other ideas. If I have a criticism it's that the show lacks heart.'

The assistants were already at the door. Mendoza crossed to join them.

'Hold on,' said Tom, 'I do have another idea.'

The producer turned, hand on the door.

'Sorry, I'm running late. But keep me posted, okay? I mean it.'

Then he and his entourage were gone. I heard a clatter of footsteps down the staircase. Silence descended on the room.

'Jesus,' said Richard softly.

I thought he was reacting to Mendoza's verdict but no – he was still scanning the red exercise book. His face was pale and there was a sheen of sweat on his brow.

'Are you okay?' I said.

He didn't seem to hear. He and Tom stared at each other. They had the weirdest expressions on their faces. What was going on? When Tom finally spoke, his voice was almost a whisper.

'I have no words.'

Richard said nothing. He stood and stretched out his arms. Tom took a step forward, into his father's embrace. Richard lost his grip on the exercise book. It fell to the floor. As the men hugged, clutching each other for dear life, I picked up the book and scrutinized the old-fashioned handwriting. The first chapter had a heading in French. '*Tout comprendre, c'est tout pardonner.*'

The Thoughts were silent as I sat down and began to read.

TOM

I followed Dad out of the pub. We left Harriet inside, reading. Out on the street corner, the rain had stopped and the night air was cold but crisp. Dad stood under a street-lamp and lit a cigarette. His hands were trembling. I felt a surge of pity course through me, constricting my throat. He turned to face me.

'Should I have told you?'

I searched for something to say. Finding my voice was hard, choosing the right words impossible.

'I can't see how there was a right thing to do.'

He managed half a smile.

'That's very gracious.'

'I mean it, Dad.'

His voice grew hoarse. 'Thank you,' he said. 'For calling me Dad.'

I opened my mouth to speak but he held up a silencing finger. We stared at each other for a moment then he cleared his throat and drew on his cigarette, exhaling twin plumes of smoke.

'You mustn't blame your mother. She wasn't well.' He sighed. 'As for George . . .'

He tailed off, allowing the sentence to finish itself. We let the silence stretch, the still of the night at odds with the emotions churning inside. Then he turned up his collar and donned his fedora.

'Did I ever tell you I hate that hat?' I said.

He smiled and took a final drag on his cigarette then flicked it into the gutter.

'So now what?'

'A walk?' I said. 'We could have a chat?'

'About anything in particular?'

It was my turn to smile. 'We'll think of something.'

He nodded. To my surprise, he hooked his arm through mine. We began to walk along the rain-slicked pavement, saying nothing. Sometimes there is comfort in silence.

ONE YEAR LATER

RICHARD

The low winter sun was setting over Terminal 5 as the taxi pulled to a halt. I paid the driver and hurried into departures. No sign of Harriet at any of the check-in desks. My pulse quickened as I scanned the crowds in vain. Starting to panic, I turned and saw her walking towards me, wheeling the pushchair we'd chosen from Harrods a week after the baby was born. It had cost a lot of money, of course, but, like all the best things in life, babies don't come cheap.

Harriet's eyes lit up as she saw me.

'Thank God. I thought you weren't coming.'

'Wild horses wouldn't keep me away,' I said. Lame, I know, but there are times when words are hard to come by. I crouched down to look at the baby. (Her name was Georgia; Harriet had insisted.) For once she was asleep, not staring in wide-eyed wonder at the world.

'I assume you've knocked her out with Valium?' I said.

Harriet nodded.

'And a pint of brandy,' she deadpanned.

I smiled.

'Her first flight. Quite a milestone.'

Harriet smiled.

'Nan's all prepared.'

I looked up to see Nancy approaching with a small case on wheels.

'Is that all you're taking?' I said. 'For a whole year?'

She shook her head.

'I've checked in my cases. This is hand luggage. Nappies, bottles and wet-wipes.'

You had to hand it to her – ever since George died she'd been a trouper. From suggesting Paddy might know someone who could discreetly launder the mountain of cash to encouraging her granddaughter to buy a flat with the proceeds then rent it out to fund a make-or-break bid to crack Hollywood, Nancy had been a cool head. She'd also encouraged Harriet to quit Silk FM in order to give her dreams a chance. Now, she was getting her reward: twelve months in a Malibu beach house, babysitting her great-grandchild while Harriet took on Tinseltown.

'No sign of Tom?' she said, scanning the crowd.

I followed her gaze. There he was, right on cue, hurrying towards us.

'Sorry,' he said. 'The casting session overran.'

'How's it going?' I said.

'Good. Paul's found a theatre in Nottingham. We open at the end of April. A three-week run to iron out the wrinkles. After that, who knows?'

I smiled.

'Today Nottingham, tomorrow the world.'

'Sorry to miss it,' said Harriet. 'You really don't mind?'

Tom shook his head.

'You're doing the right thing.'

We said nothing for a moment then Harriet started what sounded like a prepared speech.

'I only hope you and Richard can forgive me ...'

She made it halfway through the first sentence before tailing off, too choked to speak. The awkward silence that followed was broken by Nancy. She pointed to a monitor.

'Our flight's on schedule.'

Tom did his best to make his smile convincing.

'Give my love to La-La Land.'

For a moment, I thought Harriet was about to burst into tears.

'You'll come?' she said. 'Christmas?'

'Of course,' said Tom. He turned to me. 'What about you?'

I considered my options: Belsize Park or Malibu.

'I'll do my best,' I said, taking a step towards Harriet and kissing her cheek. Tom followed suit then stood at my side, watching Harriet and Nancy walk away, steering the pushchair towards departures. I thought I heard a buzzing coming from Nancy's case but perhaps it was my imagination. They disappeared from view, leaving a chill in the air. I cleared my throat.

'I'll take a taxi back to town. Can I give you a lift?'

Tom shook his head.

'It's quicker by tube.'

'Suit yourself.'

I watched as he walked away, following signs for the tube.

'Tom?'

He stopped and turned.

'Break a leg,' I said.

He smiled.

'Thanks, Dad.'

Then he was gone.

HARRIET

I changed Georgia's nappy in the departures lounge loo.
When I emerged I found Nan in Costa Coffee, talking to a
man in a suit. Mid-forties, sharp suit, black hair.

'This is my granddaughter,' she told him. 'And her little
one. Aren't they gorgeous?'

The man's handshake was firm, his eyes ice blue.

'Pleasure to meet you,' he said. His accent was American,
west coast.

'His name's William Morris,' said Nan. 'He's on our
flight. He's an agent.'

'William Morris is the name of the agency,' said the man.
'Well, sorta. My name's Jake.'

OHMIGOD HE'S GORGEOUS!

'I'll leave you to get acquainted,' said Nan. 'If you need me
I'll be in Duty Free. I need more batteries.'

We watched her go. Jake sipped his coffee.

'First time to LA?'

'Yes.'

'Excited?'
'Terrified.'
'You'll be fine.'
'How do you know?'
He grinned.
'Trust me. I'm an agent.'
OHMIGOD OHMIGOD OHMIGOD . . .

TOM

The tube train was waiting at the platform. I settled into an empty carriage and leafed through a discarded *Evening Standard* but the words swam before my eyes. As the doors closed I was aware of someone boarding the train. I looked up.

'You're right,' said Dad. 'This is quicker.'

He sat next to me. I put down the paper.

'So,' he said, 'remind me what your new show is about?'

I'd told him already, of course, but he liked hearing my elevator pitch, the one that had received the thumbs-up from Paul.

'An estranged father and son who unwittingly fall in love with the same woman.'

His lips twitched into a smile.

'As if *that* would ever happen.'

I returned the smile but said nothing.

'Hungry?' he said. 'I've made *coq au vin*.'

I raised an eyebrow.

'Made or bought?'

'Made.'

'I'm impressed,' I said.

'That makes two of us.'

We smiled then lapsed into silence, listening to Harriet on the tannoy as the train started to move and the journey began.

Acknowledgements

My thanks to Sara-Jade Virtue, Paul Simpson, Pip Watkins, Alice Rodgers and the rest of the wonderful team at Simon & Schuster. Thanks also to Annabel Merullo and Daisy Chandley at Peters Fraser and Dunlop, and to all the readers and bloggers whose enthusiasm is such a tonic. May the blue-bird of happiness fly up your nose!

Andaz London Liverpool Street is a 5 star lifestyle luxury hotel in the heart of vibrant East London.

Opened as the Great Eastern Hotel in 1884, the hotel is housed in Liverpool Streets station's beautiful redbrick Victorian building, designed by the architects of the Houses of Parliament, with interiors seamlessly blending modern and heritage designs by Conran + Partners.

Capturing the hotel's location and history, our 267 rooms and suites aim to be creative spaces where the traditionally conservative City meets the vibrant artistic vibe of East London with illustration tattoo art by local artist Sophie Mo and photography of the local area by Hoxton Mini Press' Martin Usborne.

For the foodies, there is something to suit all dining tastes at any of Andaz London Liverpool Street's 5 restaurants and bars, from specialty morning coffee and healthy breakfasts to fresh Japanese, brunches galore, traditional pub fare and perfectly grilled dishes.